PLAY OUR SONG

Sienna Waters

Copyright © 2025 Sienna Waters

All rights reserved

The characters and events portrayed in this book are fictitious. Any similarity to real persons, living or dead, is coincidental and not intended by the author.

No part of this book may be reproduced, or stored in a retrieval system, or transmitted in any form or by any means, electronic, mechanical, photocopying, recording, or otherwise, without express written permission of the publisher.

Find out more at www.siennawaters.com. And stay up to date with the latest news from Sienna Waters by signing up for my newsletter!

SIENNA WATERS

To N.–

With all my heart,
xxx

CHAPTER ONE

Chief Superintendent Ware stared Tilly up and down, and she had a momentary quiver in her stomach. She was pretty sure that she hadn't done anything wrong, but then, could one ever be certain?

The Chief Superintendent squinted at her. "The suspect is believed to be intoxicated and when tracked down, is found in a local accident and emergency department having what is clearly a whiplash injury treated, an injury almost exclusively found in those involved in car accidents. Do you perform an arrest?"

"No," Tilly said confidently. "A suspect can't be arrested under section six, paragraph five of the road traffic act 1988 when in hospital as a patient."

"Good, very good." He smiled a little. "You'll be off then?"

Tilly relaxed slightly. Well, as much as she could relax when a half-naked Chief Superintendent could barrage her with questions from the sergeant's exam at any moment. "Just about to leave, dad. Er, sir." She was technically in uniform.

"Let me change out of my pajamas and I'll drive you to the station," he said, heaving himself up from the breakfast table. "It's not out of my way."

Matilda Ware had wanted to be a police officer for as long as she could remember. Probably longer, to be honest. Seeing her dad come home in his scratchy uniform every night, hearing his stories, knowing that he was out there protecting people, she'd been fiercely proud of him and wanted nothing more than to be exactly like him. Well, minus the beer belly, maybe.

And she was firmly on her way, quite literally, as he waved from the train platform and she blew kisses from the window. With her sergeant's exam coming up, the opportunity to work in a small police station was exactly what she'd needed.

Not that she'd been convinced at the beginning. A tiny town with only one policeman? It didn't sound like the opportunity of the year. But as her father wisely pointed out, a small town with only one officer meant that she'd be called upon to do things that she wouldn't normally have the chance to do. And besides, Max Browning was one of the finest police officers that he knew and they'd been on a training course together. She had a feeling that her dad saw Max as some kind of mentee.

Tilly grinned to herself as she settled into her seat.

A few months of the kind of no-holds-barred policing she'd get in this tiny town and then she'd be moving onward and upward, well on her way to becoming Chief Superintendent, just like her dad. Or, and she shivered a little at the thought of it, maybe even Chief Constable.

She sighed in satisfaction and pulled out her copy of the police training handbook. A little light reading for the short journey to Whitebridge.

THE TOWN WAS tiny and perfect, perched in a little valley with higgledy-piggledy houses in pastel colors lining narrow streets. Tilly dragged her suitcase down the high street, passing a pub, a bookshop with a gray cat sitting in the window, a village shop, and a little cafe that smelled of roasted coffee and made her stomach rumble.

Just the place, she thought. It was pretty quiet, though. Maybe there was actually no crime at all here. She felt a bit sick at the thought of it. She couldn't afford to be stuck in a back-water, she had career milestones to hit and she had no time to waste.

Then she saw an SUV parked on a double yellow line and

calmed down. There was crime everywhere, no matter how peaceful a place looked. There'd always be a dark underbelly, a seedy side to things.

Her mum had always hated that. Always hated that she and her dad were looking for the maggots in the apple, looking for what was out of place or just plain bad. It was probably why she'd left in the end.

Tilly didn't like remembering that day, didn't like the ripping feeling she'd had when she'd had to choose, even though she knew that she'd chosen right. She'd had to stay with her dad. He'd needed her. Her mother hadn't.

Even now, her mum only rang once in a blue moon and forgot her birthday more than she remembered it.

She stopped, her case bumping to a halt behind her. A blue sign over a crooked door marked the sandstone building as the local police station. Tilly took a second to check her uniform, to square her shoulders, then nodded to herself and strode confidently in through the front door.

A man was leaning on the wooden counter inside, a pipe clamped between his teeth, and a disgruntled look on his face.

"We've already got a copper," he said when he saw Tilly.

"Well, now you've got two, haven't you?" she said.

He grunted. "S'pose." He brightened up a little. "Unless you've come to take over from Max? Like, he's going on holiday or something? Wouldn't open cases need to be suspended or something if that happened?"

"Nice try, Dave." A tall, freckle-nosed man came out from the back room. He was wearing what was possibly a uniform, but without a tie and with no jacket, and with shirt sleeves rolled up to his elbows, Tilly couldn't be quite sure.

"You've got a visit," said Dave, pulling his pipe out of his mouth. "Probably some big city copper come to reign you in, keep an eye on you and the likes."

The man turned to Tilly and grinned, light dancing in his blue eyes, and Tilly thought he looked rather handsome when he smiled. Not that she was interested in men and definitely not in her superiors.

"You must be Constable Ware, I'm Max. I'll be with you in a minute. Let me deal with this old reprobate first."

"Don't go calling me names now, young Max. It's bad enough you're taking my license away."

"I'm confiscating it temporarily," said Max. He held out a large brown envelope. "Go on, drop it in there."

With a sigh, the old man reached into his pocket, pulled out his driving license, and dropped it into the envelope.

"Right. You can have that back in two weeks. Just come down here and I'll give it to you. In the meantime, have a think about your driving skills. Dangerous driving is no joke. I can get you on a course if you need a bit of help."

"I'm a perfectly good driver," grumbled Dave.

"Mmm, that's not what McKeefe said when he reported the damage."

Tilly was getting more and more horrified the more she heard of this conversation. She was itching to say something, positively quivering with the need to interrupt. But her dad had trained her better than that. However he was dressed, Max was her superior officer and she couldn't question him in front of a member of the public.

"Go on then, off you go," Max was saying. "And if I get reports that you've been driving without a license, then there'll be trouble."

"You know I wouldn't do that," Dave said, looking hurt.

"I know, I know," said Max comfortingly as he came around the counter. "But I've got to say it just so as it's said."

Dave sniffed. "I s'pose." He straightened up a little. "And I s'pose there's nothing stopping me going to the pub for a pint or two now. Can't drive home, can I? Josh is going to have to let me sleep in the bar again."

Max shook his head. "That's his look-out, but I wouldn't count on it, not after what happened last time. You can't go around scaring tourists wearing only your pajamas. I nearly had to arrest you for lewd conduct."

Dave laughed and was still laughing as he left the station. Max turned his attention to Tilly, and she snapped off a smart salute before finally letting herself speak.

"You should have arrested him."

"What?" Max asked, looking surprised.

"Dangerous driving is an offense," she said. "That man should have been arrested."

"And what good would that do?" Max asked her, looking amused.

"He'd be punished, fined or imprisoned. He'd learn not to do it again. He'd be in custody, so reparations could be collected for any damage done. And... and it's the law."

Max leaned back on the wooden counter. "It is," he said carefully. "But then Old Dave doesn't have two pennies to rub together and putting him in prison for a few nights would only mean that someone would have to go out and feed his cows and get them milked."

Tilly opened her mouth and then closed it again, not sure what to say.

"There was no real damage. He took a corner too close and knocked over a bit of hedge in Dougie McKeefe's lower field. Nothing that won't grow back. And he wasn't drunk. Dave knows better than that." Max smiled. "This way, Dave gets a bit of a break to think about things and a bit of inconvenience, and he'll be more careful next time."

"Okay," Tilly said slowly. "But... but what about the law?"

Max shrugged. "I've got no evidence. I didn't see a thing and by the time I got up there, the rain had washed away any tire tracks. So on the whole, I think this was the best outcome, short of setting up a major incident and calling out forensics to match the mud of the field to the mud on Old Dave's tractor, don't you?"

Tilly stood, desperately trying to think of an argument to prove that she was right, and coming up with nothing. She knew that she was in the right, of course she was. And yet... and yet she found that she couldn't argue the point.

"And here's me leaving you standing around with a suitcase,"

Max went on cheerfully. "Let's get you a cuppa and then we'll get you over to the house and you can put that thing away and meet the family."

"Meet the family?" she asked, finding her tongue.

"Yes," beamed Max. Tilly was finding it very difficult to think of him as Sergeant Browning. "You'll be staying with us for the time being."

"Right," said Tilly. And she wondered just what exactly she was getting herself into here.

CHAPTER TWO

Sophie glared at her brother over the desk. Not that Gio noticed. He was busy with his head under the bonnet of a Kia, up to his elbows in oil.

It had all started last night.

Sophie had been on the dating apps for as long as she was old enough to dabble. Not that she held out great hopes. But every now and again, someone came along and she was surprised. And Katie had been the biggest surprise of all.

Not only had she lived no more than fifteen minutes away, which was a miracle because honestly, Whitebridge was so small that Sophie had set all the app filters to a hundred-mile radius, but she was nice. And funny. And she wasn't looking for a threesome with her boyfriend, which was what most nice, funny women seemed to be looking for.

So when Katie had finally suggested a date, Sophie, who'd been far too nervous to suggest one herself, had happily agreed. All of which had led to Sophie and Katie sharing a small, rickety table at the pub on the high street last night.

Things had been going quite well. Sophie had managed not to spill anything down her front, nor to say anything ridiculously stupid. To be fair, the chemistry wasn't quite as hot as she'd imagined from the messages they'd shared, but still, there was a prickling of something in the air.

Until Katie had started staring off over Sophie's shoulder

when Sophie was talking. Sophie, who'd been talking about her job as the accountant at the family garage and who was well aware that accounting wasn't particularly scintillating, took the hint.

"And what about you?" she'd asked. "What is it exactly that you do?"

"I'm a horse riding instructor," Katie had said, turning her attention back to Sophie.

Sophie had had a mental image of Katie with her thighs clamped around something that certainly wasn't a horse and had swallowed. "That sounds lovely."

"Mmm," said Katie, but she'd gone back to staring over Sophie's shoulder.

Sophie had cleared her throat and tried again. "Do you own your own horse?"

"Mmm," Katie had said again.

Sophie bit her lip. Something had changed, and she wasn't entirely sure what it was.

The messages that they'd shared had been polite, then flirty, then downright spicy. And to be completely honest, Sophie had held out certain... hopes. Hopes that maybe after a solid five-year dry-spell she might be seeing some action. Not that she expected anything, or would force anything, but all omens had seemed to be pointing in the right direction.

Enough so that she'd had time to think about where they could get some privacy. Certainly not Sophie's place, not when she still slept in her childhood bedroom. But Katie had a car and a flat of her own, so maybe...

"I'm sorry," Katie had said, interrupting Sophie's thoughts.

"Sorry?" Sophie had said, dragging herself back into the moment.

"Yeah, sorry," Katie had said. "But do you know that guy?"

Sophie had turned around and anger had flooded every cell of her body. Gio had been sitting there, two tables away, giving Katie a death stare and clearly enjoying his role as impromptu chaperon.

For a second she'd debated lying, but there didn't seem to be much point. "It's my brother."

"Right," Katie had said, looking slightly relieved but not exactly comfortable.

And when, ten minutes later, Katie had finished up her drink and said that she had to be making tracks, Sophie had known deep down what was happening. But she'd shot her shot, anyway.

"So, how about dinner? Maybe at the weekend?"

Katie had smiled a little sadly and had studiously kept her eyes away from Gio, who was a hulking, brooding shadow in the corner, and had said that it wasn't Sophie, it was definitely her, and she wasn't as in the market for something serious as she might have thought. That it had been a lovely drink and a real eye-opener and she'd definitely message Sophie when she was feeling better about dating and…

And then she was gone.

And now Sophie was glaring at Gio over her desk and wondering just when would be an appropriate time to slam the Kia hood down on his neck.

She'd been so angry last night that she'd stomped straight out of the pub and gone home without a word to Gio. Gio, on the other hand, had been whistling over breakfast while Sophie had been hatching a plot to poison his eggs.

"Soph, go and grab us a sandwich."

She looked over to her father's legs, sticking out from under a Ford. "Make Gio go."

Her father slid out and narrowed his eyes at her. "Don't start with that attitude. We're a family. Gio's working on that Kia. You can go and pick up lunch. Get sandwiches from the pub."

"Make mine ham and cheese," Gio said without looking at her.

"I thought you were supposed to be clearing out the storage shed out back," she said, fully aware of the fact that Gio was dreading the job and that her father had been on at him to do it for months now.

"It's already done," her father said. "Now, some sandwiches."

She thought about questioning that. It wasn't fair that Gio hadn't done what he was supposed to and her father had just gone ahead and done it. But that was the way of things. Gio got away with far more than she ever did. She sighed. Maybe she was better off getting some fresh air, she thought, as she pulled on her jacket and made her way out onto the street.

It was because she was a girl. A woman now, not that her father and brother had noticed. Still, with her mum so long gone, she supposed that neither of them had much experience living with a woman. Sophie walked miserably to the pub. Not that she was about to get much more experience living with a woman with her brother watching over her shoulder all the time.

"What can I get you?" asked Jules the barmaid cheerfully when Sophie walked into the pub.

"An axe to dismember my brother?" suggested Sophie.

Jules laughed. "Yeah, can't say I didn't notice. Was that her last night? The one you've been talking to online?"

"Katie," Sophie said. "And yes. Not that we'll be talking again. She's blocked me now, thanks to that great idiot."

"He's just looking after you," said Jules, wiping her hands on a bar towel. "He's protective. Your dad too. But you should hear what they're like when you're not around, dead proud of you, they are. Your dad tells anyone that'll listen that you went to college. He thinks the world of you."

Sophie smiled. "Does he really?"

"Oh, they both adore you, Soph, you know that."

"I know." She sighed and climbed up onto a bar stool. "I know they do. It's just... How can I have a life with the two of them looking over my shoulder all the time?"

"Maybe you need to set some boundaries," Jules suggested. "Talk to the two of them. You're an adult, Soph, not a little kid." She started stacking pint glasses. "It's that or move out."

Sophie thought about that for a second, then shook her head. "I don't think so. They need me. You should see the state of the place if I'm not around to take care of the house. When I was at college, they survived on takeout and cans of beer."

"You're not their housekeeper."

"I know, I know." She sighed again. She wasn't. But she also knew that her dad needed looking after. He'd not so much as looked at another woman since his wife had died, and that was so long ago that Sophie didn't even have a clear memory of her mother's face.

"Don't look so glum," Jules said. "Something'll show up. It always does. You'll be in here moaning about having no girlfriend one day, and talking about getting married the next. That's the way it always happens. When you least expect it."

Given that Sophie was almost out of hope and expecting nothing, she assumed a host of eligible, attractive lesbians would be walking into the pub at any moment. "It's a small town," she said instead.

"And you're being pessimistic, which is drastically unlike you. Pick yourself up, cheer up, and tell me what you want for lunch."

"Fine, an egg salad sandwich for dad, and two ham and cheeses for me and Gio." Jules was right, she wasn't going to get anywhere with a face like a wet weekend.

"There's only one ham and cheese left," Jules said. She grinned at Sophie, then unwrapped the sandwich and popped it onto a plate. "Go on, petty revenge is the best kind. Eat it here and I'll get another egg salad for Gio."

Sophie munched on her sandwich as Jules put the others into a bag. "Any news?"

"There's always news," said Jules. "Old Dave is having his license taken away for driving into that hedge. Oh, and speaking of McKeefe, he's had his car stolen. That's the third around these parts this month. You should tell your dad to make sure the ones he leaves outside are alarmed."

"Will do," Sophie said, swallowing a mouthful of sandwich. "Billy alright?" Billy was Jules's wife, a talented musician as well as a music teacher at the local school.

Jules rolled her eyes. "She's got a new project."

"Oh yeah?" asked Sophie, brightening up. She liked Billy, and the woman had interesting ideas, if not always successful ones. Her last plan had been to start a Whitebridge orchestra, which was all very well and good until it turned out that the only musicians in town were Billy herself, Ag, the local policeman's daughter, and Old Dave who played the spoons and couldn't count higher than four once he'd had a drink.

"Yeah, another one of her village projects," Jules said, sliding the bag of sandwiches over to Sophie.

"I don't think anyone's learned to play anything since the last orchestra attempt," Sophie said. "At least not anything useful, like a cello or a trumpet."

"No, this time there's no instruments required." Jules leaned on the bar. "This time it's a village choir."

"Huh," said Sophie. "Well, maybe that's a better idea. Definitely easier on the ears, I'd think."

"Mmm, I'm not so sure." A customer appeared at the other side of the bar. "I'd better be off. I've put the sandwiches on your tab." Jules stood up. "And don't forget, boundaries."

"Right, boundaries," Sophie said.

It was all very well giving advice, she thought as she finished her sandwich. But she didn't see her family going for it. Still, there was no harm in trying. She'd give them a talking to tonight. After all, it wasn't like she had a date or anything.

CHAPTER THREE

"Have you got a boyfriend? Or a girlfriend? Or both?" The girl looked at Tilly with her head tilted and a curious face.

"Ag, we don't ask questions like that," said a woman with blue hair, presumably the child's mother and Max's wife.

"Why not?" asked Ag. "I want to know, and it must be better to ask someone than it would be to talk behind their back. Right?" She directed the last question to Tilly, who was already feeling very out of her depth.

"Maybe," Tilly said carefully.

"See, I told you," Ag crowed to her mother. "So, which is it? I don't mind, if that's what you're worried about. My mum's married to my dad. But my auntie Ant is married to my auntie Ad, and my teacher Mrs. Brooke is married to Jules at the pub, so really, it doesn't matter. I think that when I grow up, I won't have a boyfriend or a girlfriend, though." She leaned in conspiratorially and whispered, "I'll have a piano."

"I see," said Tilly, suddenly feeling like she was very unqualified to have this conversation.

"I'm sorry," said the blue-haired woman. "I'm Mila, Max's wife, and this is Agatha. She's nine and precocious."

"Am not," Agatha said.

Mila ignored her and smiled at Tilly. "And you must be Tilly. We're glad to have you." Just as she was saying this, a small boy came rocketing into the kitchen.

"Mum, mum, mum, mum!"

"What, what, what, what?"

He stopped and then looked at Tilly. "You're very pretty."

"Um, thank you?" hazarded Tilly.

"You're welcome," he beamed. He turned to his mother. "Mum, I finished my lunch and I'm ready to go."

"And this is Dash, Dashiell technically," said Mila.

"But I can't spell that," put in the boy.

"Right." Mila pulled a face at Tilly. "They should both be in school, but we had the dentist this morning. I'm just about to take them back. Where's Max?"

"Right here," Max said, coming into the kitchen. "Sorry, I just caught Dave outside. Have we all met?"

"Yes," said Dash. "She's pretty."

"I think that might be verging on sexual harassment," Mila said. "These two need to be back at school."

"I'll take them," said Max. "You show Tilly where to put her things." He turned to Tilly and winked. "I'll be back in a jiffy."

A tornado-like moment later and Tilly was left alone with Mila who sighed and smiled. "They're a lot," Mila said. "But they're good kids, really. And I promise you won't have to see them all the time. Come on, let me show you where you're staying."

Tilly, who was starting to get slightly concerned, followed Mila through the house. This was all starting to look far too much like some kind of school exchange trip.

"Here," Mila said, opening up a door onto a small stairway. "There's a small apartment here. You've got your own little kitchen and a bathroom as well. This door locks, so you'll have your privacy, and there's a door out back to the garden, so you won't even have to come through the house if you don't want to."

Tilly lightened with relief. So she wasn't actually going to be staying with her boss's family. "Thank you," she said.

"Not at all," said Mila, starting up the stairs. "I'm sorry that you can't be a bit more independent, but there just aren't that many flats in Whitebridge. Property prices are getting quite impossible. But at least this way you'll have a roof over your head."

"It's very kind," Tilly said, lugging her suitcase behind her.

"And you don't have to come through the house," Mila said again. "But we're rather hoping you might. You're welcome for dinner any time you like, and just pop down if you need something. It's really no trouble."

She opened up another door into a small but light room with a bed in one corner, a kitchen in another, a small couch, and a very large bookcase.

"That's a lot of books," said Tilly.

Mila grinned. "I'm half-owner of the bookshop on the high street, the Queens of Crime? It's a crime only bookshop, you should pop in sometime and see if there's anything you like. Max always complains that the books aren't realistic enough. Too much murder and too little paperwork, he says."

Tilly stood her suitcase by the door. "Is there a lot of crime in the area?" she asked.

Mila sighed. "More and more, I'm afraid. We're a lovely little village, and I'm sure you'll find that everyone here is really nice. But we're not immune to the world. We have our issues just like anywhere else." She gave Tilly a shrewd look. "Worried you won't have enough to do?"

Tilly found that she quite liked Mila. She gave a guilty grin. "Maybe a bit concerned."

"Don't be," said Mila. "I've been married to Max long enough to know that there's plenty to be done here."

Tilly sort of wanted to ask what kind of policeman Max was. From what she'd seen so far, she wasn't exactly impressed. The law was the law, as far as she was concerned, and no police officer should be able to flex that law to please his own needs.

Not that she thought Max was corrupt or anything. But maybe policing here in a small community, he'd become a little lazy, a little out of touch with modern methods. She brightened up at this. She could be the one to teach him better, to show him better, she thought.

"Mil, Officer Ware!"

"That'll be Max now," Mila said. "The school's only just down the road." She turned to Tilly and grinned. "Ready for your first day of work?"

Tilly grinned right back. "I was born ready."

Mila laughed. "Get to it then, girl. I'll have dinner ready when you get home if you can deal with my hellion children for an hour or so. Nothing fancy, but it'll be a hot meal."

Tilly found herself nodding. She might not be terribly comfortable with the whole family meal idea, but she definitely saw the advantages in a solid home-cooked dinner.

"AFTERNOON, SYLV," MAX said, waving at a rotund woman outside the shop.

"Afternoon, Max. And who's this then?"

"New constable," Max said. "Constable Ware, meet Sylv, shop owner, rabble rouser, and all around hardened criminal."

The jolly looking woman laughed. "Don't listen to him," she said, shaking Tilly's hand. "But I do run the shop. Just you come in if there's anything you need." A customer rapped on the counter inside. "Best be off," she said.

They were just walking away from the shop when a harried-looking woman with a long ponytail rushed out of the post office, almost colliding with them.

"Jesus, sorry, Max."

"Not a problem." Max smiled. "Hope, this is Constable Ware, new in town. And Constable Ware, this is Hope. She's the secretary over at the school, which makes her by far the most important person in the entire building."

Hope laughed. "Have at you," she said, but she was blushing. "Pleased to meet you," she said politely to Tilly. "And I've got to be off. Ava's doing painting with the lower infants and there'll be blue walls if I'm not there to help keep an eye on things."

"Do you know everyone in town?" Tilly asked as they moved

on down the street.

"More or less," Max said comfortably. "I came here fifteen years ago now. Settled down, got married, couldn't think of leaving."

Tilly scratched her nose and then cleared her throat. She'd always been taught that asking questions was a good thing, but she wasn't sure how Max might feel about that.

"Something on your mind?" asked Max.

"Just... Well, isn't it a bit difficult to be the long arm of the law when all these people are your friends?" Tilly asked.

Max stopped in the middle of the pavement in thought. "I don't think so," he said finally. "I mean, first of all, most of Whitebridge aren't exactly criminals. Secondly, if I didn't make friends here, I wouldn't have any friends at all. And thirdly, well, I'd like to think that if the worst happened, then I'd do the right thing. I might be a more caring officer than others might like. It might sadden me to arrest someone I know and love. But if Sylv ends up murdering her lodger, I'll be the one to clamp the handcuffs on."

Tilly wasn't so sure about this, but she nodded. "Okay, makes sense."

"Policing a small community is different from policing in a city," Max said as they walked. "You'll see. It's more... flexible, perhaps, and there's more community care involved. But it's rewarding in its own way, even if it isn't all chasing bank robbers down."

"Right." Tilly's stomach tightened a little. It just sounded like a lot of paperwork and not much else. Maybe a walk every lunchtime to say hello to people. Hardly high-profile policing.

They turned a corner and were suddenly engulfed in a wave of children.

"Afternoon, Max," said a tall, bearded man.

"Ah, this is Frank Meyer, teacher of the upper Juniors, the oldest kids at the school," Max said. "And Frank, this is Tilly Ware."

"Nice to meet you. We're just off to the playing fields for a game of football," Frank said.

"I'm going to be goalie," piped up a familiar voice. Tilly looked down to see Agatha Browning bouncing up and down in shorts and a striped t-shirt. "And guess what, dad?" she said, still bouncing. "Ms. Brooke is starting a choir and I can't even join in it, even if I'm the best at music in the whole school." She looked annoyed.

Frank Meyer raised an eyebrow. "That would be the contentious point of the day," he said more quietly. "Sorry, I don't know where she heard it, but she's not happy. I'm sure that you and Mila are going to have to put up with a lot of complaining tonight."

"Is it true?" asked Max.

Frank nodded. "Billy Brooke is starting a village choir. There's a notice on the board outside the school. First rehearsal's tomorrow night at the village hall. Should be fun. Are you up for it?"

"Not me," Max laughed. "I only sing in the bath."

"And he's terrible," put in Ag.

"What about you, Constable Ware?" Frank asked.

For a second, Tilly thought about it. She did like music, she'd sung in the police choir in training college. And... and this was community policing. If that was what she was here to learn about, then that's what she was going to do. What better way to become a part of the community? If Max was right, this was how she was supposed to be doing this job.

"Yes," she said. "Yes, I think that sounds like fun."

CHAPTER FOUR

Sophie put plates down on the table.
"Thanks, love," said her dad. "You finish this month's invoices?"

"Yes," she said, taking a seat beside her dad and opposite her brother. "But something isn't adding up."

"What's that then?" asked her dad, digging into his beans on toast.

"If I knew that, it wouldn't be a problem," Sophie said. "It looks like there's more money coming in than invoices going out, which doesn't make sense, I'll have a look at it again tomorrow."

"Doesn't sound like a bad thing, that," Gio said. "Better than invoices going out and no money coming in."

"Yeah, it all needs to add up though," said Sophie picking up her fork.

Once, she'd wanted to do something else. She'd seen herself wearing a smart suit, maybe some heels, wearing her long dark hair up in a bun. Maybe even being daring and cool like those women she saw on TV. Sort of like in *Industry*, but with less sex and more accounting. Not no sex, just not every night. A girl needed her beauty sleep after all.

And then… Well, then she'd graduated and come home and just sort of not left again.

College had been fun, or fun enough. She'd worked hard, made some friends, lost her virginity, ticked all the little boxes that students were supposed to tick. It was after college that had proven to be the issue.

It wasn't so much that she thought her dad and brother would fade away without her. It was more that they needed her. She could see that. Could see that their lives were better with her in them. For the most part, she didn't resent that. Not really. It wasn't like she'd been flooded with offers from fancy companies in the city or anything.

Wearing her jeans and Adidas to a dirty garage every day wasn't quite the dream, though. Nor was picking through oil-stained receipts and booking appointments for tire rotations.

"Have a look and see that things add up," her dad was saying.

"Yeah, I will," she said.

She sniffed and then put her fork down.

Alright, so she wasn't exactly living the dream. But her life was good. She had friends; she had a job; she was paid a fair wage. Jules was right, though. If she wanted to be independent, she needed to lay down a few ground rules.

"There's something I want to talk about."

"What's that, love?" asked her dad, busy forking beans onto bread. "If it's a raise, you'll have to wait until the new year."

"Why should she get a raise and not me?" Gio complained.

Their father glared at him. "Did I say you wouldn't?" he said. "If business keeps going well, then the two of you will get a raise come the new year. But I'm not promising anything right now."

"Sweet, thanks dad," said Gio.

"I don't want to talk about raises," said Sophie.

"The last time you said you wanted to talk about something, you got all pale and sick looking," Gio said.

"Because I was about to tell two macho men that I was gay," Sophie said. "So, pretty understandable, don't you think?"

Gio snorted. "As if we'd care. You can love who you like as long as you're happy, end of story." He narrowed his eyes and looked at her. "Anyone been giving you gip about it? Want me to give anyone a seeing to?"

Sophie sighed. This was part of the problem. Laying down

boundaries was all very well, but it involved actually being listened to. More than that, she knew that Gio was deadly serious in everything he'd just said. He might be a lumbering idiot at times, but he adored her and would defend her to the death.

"No punching," she said. She took a deep breath. "But I would like a bit more independence."

Her dad looked at her. "How do you mean?"

"I mean..."

"You want to move out?" Gio asked. "But then you wouldn't be able to save any money."

"And you wouldn't have dinner on the table every night," Sophie said.

"Will you listen to the girl?" said their dad.

"Woman," Sophie corrected. "I'm a woman, not a girl. And I'd like to go on dates unmolested."

Her dad turned his attention to Gio. "What did you do?"

"Nothing," Gio protested. "I was just having a drink at the pub. It's not my fault she was on a date there."

Her father turned back to her. "See? Coincidence, that's all."

"Right," said Sophie. It wasn't like she could argue with that. She cleared her throat again. "Alright, I don't want the two of you poking your noses into my dating life."

"We don't," started Gio.

"And," Sophie said, glaring at him. "And I don't want to cook dinner every night."

Her dad nodded. "Alright then. Gio, you cook twice a week."

Gio frowned. "But—"

"No buts. Soph's right. She shouldn't be doing all the work. You cook twice a week." He looked at Sophie. "As for dating, well, there's no promises there. You're a young woman and the world isn't always safe. I won't apologize for making sure that you're not in any trouble."

"At the local pub?" Sophie asked.

"Wherever you are," said her dad with finality. "You might be a woman, but you're also my girl and I'd never forgive myself if something happened to you. Gio too. We're just looking out for you."

"Right," Gio said.

Sophie shook her head and picked her fork up again. There was no point in this conversation, nothing was going to change.

"IT'S ALRIGHT FOR you," she said to Jules an hour later, perched on a bar stool with a coke in front of her. "You're all moved out and everything."

"Whatever makes you think that grandpa Jim was any better than your dad?" Jules asked. She and her sister had grown up with their grandfather, a formidable and slightly dodgy man who now resided in the Whitebridge Residential Center, which was a posh way of saying an old folk's home.

"What did you and Amelia do about it, then?" asked Sophie.

Jules shrugged. "We got about. Grand-dad doesn't have eyes in the back of his head."

"And he doesn't have a minion to do his bidding," Sophie said.

Jules laughed. "Gio looks nothing like a minion. Besides, he's not here now, is he?"

"He doesn't need to be," said Sophie. She nodded toward a pair of men in the corner. "Stu and Del are there. If I do anything, word'll get back to Gio soon enough."

"Well, you are sitting in a public place," said Jules.

"Who's sitting in a public place?" Amelia, Jules's older sister, appeared. "And I'll have a half, please."

"I am," Sophie said.

"And what's so wrong with that?" asked Amelia. Sophie sighed and explained her woes to Amelia, who laughed. "You're just not doing things right," she said.

"What's that supposed to mean?"

Amelia looked at Jules and winked. "Remember the youth club?" she asked.

"What youth club?" asked Sophie.

"Exactly," said Amelia. "Whenever grand-dad Jim used to ask where we were off out to, we told him the youth club. He was always dead satisfied with that. Thought it was good for us to socialize, didn't he, Jules?"

"He did," agreed Jules.

"But... we never had a youth club, did we?" Sophie said.

"Depends on how you look at things," said Amelia. "I mean, technically, maybe not. But what's a youth club? A group of young people getting together to socialize, right?"

"In other words, the two of you going out with your friends," Sophie said, finally cottoning on.

"It wasn't exactly lying," said Jules.

"Plus, it was one place where he definitely wasn't going to follow us," said Amelia. "I mean, me and Cass went to the cinema once and half-way through the film I heard crunching and turned around to see grand-dad Jim sitting there trying to get popcorn out of his false teeth."

"I think what Am's saying is that if you want a bit more privacy, maybe you should be planning things in places where your dad and brother aren't going to be watching you," said Jules.

"Don't forget all of Gio's friends in that equation," Sophie said. She took a drink of her coke. "Dunno. Short of having a gynecologist appointment once a week, I can't think of anywhere that they won't be to keep an eye on me."

Jules frowned for a minute and then beamed, throwing her bar towel over her shoulder. "Can you not?" she asked.

"I just said I couldn't," said Sophie.

"Me neither," said Amelia, accepting her beer from Jules.

"Seriously? Do neither of you listen to a word I say?" grumbled Jules. "Do you not go on the Whitebridge website? Read the ads on the board outside the school? Honestly, how do either of you ever know what's going on around here?"

"Dunno," said Amelia cheerfully. "Cass usually tells me anything I need to know. Cheers for the beer, Jules. Catch you later, Soph." She went back to the table she was sharing with her best friend and business partner, Cass.

"Well then?" Jules asked Sophie.

And Sophie had a sudden flash of memory. "Right, you were just telling me at lunchtime about Billy. But... a choir? Really?"

"Think about it," said Jules, leaning on the bar. "Your brother and his friends aren't likely to join, are they? It's a safe place, so no one's going to worry about you being there. And if some nights you don't quite end up at rehearsal and end up, say, on a date or something, no one will suspect a thing, will they?"

"But... don't you have to be able to sing?" asked Sophie.

"Everyone can sing," Jules said with authority. "Billy was telling me that just this morning. She says that no one thinks they can, but everyone carries a beautiful instrument with them every day. Or something like that."

"Yeah, I'm not convinced."

"So?" asked Jules. "If you don't like singing, just mouth the words, it'll be alright. And I'll be there. There'll be loads of people, I'm sure." She winked at Sophie. "No brothers, but there might be the odd attractive woman, you never know."

"In a Whitebridge choir?" scoffed Sophie.

"Oy, there's plenty of attractive women in town."

"Yeah, and they're all taken," said Sophie.

Jules rolled her eyes. "Listen, are you coming tomorrow or not?"

Sophie sighed and glanced over to where Stu and Del were guffawing at something on one of their phones. "Yeah," she said. "Yeah, I'll be there."

CHAPTER FIVE

The windows of the little village hall were all aglow in the dark evening. Tilly wrapped her denim jacket a bit more tightly around herself. She knew where she was going, Mila had provided directions after laughing when Tilly suggested she might like to come.

"I've got enough music in my life without having to practice singing," she'd said, over the sound of Ag's piano playing from the next room. "You have fun though, and tell Billy I say hi."

It was the very beginning of autumn and the air had a distinct chill to it tonight. And Tilly had spent the day giving herself a stern talking to. Community policing was important. It might not be glamorous, but it was a large part of the job outside of the city, and she was going to be just as good at it as she was at everything else.

She excelled at taking exams, at knowing rules and regulations, at the nuts and bolts of being a police officer. And she was starting to have a sneaky feeling that her father had had her sent here to learn the more human side of policing.

Which was exactly what she was going to do. And that did not mean being a walk-over like Max was. She had no intention of doing anything other than sticking to the letter of the law. She was here to show Max how things should be done. Which definitely did not involve putting people's driving licenses in brown envelopes and confiscating them until they'd had time to think about how naughty they'd been.

She tromped toward the open doors of the village hall.

Plus, she wasn't going to be caught off guard. Every town had its secrets, and she was going to uncover Whitebridge's. Every place had its seamy side, and she was going to find Whitebridge's. She might be learning community policing, but she was going to find some juicy crime, whether that was an embezzling shop clerk or a teacher with a sordid past.

"Hello there."

She turned around to see a tall woman with red-blond hair and glasses smiling widely at her. "Um, hello?"

"You must be the new police officer. Pleased to meet you." The voice was distinctly American. That was more like it. An escaped gangster, perhaps. "My name's Ava. I'm a teacher over at the school. Welcome to town. You heading to the choir?"

Tilly nodded. "A teacher? An American?"

"They do let us leave the country occasionally," Ava said, looping her arm through Tilly's. "Besides, I'm married to an Englishwoman, so that helps. How are you liking things here so far?"

"It's fine," Tilly said as they walked toward the village hall. She wasn't used to this, wasn't used to people just talking to her, touching her, being nice to her. It made her slightly suspicious.

"Oh, you'll love it here, everyone does," Ava said as they walked in.

Which sounded almost threatening. The sort of thing people said in horror movies about small towns that sucked you in and turned you into a zombie or something.

"Are you alright?" Ava asked, looking at Tilly with concern.

"Yes, yes, fine." Stop thinking about zombies, she told herself.

"Good," Ava grinned. "Then let's start the introductions."

"Introductions?" Tilly realized that they were in the warmth of the village hall and began to take her jacket off. She looked around and saw stacks of chairs, a small stage, an upright piano, and a group of people.

"It's overwhelming at first, but you'll get used to it quickly,"

Ava said. "That's my wife over there, Hope." She waved at a woman with a ponytail that Tilly recognized. "And there's Sylv from the shop. Oh, and that's Billy over there by the piano."

Tilly looked over and felt her stomach do a flip. Billy was tall and curvaceous with long, dark wavy hair and intense dark eyes. She was undeniably attractive, even if she wasn't quite Tilly's type.

"Billy's married," Ava said, as though she was reading Tilly's mind.

"I know," said Tilly. "Ag told me."

"Ah, so you've met our prodigy," Ava said with a chuckle. "She's quite something, isn't she? What's the most inappropriate question she's asked so far?"

Tilly rolled her eyes. "This morning over breakfast she asked me if I've ever killed a man."

"And have you?" Ava asked.

"Not yet," Tilly said, finally starting to smile.

"She once asked me if I'd ever thought about eating human flesh," Ava said. "She's quite the handful. Mind you, my daughter Alice was just as bad at her age, if not worse."

"I'm not really sure that children are my thing," Tilly confessed.

"Neither was I." Ava laughed. "And now look at me. And look who we have here, who'd have thought that singing was so popular."

Tilly turned to see who had just walked in and collided with someone so hard that for a second, she saw stars. A book fell to the floor. She automatically bent to pick it up at the same time as the person she'd bumped into did, and their hands brushed, and for a second all Tilly could do was look at the pale, soft hands next to hers.

Then she looked up and her heart tumbled in her chest and her mouth went dry and deep dark eyes looked into hers and for a moment she couldn't even think.

✼ ✼ ✼

"I don't know about this," Sophie said.

"Just drink up your pint and let's go," said Jules. "And here, this is the book you wanted."

Sophie took the battered paperback and looked at the cover with glee. It showed a man's hand on a woman's bottom and promised to be a 'rip-roaring rude bonkbuster.' "You know, I can't help myself when it comes to these. I can't get enough of them."

"I know what you mean," said Jules with a grin. "I'm the same. They're quite addictive, aren't they?"

"At least it'll give me something to look forward to tonight."

Jules disappeared for a second, then came back around the bar carrying her jacket. "Stop being such a sad sack."

"What if I can't sing? What if I open my mouth and all that comes out is a frog croak or something?"

"Impossible," Jules said, taking her arm and pulling her off her barstool. "Apart from anything else, I know you did singing in school because we all did. It'll be just like that except we're grownups. It's going to be fun."

"Where are you off to, then?" Both women turned around to see Stu, one half of Stu-and-Del and Gio's friend, leaning on the bar.

"What's it to you?" asked Jules.

"Nothin'," Stu said, looking kind of hurt. "Just keepin' an eye on Soph, that's all."

"Choir," Sophie said primly. "Do you want to come? You're very welcome. Billy Brooke's set it up. It should be a good night out. 'Course, there's no beer, but I should think there'll be hymns and probably some tea in the interval."

Stu had paled more and more as she spoke, and he was now firmly shaking his head. "Nah, I'm right, thanks. You'll be up at the village hall then?"

"Safe and sound," Sophie said with a sigh. "No need to worry."

"Righty-o," Stu said. "I'll get another pint in then." And he turned back to the bar.

"Told you," Jules said as they stepped out into the autumny

evening. "Come to a couple of rehearsals and then you'll have all the excuses you need. Any time you want to go out, you just say you're going to choir and off you pop, no one the wiser. Even if you hate it, you can show up for long enough to make everyone think you're a regular, surely?"

Sophie's heart had lightened a little now that they were outside. This could actually work. "Yeah," she said, feeling better. "Yeah, I can do that. I'm pretty sure I'm going to be terrible, though. So I'm just going to stand at the back and flap my mouth open and closed until it's time for tea."

"Whatever you need to do," Jules said, turning up the path to the village hall. "Come on, we're going to be late."

They hurried inside and Sophie was tugging off her jacket with one hand and holding her book with the other when someone turned and smashed right into her. "Ow," she said indignantly, dropping her book.

She bent to pick it up and her hands touched warm, long fingers. And when she looked up, her erstwhile attacker had bent too. And she was looking into wide blue eyes, at short, curly blonde hair, at a sharp chin and a determined nose, and her heart was suddenly beating very, very fast indeed.

"I'm Tilly," said the generous mouth, and her cheeks were flushing red. "I'm a police officer."

"I'm Sophie," said Sophie. "And, um, I'm not?"

CHAPTER SIX

"You're not what?" Tilly asked, confused.

"Not a police officer," Sophie said.

"Well, I know that. I mean, I should know that. I'd have seen you at the police station if you were a police officer, wouldn't I?"

"I suppose," Sophie said. "I'm an accountant, by the way."

Tilly was watching the way Sophie's mouth moved, was looking at the soft curves of her eyebrows, was practically drinking the woman in. "Oh?" was all she could manage to say.

"Not very sexy, I know."

Tilly swallowed. "Oh, I don't know," she said. "That show *Industry* makes it look quite sexy."

"They're traders and, uh, financial advisors and stuff," Sophie said, her hands still on the book, still touching Tilly's.

Tilly looked down again to where their fingers met and suddenly saw the cover of the book she was touching. "Oh," she said again. "Oh." She pulled her hand back and looked up. Sophie was smiling and Tilly's heart started to beat funny.

"I know, I know. But don't knock it until you've tried it," Sophie said. "They're really very good. In fact, if you want, I can pass it along when I've finished reading it. There's a lot of sex in it, but it's quite well done."

Before Tilly could answer, she was rescued by Billy clapping her hands. "Alright people," she said. "I want you all around the piano. Come on, no need to be shy."

Tilly found that she was sticking close to Sophie, like she didn't want to be pried away. They joined the group around the piano.

"Quick chorus of This Little Light of Mine," Billy said bossily. "You all know the words, I'm sure. Let's really belt it out. Come on." She hit the piano keys, and they were off.

The song was so familiar that Tilly didn't have to think about the words or the tune. Instead, she could focus on the creature standing next to her. Now that they were upright, she could see that Sophie was exactly her height. She could also smell something, a sort of perfume mixed with car oil. It wasn't an unpleasant smell.

In fact, now that Tilly thought about it, she didn't think there was anything unpleasant about Sophie. She was smiley and nice and... And why had this never happened before?

Okay, so she might not exactly read the sort of books that Sophie was obviously into, but Tilly had read some books. And she'd seen films, watched TV, had a few unfortunate fumblings in the dark until she figured out what she wanted, and had henceforth not dated a single person seriously.

Well, she had a job to do and training to finish and a hundred other excuses that stopped her revealing too much of herself or making herself in any way vulnerable.

All of that came together to mean that she knew exactly what was happening here. And the thought of it made her smile a little as she sang, made her heart lighten, made the shabby little village hall seem larger and brighter and shinier.

And when she caught Sophie's eye and Sophie smiled at her, Tilly felt a swelling, bursting feeling inside that could only mean one thing. She liked Sophie. As in *liked* liked. Like, really liked. Which just made her smile more.

"Alright, not too bad," Billy said, bringing the song to an end. "But I think we're capable of a bit more than that, don't you? Let's have a go at Onward Christian Soldiers. Nice and loud, not shouting, but as loud as you can, really give it some oomph." She crashed a chord on the piano and they were off again.

Halfway through the first verse, Tilly noticed something strange. She frowned and leaned in toward Sophie, listening intently.

"You're not singing," she accused as they reached the chorus.

"I can't," hissed Sophie.

"Ridiculous, of course you can."

"How would you know?" Sophie asked, turning those dark eyes on Tilly and making Tilly's tummy feel funny.

"Everyone can sing. And if you can't or don't want to, then why are you here?"

"Long story," muttered Sophie.

"Just sing, give it a go," Tilly pushed.

Sophie rolled her eyes, but as the second verse began she opened her mouth a little wider and then she was singing and Tilly felt like she'd achieved something, but she wasn't sure what.

"Not bad," said Billy as the second song came to an end. She sniffed and stood back so she could survey the group. "Right, if we're going to do this, we're going to do it properly. I need four groups, sopranos, altos, tenors, and basses. Separate up."

Nobody moved. Billy clicked her tongue impatiently and Tilly tried not to giggle. It was pretty obvious that not a single person in the room knew what they were doing.

Finally, Billy took pity on them. "Alright, I'm going to play two notes on the piano. If they're easy enough for you to sing without straining, then come and stand on my right." She did as she'd said and Tilly sang both notes easily enough. "Come on then," Billy said. "You're my sopranos. Altos next. Sing these two notes. If they're easy for you, come stand in a separate group next to the sopranos."

And Tilly found herself leaving Sophie's side for the first time. Sophie, it turned out, was an alto. Tilly cursed her vocal chords. This wouldn't be it though, couldn't be it, because she'd felt something happening. She was absolutely sure that Sophie had felt it, too.

As Sophie and her group came to stand on the other side of the piano, Tilly looked over and Sophie was watching her. Tilly felt her cheeks get hot, and Sophie grinned and looked away before glancing back.

Yes, definitely something. Tilly wanted to laugh but didn't. This was like being a teenager with a crush, and she was loving it.

Billy started putting them through their paces, handing out sheet music and guiding them through the first two lines of a song. And Tilly had to admit that they weren't bad. Not a professional choir, but decent enough for a group of amateurs.

It probably helped that Billy obviously was a professional. She ran them through their paces until Tilly's back was aching with standing and her throat was starting to feel sore. Only then did Billy stand back and nod.

"You're all alright," she said. "Not bad at all for a first rehearsal." She nodded and surveyed them all. "Which is just as well, because we'll be having a winter concert in just a few weeks."

There was a mumbling at that.

"Well, there's no point in singing if no one's going to hear you, is there?" Billy said. "Next time we're going to work on the rest of this song, start another, and we're going to find a few soloists for the concert, so keep that in mind. Alright, off you go."

Tilly practically pushed her way through the chattering choristers until she was at Sophie's side. Then she found that she was lost for words. She cleared her throat.

"I did sing," Sophie said. "I swear I did. There's no need to arrest me."

"I wasn't planning on it," said Tilly. Why had she been worried? For some reason as soon as they started talking, it was like they'd known each other all their lives, weirdly comfortable. "Are you coming back next week?"

"Next week?" asked Sophie. "Oh, no."

Tilly's heart dropped. "You're not?" She'd have to make a move now, have to ask her out or something, and she really wasn't ready for that at all.

Sophie laughed and her eyes crinkled up in the corner. "The choir is twice a week," she said. "Billy's a real slave driver. Mind you, if she wants a winter concert, then she'll have to be." She tilted her head to one side. "I mean, yes, technically, I suppose I'll be here next week. But I'll also be here on Friday, which is our next rehearsal."

Tilly's breath returned in one big gulp, which then threatened to choke her. She gasped and coughed.

"Are you alright?" Sophie asked.

Tilly nodded, eyes streaming.

Sophie tutted and slapped her on the back until Tilly could get her breath back. "Happens to me all the time," she said, to Tilly's apologies. She looked over her shoulder. "I'm coming," she said to a blonde woman who was hovering near the doors. "Got to go," she said to Tilly.

"Right," Tilly said. "Um, bye then."

"Bye." She turned to leave.

"Don't forget the book," Tilly called after her. She cringed inside.

But Sophie just laughed. "I'll bring it next rehearsal if I'm done with it, but no promises."

And then she was gone and Tilly could breathe normally again.

"She's alright, that Sophie, isn't she?" Sylv from the shop was wrapping a scarf around her neck. "Pretty girl."

"Mmm," Tilly said, still watching the door that Sophie had left through.

"Just watch out for that family of hers," Sylv said, pulling her handbag over her shoulder.

"What do you mean?" Tilly asked, but Sylv was already leaving.

Tilly put her own jacket on and went out into the night. She smiled all the way home.

Mila had made her promise to come in through the front door so that she could know that she was home safe, which seemed like a sensible precaution to Tilly, so she did as she was told.

"Have fun?" Mila asked from the kitchen as Tilly got in.

"Yes," Tilly said. Then she grinned. "Yes, it was really fun, actually."

Mila raised an eyebrow as Tilly got closer. Papers were scattered over the table, but as Tilly came nearer, Mila scooped them all up and tidied them away. Not so fast that Tilly couldn't see they were financial papers, bank statements, that sort of thing. "Want a hot chocolate before bed?" asked Mila.

Tilly hesitated, then shook her head. "No, thanks," she said, backing back out of the kitchen. "It's been a long day. Think I might just… head up."

Another eyebrow lift, a small smile. "No news to report from choir?" asked Mila. "No… muggings or blackmail or… or attractive people?"

For an instant, Tilly considered telling her, but then she shook her head. They didn't know each other that well and the last thing she needed was gossip in a small town. "No, no, nothing like that."

"Right," Mila said as though she didn't believe her in the slightest. "Night then."

"Night," said Tilly.

And she went up to bed, clutching the memory of the touch of Sophie's fingers to herself like a soft cushion.

CHAPTER SEVEN

"You're cheerful for a Wednesday morning," Gio grumbled as he took a seat at the breakfast table.

"There's nothing wrong with facing the world with a smile," his father said.

Sophie stuck a tongue out at him. "I'm in a good mood, that's all."

"Oh yeah? Anything to do with that choir meeting last night?"

"How did you know about that?" she asked.

Gio shrugged. "Stu told me."

"You joined a choir?" her father asked. He grinned at her. "That's nice. Your mum liked to sing."

"Did she?" Sophie said. Her father didn't mention her mother often. When he did, she tried to wring every last drop of information that she could out of him. "What did she like to sing then?"

Her father screwed up his face in thought. "She liked Duran Duran," he said. "And ABBA, and anything Italian. She sang you and Gio to sleep with Italian lullabies, which was all very well until she offed out on a girl's night and I couldn't get the two of you to sleep."

Sophie smiled. "That sounds really sweet." But when she looked over, Gio was bent over his cereal, not saying anything.

It was harder for him. She knew that. He was older. He remembered better than she did. Best to change the subject.

"Better be getting into work," she said. "I've got those invoices to clear up. I'll go through them again this morning."

"I'll do it," her father said.

She stopped chewing her toast. "Sorry?"

"I did used to do all the accounting before you took over," he said. "It might do some good to have a fresh pair of eyes on things. Besides, you've probably got enough to do, don't you? There's a stack of tax forms that need to be posted. You'll need to get some shopping in 'cos there's no biscuits in the garage and we're almost out of milk. Oh, and I need a new prescription for my meds. You can pop into the surgery and get that for me, too."

For a second, Sophie considered this, then she shrugged and nodded. "Fair enough." Like she wasn't eager to go. Like she wasn't thinking about going right this second.

Ordinarily, going back and forth through town and running errands wouldn't have made her particularly happy. Today was different, though. Today she was practically bolting her breakfast in order to go out.

Because the longer she was out and about, the more chance there was that she might bump into Tilly.

Tilly with her blonde curls and long eyelashes, with her crooked smile and her peachy skin. Just the thought of her made Sophie's pulse start to race.

She finished up her breakfast. "I'll be getting on with things then," she said, getting up from the table.

Not that she was about to mention Tilly to anyone at home. Definitely not. It was very early days, but there was something there and she knew it. Something sparkly and lovely, so it was like standing on the bank of a cool lake on a hot summer day.

And if she could somehow run into Tilly without making a fuss about things, and without having to wait for another choir rehearsal, well, that was all for the better, wasn't it?

THE VILLAGE SHOP was quiet at this time in the morning. Sylv was sweeping up by the door when Sophie came in.

"What you looking for, then?" Sylv asked as Sophie craned her neck down the small aisles.

"Nothing," said Sophie. "Just, um, wondering who else might be in, that's all."

"Not a soul in here," Sylv said cheerfully. "Have a good time last night?"

Sophie felt herself blush, then she coughed as she figured out what Sylv was talking about. "Oh, at choir? Yes. It was better than expected, actually, you?"

"I like a good sing," Sylv said, taking the milk that Sophie was holding. "Nice to see so many people come out as well. Especially after the orchestra debacle. And that new policewoman as well."

"Police officer," said Sophie, leaning on the counter. This was her chance. Sylv was the biggest gossip in town. "She seems alright."

"Bit of an 'abide by the letter of the law' type, from what I've heard. Gave Adelaide Park a ticket for parking in front of the bookshop to unload her car."

"Well, Ad does insist on driving those big American SUVs," Sophie said. "Her car does sort of block the street."

"What about her telling Josh at the pub that those tables outside have to be exactly a meter from the curb, then?" asked Sylv.

Sophie sniffed. "I wouldn't know about that," she said. "But, I mean, I suppose the law's the law, isn't it?"

Sylv raised an eyebrow. "You're in that girl's corner, aren't you? Any chance that you'd be sweet on our new policewoman?"

"Police officer," Sophie said. She drew herself upright. "And no, obviously not. I mean, she's police, isn't she?"

Sylv took a look at Sophie, then obviously remembered who she was, who her father and her brother were, and nodded. "Yeah, fair point. Shall I put this on your tab?"

"Please," Sophie said, scooping the shopping into her bag. She left the shop.

Okay, so there was a small hiccup in all of this. Tilly was pretty and funny and in the choir, meaning Gio wouldn't be around to interfere. Sophie liked her, and she was pretty sure that Tilly liked her, too.

But yes, Tilly was a police officer. Not exactly ideal. But then, it wasn't like her dad had told her not to date police officers. Mostly because he'd probably never imagine that she would, but still, it wasn't forbidden.

And it wasn't like her dad and her brother were career criminals or anything. They weren't. Both had had their issues, mostly after a few beers in the pub, but they weren't the Kray Twins. They just... didn't always keep to the letter of the law. The spirit of the law, yes. But Sophie knew that there were always shortcuts and corners that got cut, and that being a hundred percent respectable wasn't really a priority.

Nobody had killed anyone and nobody had got hurt. That was the important thing. But if some rich corporation or whatever lost a few pounds, well, that wasn't so bad, was it? At least it wasn't to her dad and Gio. Sophie herself stayed well out of it. Her books were clean. Which was probably why her dad had insisted on taking over this morning.

She sighed.

This wasn't a deal breaker, she told herself. Her family might not have a fondness for the police, but they hadn't been in trouble for a long time. They were relatively clean now, and it wasn't like she was inviting Tilly over for tea.

She went into the post office, posted her letters, then made her way out and over to the doctor's surgery.

Not that she was inviting Tilly to anything, given that she couldn't find the damn woman. She'd walked all the main streets in town and there was no sign of her. Sophie sighed as she walked up to the surgery. Maybe Tilly was at the station, which was one place she probably shouldn't be seen going into.

"Morning," said Cordelia, the surgery receptionist. "What can I do you for?"

"Just a repeat prescription for dad," said Sophie.

Cordelia typed something into her computer. "Give it a minute. I've sent it through to Lydia. She'll need to sign it. She'll bring it out when she's done. Everything alright with you?"

"Not bad," Sophie said because she wasn't about to admit to being half in love with someone she couldn't find and had only met once for a couple of hours. And most of those hours had been spent singing and not even talking.

Was that it? Was she really half in love with Tilly?

Lust maybe, but love? Was that what those tingly feelings were?

"Can you fall in love at first sight?" she asked Cordelia.

"You're asking the wrong person," Cord said. "I hated Lyd at first sight though, if that's any help?"

"Not really."

"Thinking about falling in love, are you?"

Sophie blew out her cheeks. "Depends. Do I get patient-doctor confidentiality?"

"I'm only the receptionist. You'll have to talk to Lyd for that." Cordelia grinned. "Wouldn't blame you if you are, though. I thought for ages that I was happy alone. Turned out that I was lonely and grumpy and rapidly turning into one of those strange old ladies that has too many cats."

"I don't have any cats," Sophie pointed out.

"Wouldn't do you any harm to get a love interest, though," Cord said. "There's a lot to be said for having someone to cook dinner for you every now and again."

Jesus, she wasn't going that far. She'd barely met the woman. But now that she thought about it, having dinner with Tilly wouldn't be so bad.

"Here you are," Lydia said, coming out of the consulting room. "Oh, it's you Sophie. I thought it was your dad. He really should come and pick up his prescription himself, you know."

"Yeah, you know what the chances are of that happening," Sophie said, pulling a face. "He's only got the thing in the first place because you came out to him when he collapsed."

"How's he doing?"

"Alright, I think," Sophie said. "He's not had any more attacks, and I keep his diet as healthy as I can. He won't eat a salad, though. I end up having to hide vegetables under baked beans and hope he doesn't notice."

"Whatever works," Lydia laughed.

Sophie took her shopping and the prescription and walked back toward the garage. Half way there on the opposite side of the street she passed the police station. She hesitated for a second, then continued on her way.

She liked Tilly. But it all had to be a secret. She wasn't going to let her family ruin another possibility for her. And she could wait until Friday to see her again. She started whistling as she walked the rest of the way.

CHAPTER EIGHT

Tilly bent over and inspected the rear of the bike. "No," she said, straightening up again. "No, I'm afraid you'll have to get a red reflector. It is the law. Did you not do your bicycle proficiency test?"

The boy looked at her with wide eyes. At the beginning, he'd had an attitude. Well, most fourteen-year-olds had attitudes. Now he just looked scared.

"It's alright," said Tilly. "You're not going to prison or anything. Here." She took out her book and scrawled the information on the ticket. "Take this, pay it, and you'll hear no more about it. Just make sure to put a reflector on that back seat post or wheel arch before I see you riding around town again."

"Right, miss. Yes, miss," said the boy. He snatched the ticket and hopped onto his bike before Tilly could stop him.

Tilly shook her head. She hoped the kid would learn a lesson.

She continued walking, keeping her eye out at all times for any sign of crime, but also any sign of Sophie. Every time that she thought about her, she got a warm feeling in her stomach and a smile appeared magically on her face.

Okay, so there was some gray area here. Tilly had stayed awake far later than she should have thinking about it. It wasn't ideal for police officers to have a relationship in the area they patrolled. In fact, as a general rule, officers were posted away from areas that they'd grown up in, just to avoid having anyone's loyalties tested.

But she hadn't grown up here, and, more importantly, she wasn't planning on staying here. This was a few months out of her life before she moved on to bigger and better things. If she happened to meet the love of her life whilst she was here, well, that was alright, wasn't it?

Love of her life. Jesus. Not that she was overthinking things in any way whatsoever. She had the secret smile again. Alright, maybe she was blowing things slightly out of proportion. But she liked Sophie. Liked the look of her, liked her smile, liked the way she smiled, liked how she sounded. There was a lot to like.

Maybe, said the reasonable voice in her head, you'll hate her once you actually talk to her as opposed to singing at her.

Fair point. But she wouldn't know until she tried, would she?

She bit her lip. Friday wasn't that far away. Maybe she should make the first move, ask her for a drink or something?

Her phone vibrated in her pocket, reminding her of the time. She turned on her heel and walked back toward the police station.

Yes, that's what she'd do. She'd make the first move. Ask Sophie for a drink. That way, they could really tell what was what.

She was feeling quite good about herself when she walked into the station.

"Afternoon," she said to Max, who was standing behind the wooden counter.

"Did you just write Jamie Lunsdon a ticket for not having a rear reflector on his bike?" Max asked.

Tilly nodded. "It scared him a bit, but I don't think he'll do it again." She hesitated. "I did tell him he wasn't going to prison, though."

Max sighed. "Tea?"

"If there's some going."

"Right, then you'd better come around here and have a seat. I'll get the tea then you and I need to have a chat," Max said.

Tilly felt her stomach contract. "Have I done something

wrong?"

Max sighed again. "No, no, you really haven't. Maybe that's sort of the problem. Have a seat. Let me get the tea in."

He disappeared back to the small kitchen, and Tilly could hear him making the tea. She didn't like the idea of needing a talking to, but then he said that she'd done nothing wrong, so whatever it was, it couldn't be that bad.

As she was waiting, the station door opened. An elderly woman crept in.

"Can I help you?" Tilly asked.

"They've been in again," said the woman, tearfully.

"Who?" asked Tilly.

"The burglars. They've been in again." The woman sniffed and Tilly came around the counter.

"You've been burgled?"

"Yes," said the woman. "It's the third time today."

Tilly's senses prickled. She put an arm around the woman's shoulders and escorted her to one of the plastic seats. "Well, that won't do at all," she said comfortingly. "But you've come to the right place. Can you tell me where you live?"

"Of course," the old woman said. She fumbled for a purse and brought out her pension book. "Here, it says on there."

"Right," Tilly said, seeing that there was a phone number there. "You just sit here and I'll get you a cup of tea and then I'll look after all of this, alright?"

The woman nodded.

"Tea's already served," Max said, appearing with a cup of tea in his hand.

The woman took it gratefully.

Ten minutes later and the woman's son had arrived to take her home and Tilly was handing back her pension book.

"I'm so sorry about all of this," the son said.

"Don't be," said Tilly. "It's what we're here for. I'm just glad everything's alright." She closed the door behind the two of them and turned back to see Max staring at her thoughtfully. "You wanted to speak to me?"

"Come and sit down. We might actually get to drink our own tea this time." He handed her a mug and settled into his chair. "What you just did there, it was kind," he said. "It was good policing."

"It was nothing," said Tilly.

"No, it was something. Especially for Mrs. Dodds."

Tilly said nothing to this.

Max rubbed his nose. "See, policing, in the end, it's not about catching criminals and the likes. It's not about beating the bad guy. It's about people."

"I understand that," Tilly said. "The code of ethics specifies public service, specifically: 'working in the public interest, fostering public trust and confidence, and taking pride in providing an excellent service to the public.'"

"Right," Max said with yet another sigh. "It's just that, well, you've only been here a little while, but I'm a bit concerned that perhaps quotas and regulations might be getting in the way of the whole people angle a little bit."

"What do you mean?" Tilly asked.

"Like giving young Jamie a ticket for his bike. You could have given him a talking to and sent him off home. He didn't need a ticket. Or ticketing Ad Park's car. She was just unloading a box of books in front of her own building."

"So you're suggesting that I stretch the law to allow people to do things they shouldn't be doing," Tilly said sharply.

"No," said Max. He sounded quite firm about this. "I'm suggesting that perhaps you think about the human angle of things." He rubbed his nose again. "After you've been an officer for a while, you start to realize that the law is a flexible thing, whether you like it or not."

"I don't like it," Tilly said.

"And yet part of being a good officer is knowing when to let things go, knowing when to turn a blind eye, knowing when you'd be doing more harm than good by sticking to the letter of the law."

"I disagree," said Tilly.

Max nodded. "Alright, that's your prerogative. I just wanted to mention it."

Tilly nodded, took a deep breath and remembered that she was speaking to a superior. "Thank you."

"Don't mention it," Max said. "Now, drink up. We've got places to be."

"We do?"

He nodded. "Another stolen car, I'm afraid."

"Another?"

Max put down his coffee cup. "There's been a spate of them recently. This is the fifth one that I know of, though they're not always being reported, I think. Mostly because they're not luxury vehicles."

"What does that mean?"

"It means that the majority of them are just normal cars, five years old or more, nothing fancy. I've rung around the other stations in the area and there's a handful of other cases that could well be connected. We just don't have much to go on."

"Stealing normal cars doesn't seem that profitable," Tilly said.

"You'd think. But they're being stolen for parts, in all probability. There's money in that, money in scrapping them even. And it's easier to steal something old than something new. You keep a close eye on your new Porsche, but you don't on your old Ford."

"True," Tilly said. "And there's really nothing to go on?"

"Nope," Max said. "The thefts are centered around Whitebridge, so I'm thinking that someone in the local area must know something. But so far, we've got zip. I keep hoping for a CCTV camera to catch something, or a fingerprint, anything really. It's a real dead end, though."

"Sounds frustrating."

Max laughed. "You know, when I was a kid, I thought being a policeman would mean car chases and bringing gangsters bang to rights. As it turns out, it's mostly paperwork and finding lost cats. Not that I mind." He grinned at her. "I've got a family to look after now. I'm pretty happy that Whitebridge is so quiet."

"Oh, I wouldn't say it was quiet," Tilly said. She was busy thinking. Car theft? What did she know about car theft? If she was in charge of the investigation, where would she be looking? If she could make a case for herself, maybe Max would let her take charge of this car theft ring business.

"Come on then," Max said. "Best be getting on with things. I'd like you to come up with me, have a fresh pair of eyes on the business. Maybe you'll notice something that I've missed."

Maybe she would, she thought, as she followed him out of the station. Max pulled a big set of keys out of his pocket and locked the front door before leading Tilly to the squad car and tossing the keys to her.

"You want me to drive?" she asked.

"Are you trained?"

"Yes," she said. "But... well, most male officers don't like a female constable driving them, sir. That's all."

"Tosh," Max said. "Get in and drive. It'll give me time to digest my tea. Now, tell me all about this choir. Who showed up?"

"Half the village," Tilly said, starting the engine. "And maybe you should join yourself."

"Oh no," Max said. "I've got far too much going on with..." He trailed off, cleared his throat. "I've got far too much going on at home."

Tilly felt an awkwardness there, so she didn't pursue the subject. Besides, she was driving past the village hall and that reminded her of Sophie and then she was busy smiling her secret smile.

CHAPTER NINE

"If you bolt your tea like that, you're going to get indigestion," Paul Farmer said.

"Dad, I'm not five," said Sophie, stabbing three chips with her fork.

"Then stop eating like it," retorted her father.

"I'm just in a hurry. I've got choir rehearsal." She felt a shuddering down her back when she said this. Nothing to do with the thought of singing.

"Oh, do you indeed?" Her father sniffed and considered a chip. "I might pop by myself one of these days and give the old vocal chords a work-out."

"Dad!" said Sophie in horror. Then he winked, and she saw that he was joking. "Don't tease. Did you get those invoices sorted?"

"Yeah," said her dad. "Gio, what about that Renault? Could you patch the muffler or not?"

A clear change of subject then, which was fine by her. She stabbed another chip, chewed, swallowed, then got up. "Sorry, boys. I've got to get ready. Gio can clear the table, right, dad?"

"Right," said her dad.

Sophie went back upstairs, thinking how quickly she'd reverted to her old ways once she'd come home. It was all very well for her dad to tell her that she wasn't five, but sometimes it seemed like it.

It wasn't healthy for grown adults to live with their parents like this. But then, she didn't exactly have many options. Not many that would still allow her to make sure everyone was okay and work at the garage.

So maybe, the voice in her head said, you should work somewhere else.

Maybe she should. She sighed. Her dad wouldn't be happy. But more money would come in handy and then, one day, maybe she could get a little place of her own. Mind you, with property prices being what they were, it'd be one day about seventy years from now and she might move in just in time to move back out to the old folk's home.

She pulled on some jeans and surveyed her wardrobe. Something nice, but not too nice. She didn't want to look like she was trying too hard. She puffed out her cheeks, pulled out a clean t-shirt and then threw her leather jacket on top. There. Simple, classic, and... what would Tilly be wearing?

She thought about that. Then, to be honest, thought about Tilly not wearing certain things, then there was a shout from downstairs.

"Thought you were going out?" bellowed Gio.

Shit. Right. "Okay, okay, I'm coming."

"Only the bar staff are here chasing after you," he shouted back.

Sophie stuck her phone in her pocket and ran down the stairs to see Jules lounging by the front door. "Didn't know you were picking me up," she said.

"Neither did I, but it was on the way," Jules said, casting a wary eye toward the living room where Gio and Sophie's dad were now ensconced in front of the football.

"Right," said Sophie. "Bye dad, bye Gio, don't wait up."

There were a couple of grunts in response and Sophie could see through to the kitchen where dirty plates still lay on the table. She sighed, but this wasn't her problem right now. She opened the door and she and Jules went out into the night.

"So?" Jules said, when the front door was closed.

"So what?" said Sophie.

Jules clicked her tongue. "Do you really think I didn't notice you making eyes at that policewoman all night? And then you don't even come into the pub to tell me about it? I thought we were friends."

"Oh please, since when have you liked gossip?"

Jules snorted a laugh. "Right, forgot I was Mother Theresa. Go on then, she's nice, is she?"

"You can see that for yourself," said Sophie as they walked toward the village hall. "But I barely know her. I mean, it was like a thing, you know, a movie moment."

"Love at first sight, sort of thing?" asked Jules.

"Yeah. Maybe. Except love seems like a big word for it. Let's call it feelings at first sight, shall we? That sounds a bit less scary."

"Mmm. So, what's the plan, then?"

"What do you mean, what's the plan?" Sophie said. "Like I said, I barely know the woman. But she's going to be there tonight, so..."

"So? You're going to stare at her across a crowded room until she gets magically hypnotized and falls in love with you?" Jules narrowly avoided a puddle. "That sounds like a really solid plan. Very logical. Very realistic."

"No," Sophie said. "I'm going to... to talk to her. And then, well, I don't know." She hadn't actually thought any further than that. She hadn't really dared to. She definitely did want to talk to Tilly. She wasn't sure what about, though.

Actually, to really get down to things, she hadn't thought any further ahead than just physically seeing her.

"You're going to have to be careful if you want to keep Gio and his crew out of things," Jules was saying thoughtfully. "I suppose you could... I don't know, meet her in another town? Or, and here's an idea, you could invite her for a drink at the pub."

"Right, that's a great idea," Sophie said. "Because no one I know ever goes to the pub."

"Let me finish. I was going to say that you could invite her for a drink at the pub after choir and I'll go in first and..."

"And throw out any paying customers that happen to be my brother and/or his friends?"

"Yeah, doesn't sound great now you put it that way," said Jules.

"That's kind of the problem," Sophie said. "But also, you're thinking way too far ahead. Let me just talk to the woman first. It's too early to be planning dates. And even when it's not, definitely no drinking in the pub."

"Careful, you might offend me. It's practically my pub," Jules said, pulling open the heavy door of the village hall.

Sophie was so busy rolling her eyes at Jules that she didn't see Tilly. In fact, she didn't see her until she ran into her.

"Ouch."

"Oh god, I'm so sorry," Sophie said, taking a step back.

But Tilly's blue eyes were sparkling at her and she was smiling and she was, Sophie thought, just as pretty as she remembered. She could see now that there was a smattering of tiny curly hairs along her hair-line, like a child's. It made her smile.

"You know, this is the second time we've met and the second time we've literally run into each other," Tilly said. "Probably better for the future of our relationship that we try and be slightly less clumsy?"

Future of our relationship? Sophie's mouth went dry. All she could do was nod and hope that Tilly didn't think she was too much of an idiot.

"Um, I know it's a bit forward, but I don't like messing around too much," Tilly was saying now.

Sophie looked around, but Jules had made herself scarce and everyone else was gathering around the piano.

"Would you have a drink with me after choir one night?" Tilly said. "Maybe in the pub?"

Sophie took a breath. Right. No pub. No interference. No big brother spoiling things. "No," she said quickly.

But before she could say anything else, Billy Brooke was clapping her hands and shouting over the chatter.

Tilly gave Sophie one look and Sophie couldn't read it. Sad or mad or something in between. Then she left to join the other sopranos.

* * *

"Alright, I want you all to stand in a line. Here, Sylv, you go at the front. Everyone line up behind her," Billy said.

Obediently, the rest of the choir did as they were told. Tilly was close to the front, still thinking about what had just happened.

She'd said no.

Was it possible that she'd completely misread the situation? Possible that Sophie wasn't in the slightest bit interested? Or wasn't even into women?

"It's simple. You're going to come to the front, sing the first two lines of Happy Birthday, then you're done," Billy said.

A lot of people groaned. But Tilly was too distracted to think about it.

She couldn't have been that wrong, surely. But then what other explanation was there? She hadn't asked about a specific night, so it couldn't be a matter of scheduling. The only thing that she could think was that Sophie wasn't interested at all.

Sylv gave a warbling rendition of Happy Birthday, then two more people came and went. Tilly stood next to the piano at her turn and sang without thinking. Too busy concentrating on the fact that she'd been so wrong.

Person after person sang, the words to Happy Birthday starting to sound more and more nonsensical.

It was fine, Tilly told herself. Just fine. Everyone had the right to say no, and she'd never dispute that. If Sophie wasn't interested, that was okay, perfectly alright. It hurt, but she could deal with that. Really, she could.

But when Sophie sang, Tilly couldn't stop herself watching. She was the second to last person to go, and she was clearly nervous. Her voice was clear and soft though, and Tilly didn't think she was biased when she thought that Sophie really could sing quite well.

"Right," Billy said when they were all done. "You, you, you, you, and you." She pointed out a handful of people, including both Sophie and Tilly. "You're my soloists for the winter concert. Here are your lines. Learn them." She began handing out sheets of music to a group of people that looked a lot like deer caught in the headlights.

"Do we have any choice about this?" asked a small, round man.

Billy glared at him. "No. You're a good singer. Get over it."

She stopped when she came to Tilly. "You're good, come here." She took Tilly's wrist and led her over to Sophie. "The two of you are going to duet. You'll fit together well. Here's your music."

She dropped Tilly's wrist and left her standing face to face with Sophie.

A duet? Together? Practice and sing and rehearse with someone who'd just turned her down flat?

"Off you go then," Billy barked. "Disappear off to a cupboard or outside or wherever you like. You've got fifteen minutes to learn those words, then get back in here and join in with the rest."

Tilly looked at Sophie and Sophie looked back. Neither said a word.

CHAPTER TEN

The little entranceway of the village hall was less than warm. It was also less than private. Sophie wished she'd picked up her jacket before she came out, but Tilly had stalked off and she'd followed behind like a lost puppy.

"Can you read music?" Tilly asked.

"No," said Sophie.

Tilly sighed and pinched the bridge of her nose between her fingers. "Alright, give me a second." She pulled out her phone and started messing with it.

Sophie bit her lip, wondering just what to say. The problem was, she'd had no chance to explain herself. The rehearsal had started so quickly, and now that solid 'no' was hanging in the air. It seemed weird to bring it up now, but then, she had to say something, didn't she?

Unless she just left this, like everything else, unfinished and ruined. She took a hiccuping breath and glanced over at Tilly. Her curls fell over her face as she leaned over her phone screen and her profile was so angular, so perfect, that Sophie's heart stilled for a second.

Okay, alright, leaving things was not an option. She liked Tilly, she had already admitted that. There was no hurry though, surely? It wasn't like they were going anywhere. She had time to fix this. Maybe she should just give it a few days, see if Tilly forgot.

"Alright, this is easy," Tilly said, holding up a piano app on her phone. "I'll play your part first." She looked at the music Billy had given them in her other hand.

"Billy said we just had to memorize the words," Sophie said.

Tilly arched an eyebrow at her. "Really? Because if we're going to do something, we should do it well."

"Well, yeah, I guess, but maybe we should just do as we're told?" asked Sophie anxiously.

Tilly breathed out through her nose. "What's the problem?"

"There's no problem."

"I'm a police officer. You think I can't tell when someone's lying?"

"I'm not lying," Sophie said, starting to feel warmer now.

"Sure about that? Because you don't look very comfortable right now."

"Because I forgot to bring my jacket, that's all," said Sophie.

Tilly arched that eyebrow again, and Sophie's pulse pumped a little harder. "Right."

Sophie blew out a breath. She had to deal with this. Well, with the 'not going for a drink' part. The terrifying 'singing in front of someone else' part would have to wait a minute. "Listen, I'm sorry about before. I didn't get a chance to explain myself."

"No explanations necessary," Tilly said sharply.

"Yeah, but—"

"We've got fifteen minutes to learn this," said Tilly. "Are we going to actually learn it, or should we make idiots out of ourselves when we go back in?"

Sophie could feel herself go pale. "She's not going to make us sing it in front of everyone."

Tilly frowned. "Um, that's sort of the point. That's what a solo is."

"Yeah, but..." Sophie found that she was feeling a little bit sick. "But..." she tried again.

"But... you're terrified," said Tilly. The corner of her mouth tweaked up just a little, then the movement disappeared. She cleared her throat. "Nothing to be terrified of."

"There's not?" squeaked Sophie. "Because apparently I'm supposed to go out there in front of pretty much everyone I know and sing a song that I don't know." She didn't add 'with you,' even though she was thinking it.

"With me," Tilly said for her. But she was smiling now. "So you've got nothing to worry about. Well, at least you haven't if you'll actually practice right now."

"Are you sure about that?" Sophie asked.

Tilly rolled her eyes. "I was in the police choir. This is simple stuff. It's a four-line verse of Away in a Manger, it's child's play. There's like, three notes, it's easy. Listen." She played three notes on the piano on her phone screen. "Sing those."

"Sing what?" Sophie said.

Tilly sighed. "Alright, sing this." She played one note.

Sophie's mouth was dry. She opened her mouth and a strange croaking sound came out. She cringed.

"Alright, swallow, take a deep breath and try again," Tilly said.

She did as she was told. This time, the note was somewhat identifiable.

"And the next one," said Tilly.

She sang that.

"Then this one."

She sang that too.

"Right, all you need to do is sing those three notes. Let's try the first line, like this." Tilly demonstrated and Sophie closed her eyes and sang right back at her.

"Good," said Tilly when Sophie opened her eyes again. "But…"

"But what?" The faint relief that she'd felt came crashing down and now her knees were starting to shake.

"It's fine, it's fine," Tilly said quickly. "It's just that you need to sing from your diaphragm. Try again."

Sophie closed her eyes. Diaphragm? What the hell was that? She was fairly sure that Tilly wasn't talking about birth control options, but what did she know? She didn't want to look stupid, so she sang, just like she had before.

"No, no, no," Tilly said.

And before Sophie knew what was happening, Tilly had put her phone down and was walking closer, nearer and nearer, until Sophie could smell clean soap and cinnamon. Sophie took a deep breath in and then Tilly was behind her and she could feel the hairs at the back of her neck start to stand up.

"Alright, breathe out," Tilly said from behind her. "Then breathe in again."

It was definitely warm now. Uncomfortably warm. Sophie could feel her hands starting to sweat and when Tilly's words sent little puffs of air onto the back of her neck, she started to feel more than weak at the knees. She gulped and then breathed.

"Good," said Tilly. Then her hands were on Sophie, one on her back, one on her chest. "Now breathe again, feel the tension when I press."

She did as she was told. Frankly, at this point, Tilly could have told her to surrender her first-born child, and she'd have done it.

"Good, good," Tilly said.

She was even closer now, the words tickling at the skin of Sophie's neck until Sophie was breathing out and in again even though Tilly hadn't told her to. Until Sophie was breathing harder, even.

"That's enough," Tilly said.

Sophie felt the heat between her legs, felt herself start to lean back into Tilly's grasp, until Tilly stepped away and it felt like being unmoored.

"Sing from there," Tilly said. "From that place in your chest. I know it sounds ridiculous, but just do it."

Sharp blue eyes were looking at her and Sophie was so entranced that she didn't even bother closing her eyes this time. She opened her mouth and sang. A smile spread across Tilly's face.

"Better," Tilly said. "Very nice, actually. Here, take a look at the words."

Sophie flushed with color as she took the lyric sheet from Tilly's hands.

"The music itself is simple, look at the dots," Tilly was saying.

"The higher the dot is on the line, the higher the note you sing. There's only three notes, so it's not that difficult. Give it a try. Here, these are your three notes and you start on the top one, the highest." She picked up her phone again.

Frowning down at the paper, Sophie did as she was told and found that it was easy, actually. And that maybe she didn't sound too bad.

"Again," said Tilly. "Listen to your part on the piano for a second." She played it. "Now sing it again."

And Sophie did. Paying less attention to the paper this time and more to the fact that Tilly was nodding along.

"Great," Tilly said when she was done. She sniffed. "That Billy was right. You're a decent singer."

Sophie looked down at her scuffed sneakers. "Thanks."

"I'm only speaking the truth," said Tilly.

Sophie took a deep breath. "Thank you anyway," she said. "And about earlier, I just…"

"It's not a problem," said Tilly. "It's really not. I probably shouldn't have asked."

"It's not that," began Sophie.

From the hall, they heard the sound of Billy blowing a whistle. "Get back in here," she shouted.

Before Sophie could say anything else, Tilly was walking away, back into the hall. With a sigh, she followed. Had she really blown all this so fast? And why was it so impossible to tell what Tilly was thinking?

"Alright, recite your words to me," Billy said when they rejoined the rest of the group. "Let me see you've put the work in."

"Actually, we can sing ours," Tilly said primly.

If she hadn't been busy being terrified, Sophie would have rolled her eyes. She should have guessed that Tilly was the kind of person who reminded the teacher that the class had homework.

"Good-o," Billy said, moving to behind the piano. "Go on then."

Which was when it occurred to Sophie that she wasn't

supposed to sing alone. She was supposed to sing with Tilly, and that the two of them hadn't sung together at all.

"Trust me," breathed Tilly.

Sophie swallowed, bit her lip, then nodded. For some reason she did trust her.

She opened her mouth and the first note came out and then Tilly did the same and suddenly... suddenly this was the easiest thing in the world. Suddenly their voices were twining together, and it was effortless, and Sophie was smiling as she sang. Doing this with Tilly rather than just alone made it so much less terrifying.

"Alright," Billy said when they'd finished. "Not bad." But Sophie knew that Billy didn't offer praise easily, and that she had been just the tiniest bit impressed.

The rest of the practice rolled along until it was late and people were yawning and it was really time to go home. Finally, Billy released them.

Sophie grabbed her jacket and looked around, desperate to find Tilly. Desperate to explain herself, to make Tilly listen to her, to set things right. But Tilly was nowhere to be found.

CHAPTER ELEVEN

Tilly had had a sleepless night. She'd fled from choir practice just as soon as she was able, not wanting to have to face Sophie again. No was no, and she was fully comfortable with that. But she didn't want to have to look at her for longer than she had to.

She could bite her tongue when she thought about touching her. When she thought about how warm and soft Sophie's chest had felt, how her breath had filled her up. Tilly had barely been able to stand up straight. Yeah, she needed to not do that again. There was no point dancing up to the line. The line had been drawn; it was clear; she had to respect it.

The flip side of all of this was that she'd had plenty of time to think about work. So, once she was showered and dressed the next morning, she went down into the main house.

"This is a surprise," Mila said. She was dressed in jeans and a t-shirt that already had an orange juice stain on it.

"You don't mind, do you?" Tilly said, suddenly thinking she might be intruding. "Only you did say…"

"Mind?" Mila laughed. "It's a joy to have someone at the table who can talk about things other than piano playing and Pokemon. Take a seat. I'll get you some coffee. Want some toast?"

"Just cereal is okay."

"Then help yourself," Mila said.

Tilly, who had been hoping to talk to Max, found herself

sitting down at a sticky table opposite Dash and next to Ag. "Good morning," she said politely.

"Would you rather have Kartana or Koraidon?" Dash demanded as she sat down.

"Um, I'd rather have Cocoa Pops if you've got those?" said Tilly.

Ag rolled her eyes. "He's talking about Pokemon. Again." She handed Tilly a yellow cereal box. "Did you do choir last night? What are you singing? Was it good? Isn't Billy lovely?"

"Ms. Brooke," Mila said firmly. "Please don't use her first name without permission. It's rude."

Ag rolled her eyes again. "So?" she asked Tilly.

"Ms. Brooke is very nice, we're singing lots of things, and choir was... very nice, thank you," said Tilly.

"Can I come with you next time?" Ag asked, making her big blue eyes wider and fluttering her lashes. "Please?"

"No kids," Tilly said gravely. Ag's face fell. "But I can get you VIP seats to the concert," added Tilly.

Ag grinned. "That'd be ace, thanks. And if you want, you can come to one of my concerts. I'm going to have a big competition soon."

"Maybe," Mila said.

"Maybe," said Ag, but she didn't look like that was a maybe.

"Really?" asked Tilly, pouring milk over her cereal.

"Yeah, it's really cool and maybe I could win a big grand piano and maybe go to the conservatory school even though mum and dad say that it's better to be on the ground or something."

"It's better to stay grounded," Mila said, putting coffee in front of Tilly. "As in, we need to keep our options open and not spend all day, every day, playing the piano."

"Which sounds awesome," said Ag dreamily.

Tilly glanced at Mila, who looked suddenly tired and a little pale, worried perhaps. Bringing up two such energetic kids must be pretty draining, she thought. The Brownings had been kind to her, they didn't have to put her up in their home. She could have been in one of those horrible business hotel places.

She coughed and dug her spoon into her bowl. "Um, if you

and Max want to go out one night, I could babysit," she said. She looked over at the two kids. "Once these two are in bed, of course," she added, because she wasn't sure she could handle them both awake if she was alone.

"That's very kind," Mila said. "We might take you up on that." She turned to her children. "Come on, I'm going to change this shirt and then we're out of here. Leave the table and get your school things ready. Two minutes, chop-chop."

Mila and Max passed each other as she left and Max came in. He swooped down and kissed both his children before ruffling their hair and sending them out to get their schoolbags. Then he sat down at the table and pulled cereal toward himself. "Sleep alright?" he grinned at Tilly.

"Great," Tilly lied. "I've been thinking."

"Oh yeah?" asked Max, busy getting himself some breakfast. "What about?"

"Stealing cars."

"Um, wouldn't advise it," Max said. "It can be dangerous and you'll probably end up in trouble with the police."

"Ha ha," Tilly said. "No, I was thinking about your stolen car problem. And I think you need to pursue it from the other side."

Max put his spoon down and looked interested. "How do you mean?"

"Well, we're not getting anything from the theft sites," Tilly said. "So perhaps we should look at where the cars might end up. I mean, you don't steal a car to do nothing with it, do you?"

"I could add them to the port watchlists," Max said doubtfully. "I mean, a lot of cars get shipped out to Europe and then sold. But those are luxury vehicles, not the kind of cars that are being stolen around here."

"No, you were right before," said Tilly, warming to her theme. "They're being stolen to be scrapped or for parts or whatever else. I doubt they're going far afield. In fact, I'd be willing to bet that all the cars are staying pretty local. There's no point wasting time and petrol money taking them anywhere, is there?"

"Fair enough," said Max. He poured milk on his cereal. "So?"

"So, I think we need to start looking at local garages. Those seem the most likely places that the cars are going to end up. Not the chain places, but small, family-run, independent places. Have a look around, see what's what, keep an eye on them. Ten to one, the cars are going to pass through somewhere like that."

Max nodded, looking impressed. "Good thinking. Yeah, I like that." He looked at Tilly, then grinned. "How about you take over the investigation, then?"

"As in, it's my case?" Tilly asked, stomach flipping over.

"All yours," said Max. "I'm here to consult when you need me, but this one can be yours. Give it a go and see what you find out."

Tilly was smiling so hard her face might break in half. Only a constable and trusted with her own investigation? That was unthinkable. Except maybe in a small place like this. Which was why, she realized, her father had been so gung-ho about her taking the assignment. Unusual opportunities. "Thank you," she said earnestly. "I won't let you down."

"I'm sure you won't," said Max. He sipped at some juice. "There are a few garages around town, though, so this won't be easy."

"Anyone in particular I should know about?"

Max shrugged. "There's always the Farmers, over on the east side of main street."

"Yeah?"

"They've danced on the wrong side of the law in the past, father and son out there, but nothing recent. Bit of a sad story, really. He, Paul, the father, was married to an Italian. Carmella, her name was. Good singer, by the way. She died young, ovarian cancer. They caught it when she was pregnant with their youngest and she refused treatment until the kid was born. Made it another handful of years then, well… Paul was left with two young kids to bring up and a business to run."

"Which doesn't excuse law breaking," Tilly said tartly.

"It doesn't," agreed Max. "But it does put a human face on things. You can be as by the book as you like, but don't forget that these are people that you're dealing with."

Tilly nodded. "I know. I got the message. I'll look into these people. Farmer is the last name, right?"

Max nodded. "It's only a tip, though. I haven't seen anything to make me suspicious. If this is going on somewhere local, isn't it more likely to be somewhere outside of town, more isolated, easier to hide things?"

"Good thinking," Tilly said, nodding and mentally moving the Farmer garage down her priority list a couple of spots.

"Go on then," Max said with a grin. "I know you'll want to phone your dad with the news. Give him my regards and don't be late to the station."

Tilly jumped up from the table. "I won't be," she promised as she rushed upstairs to get her phone.

"Excellent work," her father said when she told him. "I'm proud of you. Nothing less than what I expected, of course."

"This is turning out better than I thought," Tilly confessed.

Her father laughed. "Now you just need to run a clean investigation. I know you've got the knowledge, but you don't have the experience yet. So don't be afraid to ask for help. Make sure everything's documented and don't be tempted to cut corners or mess around in gray areas."

"Right," said Tilly, who knew all that but didn't mind being reminded. "I'm on it."

She was so pleased that when she put the phone down, she gave an uncharacteristic squeal of joy. Her very own investigation. She sat on the edge of her bed and tried to calm down. The same bed where she'd spent a sleepless night thinking about Sophie turning her down.

Maybe that had all been for the best, though. After all, there should be no gray areas, as her father said. Sophie could well be one of those. She had friends in town, she could forewarn people or hide information or any one of a number of complications. At the very least, she'd be a distraction, and Tilly didn't need any of that.

So maybe it was better that Sophie had turned her down flat. Tilly tried very hard to believe that. But it didn't take the sting out of what had happened. Enough so that she wondered if she really wanted to go back to choir. Maybe she should just concentrate on her new investigation.

CHAPTER TWELVE

"Let me get this straight," Jules said, leaning on the bar. "She asked you out, you said no, Billy interrupts everything, and you... You just stand there mouth opening and closing like a fish and don't explain yourself?"

"Pretty much," Sophie said miserably. "Well, except for the fish part. I don't think I was particularly fishlike. More... more stunned, actually. Also, to be fair, I did attempt to explain, but every time I did, she just interrupted me."

"She probably didn't want to talk about something that was so awkward and painful," said Jules, rolling her eyes. "Honestly, Soph, I don't know how we're ever going to marry you off."

"I don't need marrying off," said Sophie.

"What do you need, then?"

"I need..." She sighed. "I need someone nice and comfortable to curl up on my couch with."

"Right, your couch. As in, not your dad's. You need someone to take you away from all this. And that's not going to happen if you keep turning down every available woman in town."

"I have not turned down every available woman in town," Sophie protested.

"Just Tilly then," said Jules.

"Yes."

"The one that you actually want to date."

"Yes," said Sophie again. "I think."

"You think or you want?" asked Jules. "Because before you make the effort, you really should know."

Sophie blew out a breath. Try as she might, and she had tried over the intervening two and a half days, she couldn't forget about Tilly.

At first it had seemed the easiest thing. Just put it all behind her, pretend that the embarrassing incident never happened, tell Jules that she wasn't going to choir anymore. Except that would be letting Billy down, and Sophie really didn't want to do that.

Oh, that, and also every time she closed her eyes, she saw Tilly's face. There was that too. She sighed into her beer. Why did she feel like this? Was it just because Tilly was the first available woman to appear in town in forever? Or was it something more serious?

"You really like her, don't you?" Jules said, interrupting her thoughts.

Sophie looked at her pitifully. "I think so."

"Right," said Jules. "Does she make your tummy feel funny?"

Sophie nodded.

"Do you want to kiss her?"

Sophie nodded again.

"If there was a fire, would you pull her out of a burning building?"

"What kind of question is that?" Sophie asked. "I'd like to think that I'd pull anyone out of a burning building."

"Fair," said Jules. "But on the whole, I'd agree that you like our new police officer. And I don't think she's a bad choice. She was in here the other lunchtime with Max, talking about some big new case she's working on. She was… cute. All flushed and excited."

"You're married," Sophie said.

"And you're getting jealous, which is also cute," Jules said. "But if you actually do have some kind of feelings for her, there's really only one option here."

"Which is?" asked Sophie anxiously. "I mean, maybe there's some kind of rehab program? Or perhaps I could just run away. Move to South America or something."

"You could, but then Billy would just hunt you down and kill you," Jules told her. "She's got this winter concert planned to a T, and like it or not, you're now a part of it. I don't think there's anywhere in the world that you could hide from an angry Billy."

"No leaving the choir, then?"

Jules shook her head. "In fact, you're in for a surprise in the next few days."

"What kind of surprise?" She was suspicious now.

"Can't tell you," said Jules. "It's Billy's business, not mine. Just don't go moving to Buenos Aires yet."

"What's the other option, then?"

Jules lifted her eyebrows. "You could stop being an idiot and find the woman and explain yourself? That seems the simplest plan. Don't let her interrupt you, make sure you can say what needs to be said, and if she's still butt-hurt after that, well, I don't know. Buy her some flowers, maybe?"

"Do you buy Billy flowers when she's mad at you?"

Jules snorted. "If I did, she'd hit me with them. No, I just lay out my feelings and we talk about stuff. You know, communicate? It's what adults in relationships do for the most part. I can highly recommend it."

"Fine," Sophie said.

"No movie moments," Jules reminded her. "You're a grown woman with your own voice. Please use it. If you go around having these misunderstandings at the beginning of a relationship, they'll get out of control and ruin things. And unlike in the movies, most relationships don't recover from that kind of bullshit."

Sophie finished up her pint. "You've suddenly turned into a relationship guru."

"One of us here is actually in a relationship," Jules reminded her.

"Fine, fine, I'm on it. No more silly misunderstandings," Sophie said. "And now I'd better get home. Gio was supposed to cook dinner tonight, and I only stayed out this long in case he burned the place down."

Jules laughed and Sophie left the pub.

SHE MADE FAIR points, Sophie thought as she turned into her street. Maybe she hadn't tried hard enough to explain herself to Tilly. She'd been rather in shock, to be honest. And she should try harder. She wanted to try harder.

They barely knew each other, but Sophie was certain in a way she rarely was that she wanted to know Tilly better, that she wanted to see what could happen here. There was an attraction, and maybe, just maybe, that attraction could grow into something more.

Even if it didn't, it could be fun finding out, she thought as she walked up to her front door.

She opened the door to a puff of smoke and the smell of burning.

"Jesus," she said, starting to cough.

"It's alright," said her dad, coming out into the hall and flapping a tea towel around. "It's all alright, don't panic."

"Do we not have a smoke alarm?" asked Sophie, still coughing.

"That eejit in there turned it off," said her father. "Because the beeping was annoying him."

Sophie would have sighed if she could have taken a deep enough breath to do so. "What the hell happened?"

Her father stood at the front door, rapidly opening and closing it, getting the smoke to clear. "It's this thing called 'weaponized incompetence,'" he said.

"What?"

"Weaponized incompetence," he repeated. "It's where—"

"I know what it is," Sophie said. "I'm a bit surprised that you do though."

He looked sheepish. "I read about it in one of your mum's magazines once." He sniffed. "Didn't want to be an arse of a husband. Mind you, looks like your brother isn't going to be marrying anytime soon."

"Dad," Gio said, coming to the kitchen door in an apron. "Dad,

I'm just ordering some pizza."

"No way," said his father. "You're going to do it again and do it right this time. You're not spending hard earned money whenever it's your turn to cook and you're not getting out of your cooking duties. Bacon and sausage isn't exactly a gourmet dish, get back on it and try again. This time keep the heat on medium and turn the fan on over the stove."

Gio stood there for a second, a truculent look on his face, then he caved and nodded. "Right then."

Sophie closed the front door and followed them both into the kitchen. The window was wide open and the last of the smoke was leaving. She helped herself to a seat at the table, her father sat too, and Gio took more bacon from the fridge and started again.

"Get it right and I'll show you how to make spag bol for next time," Sophie said.

"Really?" Gio asked. He was grinning at that. It was his favorite meal.

"It's not hard," said Sophie. "I'll get the ingredients in and then you can make it, alright?"

"Yeah," he said, concentrating harder now. "Yeah, alright."

Their father shook his head. "Not been the best of days, has it, lad?" he said.

"Has it not?" asked Sophie. "What's gone on then?" It had been her afternoon off from the garage and she'd spent most of it hanging around the pub and complaining to Jules and whoever else had come in.

Paul folded his arms. "Police around asking questions."

Sophie felt her stomach contract. "Yeah? About what?"

"Nothing," Gio said, bacon starting to sizzle in the pan. "Because we've done nothing."

"Nothing for you to worry about," Paul said.

"You sure?" asked Sophie.

"Don't you start," said her father. "It's bad enough that the police harass us when we've not been on the radar for years. It's some stolen car ring they're after."

"And we've got nothing to do with it?" Sophie said.

Her father looked at her.

"Fine, we've got nothing to do with it."

"Could do without them poking around though," said her father. "Incompetent idiots that they are."

"Max is alright. You see him at the pub all the time," said Sophie. She didn't mention Tilly, hoping that Max's more familiar name would help matters more.

"Yeah, well," her father started.

But Sophie's phone rang and cut him off before he could say anymore.

"Hello," she said, not recognizing the number.

"Sophie? It's Billy."

Sophie couldn't remember Billy calling her before. They knew each other well enough because of Jules, but it was Jules that arranged drinks and parties, not Billy. "This is a surprise."

"I don't have a lot of time," Billy said. "But I'd like to know if you could make it half an hour earlier to choir tomorrow?"

Sophie blinked. "Um, what's this about?"

"I'd prefer to tell you in person."

Sophie took a breath. "Alright, yeah, shouldn't be a problem."

"Wonderful," said Billy. "See you there."

She hung up before Sophie could say anything else.

"Problem?" asked her dad.

Sophie shook her head. "Just a choir thing."

The sizzling from the stove took on a more sinister tone. "Turn the bloody heat down," barked her father.

"Right," Gio said. "It's alright. I've got it this time."

Just as he said that, a splash of oil burst into flame and Sophie got up to get the kitchen fire blanket just in case she needed it. She'd worry about choir later, once she hadn't burned to death.

CHAPTER THIRTEEN

Tilly showed up thirty minutes early, as requested. Well, twenty-nine minutes, to be precise. She'd just been walking toward the village hall when she'd seen a car parked on double yellow lines. The lines were protecting a fire exit, so she wasn't prepared to play around.

She'd spent a couple of minutes writing a ticket and then dealing with an irate takeout delivery person, so she had to run into the hall and arrived one minute late and sweating.

Sophie was already there.

Tilly had to catch her breath before she could even look at her properly. For god's sake, she told herself, she's an attractive woman. Get over it, you can't go into cardiac arrest every time you see someone pretty.

An attractive woman that wasn't interested.

She finally managed to take a full breath.

"Not dying then?" Billy asked from behind the piano.

"Not quite," said Tilly.

"Right," Billy sniffed. "Enough with the mystery, then. You two are good. I liked what you did last rehearsal, you can buckle down and learn things, you can read music."

"Actually, I can't," Sophie said.

Billy waved a hand. "One of you can, that's enough. So here's what I need. Ditch that last solo. I want a new one."

"You... what?" asked Sophie.

"A new solo," Tilly said, feeling rather pleased. She'd enjoyed the last one, but it had been quite easy. She thrived on a challenge.

"Right. I'd given up hope of including this in the concert, but with you two, I think we might just get away with it." Billy handed them both a sheet of music. "The Coventry Carol, you know it, I'm sure." She played a few notes.

"Yes," Tilly said. "Yes, this looks good." It was infinitely harder than the last one, longer too.

"I can't do this," Sophie said. She was looking ashen.

"Of course you can," said Billy. "You've got a good voice."

"Yeah, but… but I can't read the music and it's long and… And I can't."

"The constable over here will help, won't you?" Billy said.

Tilly was about to agree, then something stopped her. Did she really want to do this? It would mean spending time with Sophie outside of regular rehearsals. It would mean spending time away from her investigation. Could she spare that time? Did she want to be around someone so uninterested in her?

"Um, I don't know. If Sophie can't do it, then…"

"You don't think I can either?" Sophie wailed.

"I didn't say that," said Tilly, though she had said exactly that. "I meant if you think you can't do it, then maybe we shouldn't."

"Claptrap," Billy barked. "Here, we've got time. Let's do the first line together, all three of us. Get a feel for it before you decide. Tilly, this is your part." She played a simple ten-note melody. "And Sophie, this is yours, same thing, just a tad lower." She played again. "You know the tune. It should start off simple enough."

Tilly took a breath, then nodded. "Ready."

Billy gave them both a starting note.

A moment later the beautiful, lulling first line of the carol rang through the empty hall. It was too short, and so lovely that it hung in the air over them. When Tilly turned to Sophie, she saw that she looked like she was in shock.

"Easy," Tilly said.

"Perfect," Billy said.

"Wow," Sophie said.

"That's settled then," said Billy. "The two of you can work on that together, I assume?"

And it had been so beautiful that Tilly couldn't help but say yes.

"Sophie?" asked Billy.

Sophie hesitated, then nodded. "If Tilly will help."

"I'll help," Tilly said.

"Good," said Billy. "Right, get out of my way for ten minutes so that I can prepare the rest of the rehearsal. Off out into the entrance hall or something. Learn your words. I need a bit of time before everyone else floods in."

Tilly grabbed her jacket and went out, thinking that she'd get some fresh air, have a look around, see if she could spot anything else while she was here. A police officer never slept, her father always said.

Not literally, of course. But a police officer was never really off duty, especially in a small town like this. She stepped out into the cool of the evening, letting the door close behind her, turning only when she heard a muffled sound.

When she looked back, Sophie was pushing the door open again and rubbing her nose. "You just closed that door on me," she said.

"Unintentionally," said Tilly.

"It still hurt."

"But I didn't mean to."

Sophie rubbed her nose again and then sighed. She closed her eyes for a moment, appeared to come to some kind of decision, then opened them. "Can we talk for a minute?"

Tilly looked out toward the road where any number of bad parking jobs and out-of-date tax stickers and the like awaited her. A myriad of tickets to write. Then she turned back to Sophie, her dark hair loose over her shoulders, her nose still a little red, her eyes dark and serious.

"Fine," Tilly said with a sigh. "Just for a minute."

* * *

It had taken everything Sophie had to run after Tilly like that.

After a lot of thought, she'd come to the conclusion that perhaps, just perhaps, there were reasons other than her brother and father that stopped her from dating so much.

The thing was, it was easier to live her life the way it was. She might not be happy, she might not be fulfilled, but she was comfortable. There was no angst, no drama. And alright, she might blame Gio for ruining her date with Katie, but, and here was the thing, Sophie wasn't entirely sure that she'd have called Katie for a second date as it was.

Sure, a first date, a bit of fun, something unofficial perhaps. But a second date? That would make things serious and serious was scary.

Which meant that even though Sophie was chasing after Tilly just at the moment, she wasn't completely sure why she was doing it. It would be easier not to. It would be easier to let things go. Even if they did have to sing together.

But, and here was the thing, Tilly did deserve an explanation. She'd had her feelings hurt, and that was unacceptable, Sophie decided. That was just not okay. And then a door had hit her in the face and Sophie had had more than her feelings hurt.

She touched her nose again gently, experimentally.

"Are you going to talk, or are you just going to rub at your nose?" asked Tilly, somewhat sharply.

Sophie swallowed. "Fine. Yes. Talk. I just…" Her stomach felt weird and watery. "I just wanted to say that I didn't mean no."

"You didn't mean no," Tilly said slowly.

"Yes. Right. I mean the other day. I didn't mean no. Except I sort of did. I mean, it's complicated." Shouldn't have started this, she said to herself. She was screwing it up big time.

Tilly frowned. "So you didn't mean no, but you did mean no?"

"Yes," said Sophie.

Tilly thought about this for a second. They were standing just in front of the village hall, under the large light, and it shone orange on Tilly's curls. "I think we might have to talk for more than a minute," she said finally. "I don't really know what's going on."

Sophie swallowed. "Um, yeah. Okay. Here's the thing. The other night you asked me if I wanted to go for a drink with you at the pub and I said no. What I meant was 'no, I don't want a drink with you at the pub.'"

"Lovely," Tilly said. "That clears everything up. It helps so much to hear it a second time in more detail." She turned as if to leave, and Sophie clutched her arm.

"Not at the pub," she repeated. "But maybe something else? I don't know."

"You don't drink?" Tilly asked, eyes widening a bit.

"I do," qualified Sophie. "But…" She sighed and looked at the ground. "I'm really making a mess of this."

"You are," agreed Tilly. But her voice was softer, kinder. "You could try telling me why you said no. That might help?"

Sophie took a deep breath. "The thing is," she said. "The thing is… my family, my brother, my father, they're a bit… protective." She saw a look of shock pass over Tilly's face. "No, nothing terrible. They don't stop me going out or anything, but they do… they interfere."

"Ah," Tilly said.

"And if we went to the pub, and it was all full of my brother and his friends, then probably we wouldn't have a great time."

Tilly's face was looking clearer now. She was smiling a little. "Okay, I see," she said. She took a step in. "I can understand that."

For a second, Sophie was caught up in her eyes, the way the light sparkled in them. "I'm sorry," she said softly. "I didn't mean to hurt your feelings or anything. I wanted to explain before, but you wouldn't let me."

"I thought you were just trying to let me down a bit easier," Tilly said.

The light really was sparkling in those blue eyes. And Tilly's lips were just right there in front of her own. If she leaned in just a little, she'd be able to kiss them. Sophie's heart hammered hard in her chest.

She made the tiniest of movements.

A car turned into the street.

She tilted her head.

The car drove into her field of vision. She could see the familiar shape of the headlights over Tilly's shoulder.

She took a step back just as Gio drove past.

"I'm sorry," she said again.

"You don't—" began Tilly.

But a chattering group of people had rounded the corner, Jules among them. "Hey, Soph," Jules shouted.

Sophie waved at her, and when she turned back, Tilly had gone back inside.

CHAPTER FOURTEEN

Tilly printed out the report and then tapped the pages on her desk to straighten them up. Not that she had a whole lot to say, but she was going to do things properly.

Anyway, writing reports took her mind off Sophie. Sophie, who she'd almost kissed last night. If it hadn't been for the interruption of the others, she was pretty sure that they would have. What she wasn't sure about was how she felt about that.

On the one hand, she was police; she had a job to do, she shouldn't be distracted. On the other hand... well, there was so much. There were Sophie's big, dark eyes for a start. And then the curve of her neck into her shoulders. Not to mention the curve of her waist that was begging to be held. And then, a little weirdly perhaps, was the fact that Sophie sang like a little angel and didn't appear to know it.

Tilly's heart had soared when she'd heard Sophie singing last night, and even thinking about it now brought a smile to her face. Mind you, thinking about parts slightly less internal than her voice did things to her too.

She groaned. The one time she really needed to focus and all she could think about was Sophie... It occurred to her that actually, she didn't know Sophie's last name. Something Italian probably. No, wait, Max had said her mum was Italian, so maybe not.

Whatever her name was, Tilly had the feeling that a few extra rehearsals weren't going to make things better. It seemed that the closer they got to each other, the more inevitable it became that something was going to happen.

Which made Tilly feel all warm inside.

Yes, she had a career. But that didn't mean a personal life was out of bounds, did it? Except that all too often, relationships with officers just didn't work out. Look at her mum and dad. Long hours, promotional moves, a stressful job that the officer couldn't always talk about at home. It wasn't the recipe for a happy marriage.

Max and Mila seemed to be doing alright though. Well, mostly. She'd definitely heard a strained conversation this morning as she'd come down the stairs. But everyone argued. In fact, it hadn't even really been an argument, more like a stressed discussion.

"Is that for me?" Max grinned cheerfully and slid the report out of Tilly's hands.

"Yes, sir," she said, wondering how long he'd been standing there and whether she'd been sitting around with an embarrassingly vacant look on her face. Or, worse, a love-lorn smile.

"Why don't you fill me in on the highlights?" Max said, laying the report on the desk and taking a seat opposite Tilly.

"Sir, yes sir." Tilly took a second to gather her thoughts, then began. "As part of an ongoing investigation into possible infractions regarding—"

Max coughed a cough that was obviously covering a laugh.

"What?" asked Tilly.

"Nothing," Max said. "Go ahead."

Tilly cleared her throat. "Possible infractions regarding—"

Max coughed again. "Um, do you think maybe we could do this in plain language? It's been a long day so far and I'd like to get home at some point."

Tilly blushed. "I mean, yes, if that's what you want."

"Unless you want to go the whole formal route," Max added quickly. "If you need the practice or something. Otherwise, well, communication is key and we'll probably understand each other a lot better if we just, um, speak normally, rather than using all the jargon."

"Right, yes, sure." She took a breath. "Well, um, in that case, I visited a bunch of places, had a look around as best as I could, though I didn't cross any property lines obviously, and didn't find anything incriminating. That about sums things up."

Max eyed her. "You don't have to look so disappointed," he said.

"Do I not?" In truth, she was a little disappointed with herself. In her head she'd solved this case in the course of an afternoon. But the reality of police work was a lot different.

"These things take time," Max said comfortingly. "Besides, think how awful it would look if I had this case for weeks and then you swooped in and solved it in an afternoon. I'd have to start looking for a new job."

Against her will, she grinned a little at this. "Fair enough," she said. "So, what do you suggest I do next?"

"Observation is good, key even, but what do you think you should be doing?"

"Asking questions," she said immediately, without thinking. It was the natural answer.

"Right," Max said. "Have a poke around. Whoever these people are, they're good. We know that much. They're not leaving a shred of evidence at the scenes, so they're not likely to be leaving scrapped cars sitting around their garage either, are they?"

"Suppose not," said Tilly.

"Right, so look for other things. Maybe staff will talk to you, maybe someone's been overworked, asked to work night shifts which would be unusual, for example. Or maybe there's extra money lying around where it shouldn't be. Or someone's wearing a watch that they shouldn't be able to afford, that sort of thing."

"Right," Tilly said, getting the idea. "Yeah."

"Observation is good," Max said again. "But you need to go a bit deeper than the surface. You got any gut feelings about this that you didn't put into the report?"

Tilly scratched her nose. She hadn't been going to say anything, but Max had asked. "At most places I just had a wander around, maybe a chat to a mechanic or something if someone was around. Nothing official and, for the most part, people were friendly. But…"

"But?" asked Max.

She sighed. "I know you said that more than likely these cars are getting chopped outside the village. But from the second I stepped foot in the Farmer garage they knew I was police, and the father confronted me before I even opened my mouth, told me there was nothing there."

"Right."

She shrugged. "He was defensive. People aren't usually defensive unless they've got something to be defensive about. It just struck me as odd."

Max nodded. "Could be. On the other hand, he might just have had bad experiences with police in the past. You can't assume too much from all this."

"I know," Tilly said. "I know. But you asked, and that's the best I've got."

"Fair enough," said Max, getting up. "Now, I need you off to Mrs. Dodds' place, please. It's just off the high street, turn right out the door and take the first right. Number thirty-six. She wants some new locks fitting and a basic security system, chains, that sort of thing. No alarm, her son says."

"Okay," said Tilly, confused. "And I need to be there because?"

Max sighed. "Because this is community policing. Because preventing crime is just as important, if not more important, than catching criminals, and because this is the part of the job where, if you'll excuse me saying so, you're not so hot."

"Not so hot?" Tilly squeaked.

"It's not all big cases, Till. You need to focus on the people. I keep telling you that. Think about the people involved, they're not numbers, they're not names in a report. Policing is about humanity, and if you overlook that, you'll never be the kind of officer I know you want to be."

Which stung, she wasn't going to lie. She wasn't used to being criticized. She was used to being number one, top of the class. But she looked at her desk and nodded. "Yes, sir."

"Hey, cheer up," said Max, patting her shoulder. "You're here to learn. And if it's any consolation, I don't think anyone's ever given me a typed up report before. Mostly people just bend my ear about things."

She gave him a smile. "You're welcome."

"And so are you," grinned Max. "Now off you go, there's work to be done."

"ARE YOU SURE the burglars won't get in now?" Mrs. Dodds was saying.

"They won't," said Tilly, who was unsure whether or not Mrs. Dodds herself would be able to get into the small house. "Can you show me how you unlock the doors from the inside?"

"I'm no fool," grumbled Mrs. Dodds as she unlocked the new locks.

Tilly picked up the bunch of keys that the locksmith had left and stepped outside with Mrs. Dodds. "Alright, now lock up." She waited and watched as the old woman fumbled with the keys and locked the door. "Now unlock again."

Another palaver and they were back inside the house.

"Now, lock us in safely," said Tilly.

Mrs. Dodds clicked the locks back to closed. "See?" she said. "I told you I'm no fool. I know how to lock a door, young lady."

Tilly, who'd thought Mrs. Dodds was a frail and slightly demented old woman the last time she met her, was revising her opinion. She'd spent the afternoon mediating between a tired locksmith and a demanding Mrs. Dodds, and all she really wanted was to go home and take her shoes off.

But it wasn't to be. She checked her watch, almost time. "I have to be leaving now," she said. "Are you going to be alright?"

"Better now that the burglars are on the outside," Mrs. Dodds said, and tottered off toward the living room.

"Don't forget to lock up after me," Tilly shouted, shaking her head.

She left quickly. Billy had said that the village hall was free from five until six if she and Sophie wanted to use it, and it was quarter to five now. She didn't want to keep Sophie waiting. Actually, she didn't want to miss a second of being in Sophie's company.

She was walking fast and was distracted trying to message Max at the same time as walking, so she didn't see the shiny red car drive past her and then pull up to the curb. The window slid down and someone shouted at her.

"What? Sorry," she began, getting closer to the car.

A young man was glaring at her through the window. "You stay out of things," he said, pointing a finger at her. "Stay away from my garage and stay away from my family."

It was only then that she recognized him as the Farmer son. He'd been in the background when his father had been trying to throw her out of the garage. "If you've got nothing to hide, there's no reason to threaten me," she said, holding her head up high. She was no coward.

He just stared at her. "Stay away from my family," he said again, voice loaded with meanness.

Then he revved the engine and left, and Tilly watched him go.

CHAPTER FIFTEEN

"Now I'm really confused," Jules said.

They were sitting at a small table close to the counter of the cafe owned by Jules's sister Amelia and her partner Cass.

"What's to be confused about?" Cass asked from behind the counter. "Your girl's got a crush and got it bad. Not that I blame her, that policewoman's a looker alright. And she's all strict and in a uniform." She gave a little shiver of delight.

"Enough from you," Amelia said, putting coffees on a tray and carrying them to the table. "I think the question is, if Soph's got a crush and the constable is so pretty, why didn't that smooch happen?"

"Easy," Cass said. "Because Gio drove by in that banger of his." She rolled her eyes at Sophie. "Forgive Am, she's not always on the ball. Here, get one of these down you." She pulled a plate out and then got something out of a machine that looked like it might be used for medieval torture.

"What is it?" asked Jules.

"A Paganini," Cass said proudly.

"She means a Panini," said Amelia. "We just got the machine. Rented for now, of course, but we thought we'd give it a go."

"This one's ham and pineapple," Cass said, putting the plate in front of Jules. "What do you want, Soph?"

"Not ham and pineapple," she said quickly. "What about, um,

cheese and..."

"Salmon?" Cass filled in.

"God no, cheese and ham will be fine."

"Boring," said Cass, but got to work anyway.

"So you didn't kiss the constable because of Gio?" Jules asked her, getting back to the point.

"Her name's Tilly," Sophie said. "Kiss the Constable sounds like a dirty film."

"Not a bad one either," Cass said from behind the counter. "What do you think, Am? We could shoot it in the cafe when we're closed."

"I'm not being in a dirty film," Amelia said immediately.

"Did I ask you to? We'd get professionals for that."

"Where from?" asked Jules, honestly curious. "Do you know many professional adult actors in the area?"

"There must be some," said Cass, looking thoughtful. "I mean, you might not know just by looking. Like spies. Probably there's loads."

"We don't have filming equipment," Amelia said. "So it's a no on that for the time being. I like the idea of the cafe being used at night, though."

"If you open at night, you'll be treading on the pub's toes. Josh'll go mad," Jules said.

Amelia and Cass were always looking for get rich quick schemes, though they'd calmed down slightly since getting the cafe. Sophie tuned them out as she drank her coffee.

They'd almost kissed. She knew that, could almost feel it now, the brush of Tilly's lips. For a moment there, the whole world had distilled down to those lips and nothing could have pulled her away from them.

Then Gio had driven by in his decrepit old car. So she hadn't done it. She'd lost her nerve, lost her focus, and then Tilly had been gone.

"So was it because of Gio, then?" Jules said, tapping on the table to get Sophie's attention as Cass and Amelia argued over plans to turn the cafe into a club at night.

"Sort of," Sophie said. She swirled her coffee in her cup miserably. "I mean, it's kind of complicated."

"Not really," said Jules. She was always the practical one. "You like her, kiss her, give it a go. If it works, well, you can deal with all the rest later, can't you?"

Sophie twisted her face into a grimace. "Um, maybe a bit more complicated than that."

"Why?" demanded Jules.

She blew out a breath. "Because Tilly's been asking questions at the garage. Professional kinds of questions. I mean, I wasn't there, but dad and Gio said she was poking around and then..."

"And then?"

She shrugged. "And they went off on their normal anti-police thing and, um, yeah."

Jules shook her head. "You can't date to please the two of them," she said. "The only way they'll be pleased is if you either don't get married at all, or you get together with someone just like you, so they have someone else to look after them."

"Harsh," Sophie said. "I don't think it's like that. I think they want me to be happy."

"So what's the problem, then? If Tilly is the one that makes you happy."

"She's investigating the garage," Sophie said quietly.

"So? Have they done anything? Your dad and Gio? Anything untoward?"

Sophie gritted her teeth and then shook her head. "No." Even though she wasn't completely convinced, she wouldn't say anything against them.

But Jules was frowning at her, leaning in closer. "Soph, have you not told her who you are?"

"What?" Sophie asked in a desperate bid to play for time.

"You heard. Tilly, have you told her who you are?"

"Not exactly," sighed Sophie. "See? I told you it was complicated. I almost kissed her, and I wanted to, but then Gio came by and it reminded me that I should be more loyal to my family, and then I thought that if she knew who I was, she might not want to anyway and then—"

"Jesus," Amelia said, interrupting the cycle. "You need to get a grip. You can't have any kind of relationship based on all that stuff. Not based on a lie, even one of omission. The first thing you need to do is tell this Tilly who you are."

"She's right," said Jules. "Come clean, see where you go from there."

"And if she doesn't like it? Doesn't want anything to do with me?" asked Sophie.

"Her choice," said Amelia. "You can't decide things for other people. It's not fair."

"Here you go," Cass said, putting a plate down in front of Sophie. "Ham and cheese, and I threw in a bit of pineapple 'cos the tin was already open."

"What did I literally just say?" Amelia said. "You can't decide things for other people."

"Fine," said Cass, sitting down. "I'll have it then."

Sophie slid the plate toward her just as the cafe door opened.

"We're closed," Amelia said, but she turned anyway. "Oh, it's you, Gio. Come in. Want a panini? I'd advise making it yourself, to be honest."

"Nope," Gio said, his face split apart by a wide grin. "I just wanted to show Soph this. Come on, come have a look. All of you, in fact, outside."

Obediently, they trooped out to see a shiny red car parked carefully on the curb.

"What's this?" Sophie asked.

"Present from dad," said Gio proudly. "He said I'd been working hard and that the VW was on its last legs, so he let me have this. Nice, isn't it? Hop in, I'll give you a ride home."

"Can't," Sophie said, looking at the sheen on the car, her heart sinking a little. A new car. How much had that cost? More importantly, where had the money come from? "I've got a choir thing."

"Again?" Gio moaned.

"I'll have a ride," Cass said, trying the door handle.

"Yeah, go on, give us a go," said Amelia.

Gio unlocked the doors, and they all got in. Sophie checked her watch and decided she'd better go. She didn't want to be late. Actually, she just didn't want to miss a millisecond of being in Tilly's presence, which was pathetic but true.

"Tell her," Jules said.

"Tell her what?" asked Sophie.

Jules glared at her. "Tell. Her."

IT WAS ONLY five o'clock, but it was already dark enough that Sophie had to flick the light on at the entrance of the village hall. She'd just figured out which switch it was when Tilly came through the door.

"I'm not late," Sophie said even though she'd been the first one there.

"Neither am I," said Tilly.

Her face had flushed with the chill air outside and the contrast between pink cheeks and blue eyes was so pretty that Sophie was momentarily jealous that she had such dark eyes.

"Um, I was just looking at the light switches, trying to get us illuminated."

"Right," said Tilly.

This was going so well. Sophie gritted her teeth. How was she supposed to start this conversation? 'Yeah, I know we nearly kissed the other day, but I freaked out because my brother drove by. Oh, and by the way, you know him since you're investigating him for some random police reason.' She snorted a laugh to herself.

"Something funny?" Tilly said.

Sophie bit her lip. "No."

"Here," Tilly said. She reached over to flick a switch on the big bank of switches and her hand brushed Sophie's.

Sophie swallowed quickly, almost choked, and then started coughing.

"You alright?" asked Tilly.

She was close, really close. Sophie could see her through tear-filled eyes as she nodded. Tilly's hand patted her on the back and Sophie found she could take a breath.

"You go into the hall and I'll flick switches. Tell me when the lights are on," Tilly instructed.

Glad to be able to step away for a second, Sophie did as she was told. She needed to be able to breathe, needed to be able to think so that she could say what needed to be said. She stood in the dark coolness of the village hall and waited.

"That should be it," Tilly shouted through.

"It's not," Sophie said.

"Yes, it is."

"Um, it's still dark," said Sophie.

"Can't be," shouted Tilly.

Sophie sighed and turned to go back out to the entrance hall just as Tilly came in. The door swung open, just missing Sophie's nose in the dark, and then their bodies were colliding together.

For a second, Sophie clung on to anything she could, then she was holding cloth, then she was touching skin. Then her breath was coming faster and all she could hear was Tilly's breathing in the darkness.

She didn't even have to search her lips out. They were just there. There ready and patiently waiting when Sophie tilted her head in the right direction.

There was the faintest brush of contact, and Sophie's heart throbbed in her chest. With desperate hands, she reached up and grabbed hold of Tilly's jacket, forcing herself to stop.

"Tilly," she began.

But it was too late. Far too late.

Tilly didn't say a word. She moved a millimeter and then any semblance of logical thought was gone.

Their lips crashed together, the breath left Sophie's body, and her eyes closed as Tilly's mouth met her own, as Tilly's tongue explored her own, as they tasted each other, touched each other, crammed as closely together as they could in the darkness.

They were kissing. Finally. And nothing else in Sophie's world

SIENNA WATERS

seemed to matter.

CHAPTER SIXTEEN

Tilly had never wanted to meld into someone more. She pressed her body against Sophie's and reveled in the taste of her, the feel of her, not caring that she couldn't breathe. Sophie's hands clasped the back of her neck, pulling her even deeper in.

She backed her against the wall, not wanting this to ever stop, not wanting to be alone ever again, just wanting this to go on and on forever.

Only after a long, long time, did she finally pull away, tilt her forehead against Sophie's, and take a deep breath. "Thank you." It was all she could think of to say.

"You're welcome, I guess?" Sophie said. In the shadows Tilly could see a small smile on her mouth, her lips swollen.

"I've wanted to do that since the first time I saw you," Tilly admitted.

Sophie laughed. "Me too."

"I thought you weren't interested," said Tilly. "You turned me down, and I thought I needed to forget all about you. And then I got this investigation and thought maybe it's for the best, maybe I shouldn't have any distractions. And now this."

Sophie turned her head a little. "What investigation is that?" she asked, perhaps not as casually as she'd meant to.

"Some stolen cars," Tilly said with a shrug. "Someone or someones are stealing cars in the area. I'm looking into it. That's all." She moved her hands, stroked back her hair, moved an inch away from Sophie. "It's not a murder or anything, but… But it's my first real case and it's a good opportunity."

Sophie was sliding away from her now, moving so that she was standing properly, not backed up against the wall. The lights from the entrance hall gleamed in through the windows in the door, catching in her dark hair. "Tilly."

It was just one word, but it sounded so ominous. "Yeah?" Tilly asked cautiously. If this was it, she promised herself, if Sophie was calling things off now, she'd be fine with it. Hurt, but fine. She could do this. She'd had that kiss and what right did she have to expect more?

"I have to tell you something."

Tilly bared her teeth in a grimace. "Oh god, are you married? Dating?" Her heart plunged. She hadn't even asked if Sophie was single. Hadn't suspected a thing. Christ, she should really be more careful.

"It's not that."

"What is it then?" Her heart was beating fast now, her mouth getting dry. What could be worse than being married? The tone of Sophie's voice told her this was going to be something bad.

"Um, my name," Sophie said.

"I know your name. It's Sophie." Tilly was confused. "It's a beautiful name. Do you not like it?"

"Not my first name. My full name." Sophie was looking out toward the entrance now, looking like she was wishing she could run away. She took a deep breath. "It's Sophie Farmer."

It took a second. A second of seeing the light gleam in Sophie's hair, a second of tasting that kiss, a second of slow thought, until… "You… you what?"

Sophie turned back. "Sophie Farmer," she repeated.

Tilly shook her head. "No."

"Yes."

"But… You should have told me, you should have said something." Tilly backed up further, as though physically distancing herself could make everything un-happen. "You…

you're… But I can't, and…"

"It's alright," Sophie said calmly. "It's alright. I can see that you're angry."

"Angry?" Tilly said, feeling the beat of it inside her. "Angry? I can't even…" She took a breath and another breath, trying to make some sense out of all this.

Sophie was a Farmer. As in the Farmers that she was pretty sure had something to do with the car theft ring. And she'd… she'd kissed her. Another very shaky breath. Then Tilly did the only thing she could think of doing.

"I can't be here," she said. "I can't be this close to you." And she walked out without looking back.

THE HOUSE WAS quiet went she got back. She'd gotten into the habit of coming in through the front, rather than using her own door. It felt strange to feel such silence in this house, and she thought she was alone until she heard a rustle of papers from the living room.

Out of politeness more than anything, she stuck her head around the door. Mila was sitting on the floor, the coffee table covered with papers, a calculator in her hand. She looked up in surprise. "I wasn't expecting you."

"I'm not supposed to be here," Tilly said. She was still in shock, she supposed, still not able to believe that Sophie hadn't told her before, that she hadn't figured it out herself, that she'd practically thrown herself at the daughter of what could be Whitebridge's biggest crime family.

"Oh dear," Mila said. "You look like you've had quite the day." She put her calculator down. "How about a drink?"

"A drink?" Tilly said, like she'd barely heard of the word.

Mila laughed. "Sit down on that couch right there. Max has taken the kids to see a film. They won't be back for ages. I'll be right with you."

Tilly did as she was told. How could she have kissed Sophie? How could she not have known? How could she have potentially compromised her investigation like that? But it wasn't her fault, was it? Not that that would wash in any kind of internal investigation. She couldn't prove that she hadn't known who Sophie was.

But then, maybe Sophie knew nothing about anything. Or perhaps she knew everything, and she was just stringing Tilly along, trying to find out how the investigation was going. Maybe this was all a set-up.

Tilly blinked away hot tears. She wasn't going to cry over this. She just wasn't.

"Here," Mila said, coming back in and handing her a glass. "Drink that." She clinked her glass against Tilly's and then sat back down on the carpet in front of the coffee table. "Want to talk about it?"

"I don't think I can," Tilly said.

Mila blew a raspberry. "Course you can. You can do whatever you like. Would it help if I agreed to be sworn to secrecy? I won't tell Max, if that's what you're worried about." She considered this for a second. "I mean, as long as he doesn't need to know, that is."

Tilly looked at her glass, it was filled with a dark-colored liquid that smelled suspiciously sweet. Glancing over at Mila, she could see that her glass was a much lighter color, something else entirely. "What is this?"

"Gin and Dubonnet," Mila said, pulling a face. "It's too strong for me, but Max likes it when he's had a long day. And you can tell me things if you need to. There's no need to keep things bottled up."

Tilly sipped at the drink. It was strong. But it was sweet and sticky and quite satisfying at the same time. "I think I might be involved in a conflict of interest," she said.

Mila raised an eyebrow. "That doesn't sound at all like you, at least from what I know about you."

"It wasn't an intentional one," said Tilly firmly. She sighed and tried a different tack. She wasn't sure how much she wanted to say. "How do you do it?" she asked.

"Do what?"

"Stay with Max. When he's a policeman and you're not, and you live in this town too and... And just how does it work?"

"Well, I'm not exactly a criminal mastermind," Mila laughed. "It's not like Max has to arrest me once a month."

"Isn't it hard though?"

"Of course it is," Mila said. She was looking down at the papers as she said this and Tilly could see that they were the bank papers she'd seen Mila with before. "But there are advantages. Besides, neither of us wanted to move away from here. This is where I was born, where I want to bring up my children."

"But what if, say, your business partner was a criminal?"

"Ant?" said Mila. "She wouldn't hurt a fly. Anyway, she's far too busy for committing crimes. Plus, her favorite crime is murder, so that's the one she'd want to do and I don't think she's got the stomach for it, to be honest."

"Murder?" Tilly asked.

"We run a crime bookshop," said Mila. "And Ant knows a lot about crime. Maybe even more than Max does."

"Okay, but hypothetically, that would be a conflict of interest, wouldn't it?"

"I suppose," said Mila. "But I don't think it would really reflect on me. I mean, Max knows who I am, what I wouldn't do. I think it would just be one of those things. This is a small town, Tilly. It's impossible to avoid everyone just because they might be involved in something unsavory. Max has a pint with Old Dave at the pub all the time."

"The one that had his driving license taken away?" Tilly asked.

"That's the one," agreed Mila. She bit her lip, then looked at Tilly. "Is this about Sophie Farmer?"

Tilly spluttered on her drink, almost choked, then managed to swallow. "What?"

"Sorry," said Mila, holding up her hands. "It's absolutely none of my business. But..." She blushed. "But like I said, it's a small town. Billy was in the bookshop yesterday and mentioned something about the two of you making eyes at each other and I just thought... Nothing, never mind."

With a sigh, Tilly nodded sadly. "It is."

"She doesn't like you back?" asked Mila gently.

"No, no, that's not the problem." The admission made Tilly's heart give a quick extra beat. No, she was sure Sophie liked her back.

"So the problem is that she's a Farmer."

Tilly nodded.

"She's a good girl," said Mila. "Never been in any kind of trouble that I know of, and I would know. That brother of hers can be a handful, and Paul went off the rails a bit when his wife died, not that you can really blame him for that. Sophie's fine though, she's a hard worker, went away to college but came back to take care of her dad and that Gio."

"But I think they might be involved in this car theft ring," said Tilly slowly. "I've got no proof, but I think it's heading that way."

Mila shrugged. "I'd be surprised," she said. "But on the whole, even if they were, I doubt Sophie would know anything about it. The way those two protect her, I don't think they'd tell her anything, even if they were involved."

"Be that as it may," Tilly said. "I don't think it's a good idea to get involved. I've got my career to think of, after all." She took another hearty mouthful of her drink. "I think I might go and take a bath."

"Go on then," said Mila. "Have a good think. Baths always help with that sort of thing."

But Tilly didn't think there was that much more to think about.

CHAPTER SEVENTEEN

Slowly, Sophie walked toward the cafe. She didn't know where else to go. She definitely didn't want to go home. If she saw her brother and dad right now, she might say something she regretted.

She desperately didn't want to think they were involved in anything, but how could she be sure? With the promises of raises in the new year, and Gio's shiny new car? She did the accounts. There was nothing on her side that looked fishy. But then her dad waded in sometimes, and, to be honest, if there was anything that wasn't quite right, he was unlikely to run it through the books.

But car stealing?

She knew that both her dad and Gio had been in trouble with the police before. Her dad after her mum had died. He'd had anger problems, had drunk a bit too much, had got into the odd fight. And Gio, well, Gio was just a big ball of testosterone looking for trouble sometimes. But he'd been good recently, and again, it had been drunken fighting.

She couldn't put the two things together.

And she supposed she couldn't blame Tilly for not wanting to get involved. Not when her job was on the line.

Which didn't make any of it any easier. Yet again, Gio and her dad had ruined a dating prospect. And yet again, she was forced to look after their interests at the expense of her own.

She just hoped that Jules was still at the cafe, maybe even with Amelia and Cass, so that she'd have someone to commiserate with.

Two minutes later, she pushed open the door to find Jules, Am, and Cass sitting at a table with several uneaten paninis in front of them.

"Soph?" Jules said in surprise. "I thought you were singing?"

Sophie opened her mouth, but nothing came out. Then the sobs started and she couldn't say a thing.

"Wine," Jules ordered. Amelia and Cass got up immediately and Jules went to put her arm around Sophie. "Come on, love," she said, ushering her into a chair. "It can't be that bad."

But Sophie couldn't answer. She was too busy crying.

"Here you go," Cass said, shoving a box of tissues in front of Sophie and clinking four beakers onto the table.

"I got this," said Amelia, and there was the sound of a cork popping and then wine glugging into glasses.

"Now," Jules said. "Stop this crying and tell us what happened."

"I kissed her," wailed Sophie.

"She what?" Cass asked.

"She kissed her," said Amelia.

"Who?" asked Cass.

"The policewoman," Amelia said.

"Police officer," sobbed Sophie.

"Then why's she crying?" Cass asked. "I think we're going to need more than one bottle of wine for this."

"There's a whole box left in the back from when we catered that wedding," Amelia said. "So there's plenty."

"Here, drink," said Jules, pushing the beaker of sticky red wine in front of Sophie.

Sophie took a sip, then a mouthful. Drinking stopped her crying. She couldn't do both at once. She chugged half the glass, then pulled a tissue out of the box, blew her nose, scrubbed at her eyes, and finally took a breath. "Sorry."

"Nothing to be sorry about," Jules said gently. "Now, why don't you tell us what happened?"

Sophie nodded. "We kissed. It was… amazing."

"So amazing that it made you cry," Cass guessed.

"I don't think you're helping," said Amelia.

"I swear, if the two of you don't shut up, I'm going to throw you out," said Jules.

"It's our cafe," said Amelia.

"I don't care," Jules said. She turned back to Sophie. "Let me guess. You kissed first and then you told her who you were?"

Sophie nodded again, more miserably this time. "She, um, didn't take it well."

"Probably because of Gio," said Cass darkly. "He's an eejit. Your dad's always saying so."

"It's not," said Sophie. "Well, maybe it is a bit. It's because she's got a case, an investigation. I think it's like her big break or whatever. She's looking into all these cars around here getting stolen."

"Yeah, Dougie McKeefe got his nicked the other day," said Amelia. "Dunno why, it was a piece of crap."

"Probably for parts," Sophie said.

The others looked at her.

"What? I'm not supposed to know what goes on in garages? There are places called chop shops. The stolen cars get driven in, the mechanics there strip them for parts or rebuild them, depending on how good the chassis is. Then they get sold on."

"Oh," Cass said, turning to look at Amelia.

"No," said Amelia. "We're not a garage, we're not car thieves, and we don't know the first thing about cars. We're not opening a chop shop."

"It's a good way of stealing cars 'cos it means you're not stealing expensive new ones with fancy alarms and trackers and stuff. You're stealing older ones that go under the radar. You're only driving them as far as your chop shop and by the time they come out again, they're unrecognizable," said Sophie.

"Huh," Jules said. "And Tilly thinks that your dad and Gio are involved in something like this?"

Sophie nodded.

"So she can't date you," guessed Jules. She sat back in her chair and drank some wine, finishing up quickly and topping everybody's glasses up. "Are they?" she asked finally.

Sophie shook her head. "No. At least, I don't think so."

"They could be," Cass said. "Would you know?"

"I think so," said Sophie. "I mean, they'd be working nights, so I'd have to know, wouldn't I. It's just…"

"What?" prompted Amelia.

Sophie sighed. "There's a bit more money floating around than there should be, I think. It could be nothing. It could be something. I'm not sure. But I do know that the garage isn't being used as a chop shop."

"Honestly," said Cass. "Women. Can't live with them, can't live without them, not allowed to kill them." She drank.

"I don't want to kill her," Sophie said, drinking again too. The wine was sticky on her lips and her legs were starting to feel heavy. "I want to date her."

"Are you sure?" asked Amelia. "I mean, she's just practically accused your family of being car thieves and then walked out on you. That doesn't sound terribly romantic to me."

"Pretty sure," Sophie said. She closed her eyes for a second and could feel Tilly's lips on hers, could feel the heat of her body. She opened her eyes again and looked for her wine. "She's really attractive. And she's smart."

"And she thinks you're part of some sort of criminal family. Like in The Sopranos," Cass said. "Mind you, that sort of thing can work, can't it? You know, warring clans and the like. It's dead romantic."

Jules turned to her sister and Cass. "The two of you have very odd ideas of what's romantic and what's not."

"Give me a break," Cass said. "I'm aromantic, I'm playing guessing games at all this stuff, but I'm trying to be helpful."

"Fair," Jules said. She sat back in her chair again, a thoughtful look on her face. "You really sure that you're interested in this Tilly, even after this?"

Sophie nodded. "I know it's weird. I know I probably shouldn't be, but there's something there. I can't help having feelings for her, can I? It's some sort of hormonal thing or something."

"Or love at first sight," Amelia said, raising her glass and drinking. This time she was the one that refilled the glasses.

"That happens," Cass said wisely. "It's in the films all the time."

"I think it's biological," said Amelia. "Something to do with pheromones or something? I don't remember. But it's definitely a thing."

"I'm not saying I'm in love with her," Sophie said, drinking again. How would she know? Maybe she was. She thought about her a lot. She definitely wanted more of the kissing. And maybe some other stuff, too.

"Can you imagine the world without her in it?" asked Cass.

"What?" Sophie said. Her eyelids felt heavy. The wine was getting to her.

"That's supposed to be the test, I think," Cass replied. "Like, imagine the world without her in it and it gets all black and depressing and stuff and that means that you must be in love with her."

"What?" Sophie said again.

"Ignore her," said Amelia. "She doesn't know what she's talking about. Do you feel all funny when she's around? Like you can't control your own body?"

Sophie thought about the number of times she'd bumped into Tilly. She definitely did seem clumsier when they were together. "Maybe?" she hazarded.

"Then you're probably in love," said Amelia. She grinned and poured more wine into Tilly's beaker. "We should drink to that."

"Drink to me being in love with a policewoman who thinks I'm a criminal? Police officer," Sophie corrected herself.

Jules slapped a hand on the table and Sophie nearly dropped her drink. "There's only one thing to do," she announced.

"What's that?" asked Sophie, slightly suspicious now that the wine might be getting to everyone, not just her.

"It's simple," said Jules. "If you like Tilly and still want to date her, but she doesn't want to date you because she thinks you're a criminal. Or thinks your family's the Sopranos or whatever—"

"I'm an alto," Sophie felt the need to add.

"Fine, your family's the Altos," said Jules. "Well, there's only one solution to all this."

"We take out a hit on her," said Cass.

"What?" Both Amelia and Jules turned to her.

She shrugged. "It's what they'd do in The Sopranos. Sorry, the Altos."

"No," Jules said. "The only thing we can do is clear Sophie's name. If we do that then Tilly won't have an excuse not to be interested, will she?"

There was silence while they all digested this.

"Actually," Amelia said after a minute. "That's not a bad idea."

"It's... not," Sophie said, trying to think clearly and not succeeding terribly well. Then she did come up with something. "How are we supposed to do that, though?"

Cass was opening another bottle of wine. "Easy," she said. "We find the real chip shop."

There was another moment of silence, more confused this time.

"I think she means chop shop," Amelia said finally.

And Sophie grinned. "That's it," she said. "We find the real chop shop and Tilly won't be able to blame our place anymore." She stood up and her legs were a bit wobbly. She'd drunk a lot of wine quite fast.

"I've just opened a new bottle," Cass complained.

"We can go in a bit," said Jules. "We should eat something first, too. It might be a long night."

"Fine," Sophie said, sitting down. "But nothing with pineapple in it."

It felt better to have a plan.

CHAPTER EIGHTEEN

There was a knock, then another, then a very polite voice saying, "Sorry, sorry!"

"I'm in the bath," Tilly said. She had, in fact, been in the bath for nearly two hours. She wasn't sure if it was helping. She had imagined various scenarios in which Sophie had, for a variety of reasons, lied about her identity.

All of the scenarios had involved them kissing again.

"I know," Mila said from outside the door. "And I'm really sorry. But there's a problem. Dougie McKeefe thinks he's got the car thieves and Max is still at the cinema."

But Tilly was already getting out of the bath. She started toweling off. "What do you mean he's 'got' the car thieves?"

"Um, I don't really know," Mila said. "But he's a farmer. He's got a shotgun, I'm sure."

"Oh god," Tilly said, abandoning her towel and pulling her clothes back on. Her trousers stuck to her wet legs. "You'll have to tell me where to go."

"It's... Crap, I'll have to come with you," said Mila. "It's right outside of the village. You'll never find it by yourself. Come on, I'll find the car keys and keep trying Max. I'll meet you outside."

Three minutes later, Tilly was pounding down the stairs, throwing the front door open, and then skidding to a halt as she saw Mila sitting in the driving seat of a tiny, red Renault Clio. "What the hell?"

"Max has the police car," said Mila. "Get in!"

It was hardly the glamorous arrest that she'd hoped to be going to. And her legs were still kind of slippery with soap. "Okay, fine," she said, getting in. "But you must have a blue light attachment in here."

"Why would I have one of those?" Mila said, starting the engine.

"Because you're using this as a back-up police car," said Tilly.

"I use it mostly to pick the kids up from field trips and do the shopping," said Mila, pulling away from the house. "And I got hold of Max. He's going to meet us there after he's dropped the kids off with Ant and Ad at the bookshop."

Tilly looked out of the window, her stomach tightening. This could be it. Her big break and she was riding in a Renault Clio. With little to no back up. God knows how long it would take Max to get there.

She went over things in her head.

Ensure that the firearm was out of the picture. That was priority number one. Then what? Well, it depended on the circumstances, really. Part of being a good police officer was flexibility. She'd need to secure the suspects if she could. There were suspects plural, and she only had one set of cuffs, which might be a problem.

The car screeched around a corner.

A problem she'd have to deal with. She took a shaky breath. Alright, she had this. Technically, she was very well trained. She might not have much experience, but her brain would know what to do, she was sure of it.

Sure enough, that when the car pulled to a halt in front of a farm gate, she leaped out, ready for action. Mila stuck her head through the driver's window. "Can you just open the gate, love?"

Tilly sighed. Not quite the action she'd expected. She opened the gate, waited for Mila to drive through, then closed it again before getting back in the car. They bumped up the drive to the farm, the car headlights illuminating a man with a shotgun as they turned into a courtyard.

This time Mila stopped smoothly and Tilly was out almost before the car came to a halt. "Lower the weapon please, sir," she said as loudly as she dared. Then she remembered to add, "Police." Damn it, she should have said that first.

"Max?" the man asked, squinting into the car headlights.

"This is Constable Wade," Tilly said. "And I need you to lower the shotgun, please."

"They're in there," the man said, gesturing with the gun and forcing Tilly to shelter behind the open car door. "Four of 'em. I locked 'em in, so they won't be getting away."

"Very good, sir," Tilly said.

"Max is almost here," Mila said, poking her head out of the window again.

"Get down," hissed Tilly. "This could be dangerous. He's got a gun."

"Evening, Dougie," Mila said to the farmer conversationally. "Deidre alright?"

"Oh, good days and bad," said the farmer.

Tilly groaned and then saw blue lights at the end of the driveway. Half of her was disappointed. She'd wanted to make these arrests. The other half was heartily relieved. She had no idea what she was doing. Her training had in no way prepared her for chatty booksellers and armed farmers. And anyway, she didn't have enough cuffs for four suspects.

"Evening, Dougie," Max said when he drew up. He got out of his car. "What have we got here, then?"

The farmer explained himself, and Max nodded.

"Are they armed?" he asked.

Dougie shrugged. "Ain't heard no shooting, so probably not."

"Right then." Max looked at Tilly. "Stay here. I'm going to the barn. If anything happens, you get on the police radio and call for backup, understood?"

"But—"

"You heard me, and that's an order," Max said, sounding sterner than she'd ever heard him.

She nodded.

Cautiously, slowly, Max began to walk toward the barn. "Police," he shouted. "Police."

There was no answer until… until music began to drift through the air. It took a second, maybe two, and then Tilly was running toward the barn, toward Max.

"Sophie," she shouted.

"Tilly?" cried a voice from inside.

"That's Sophie Farmer," Tilly said, catching up with Max.

"What's she doing in there?" Max asked, confused.

"Not a clue," said Tilly. "But I'd recognize that voice anywhere. Maybe she's being held hostage?"

The sweet sounds of the Coventry Carol were drowned out by two voices singing what sounded like a very rude song about a young man from Venus. Max coughed. "Um, being held hostage by Amelia and Cass from the cafe? Seems unlikely."

He gestured to Dougie, who came over and handed him the key to the barn.

"Still, stand back," Max said. "Just in case."

But the only thing that came out when Max unlocked the barn were the strains of a song about a monkey doing something very untoward with a bowling ball.

"WHAT WERE YOU thinking?" hissed Tilly as she bundled Sophie into the police station.

"We were looking for car thieves," Sophie said miserably.

Tilly rolled her eyes. "Where do you want her?" she asked Max.

"We'll put the four of them in the interview room back there. The one that's for families," he said. "Give them a chance to sober up a bit before we ask too many questions."

When the four were locked away safely, complete with a pot of coffee that Max had made, Tilly finally collapsed onto her seat. "I should have known better," she said.

"Better than what?" asked Max, sitting down at his own desk.

Tilly took a breath and then explained. It was better to be open about these things, she'd realized. She'd made a mistake getting anywhere close to Sophie Farmer, a mistake she wasn't about to make again. Which was exactly what she told Max.

"Why not?" Max asked.

"What?"

"She's a nice girl," Max said. He glanced over at the interview room. "Well, mostly."

"She's just got arrested," said Tilly.

"Not a usual occurrence," he said. "Is it just because she's a Farmer?"

"Obviously."

Max shook his head. "You can't do that. These are people, remember? You can't judge someone on their family, it's not fair."

"Is it not?" Tilly said, nodding toward the interview room.

"I don't expect you to be a chief superintendent," said Max. "I do, on the other hand, expect you to give people a decent chance and to behave like a decent human being. Not too much to ask in an officer."

"But... Well..." Tilly didn't quite know what to say to that.

Max was looking quite cross. "Has it occurred to you at all to question what they were doing up there and why they were doing it?"

Tilly rolled her eyes. "Sophie said that they were looking for car thieves."

"So not actual car thieves then, just looking for them," said Max. "And why?"

Tilly opened her mouth to answer his question and then realized that she didn't actually have an answer.

"Isn't it obvious?" Max said. "Jules, Amelia, and Cass are all her friends. It might have been a crazy, drunken plan, but they had a reason. If they all went out and tracked down some car thieves, then you wouldn't be able to blame Sophie and her family."

Tilly closed her eyes. "And then there'd be no reason..." She trailed off.

Max sighed. "I'm not arresting them. Dougie doesn't want to press trespassing charges, so there's no real reason to. They weren't doing any harm. But I suggest that you have a think about what it is that you want and what you're doing here. Like it or not, that girl has feelings for you. And if you don't return them, you owe her the courtesy of being honest about that, and not hiding behind excuses about who her family are."

She opened her eyes again. "I'm confused," she confessed miserably.

Max's face cleared a little. "You're going to be a good police officer one day, Tilly. But you won't do it alone. I swear to you that without Mila there to back me up, I'd have burned out long ago. Having someone at home makes a big difference. It's not a weakness to have feelings."

"I do have feelings," Tilly said, stung.

Max grinned. "Then if I were you, I'd tell Sophie because she apparently has feelings, too."

"What about the car thefts?" began Tilly.

Max shrugged. "As long as you're not giving her privileged information, which you shouldn't be giving to anyone, then I don't see a problem."

Tilly glanced over at the interview room.

"Till, she likes you enough to go on some kind of personal vigilante mission to give you a reason to be with her. Whatever doubts you have, Sophie deserves someone to at least hear her out."

Tilly thought about how she'd felt when she heard Sophie's voice. Thought about the kiss, a kiss she'd never wanted to end. Thought about how Sophie had felt in her arms. Thought about how definite Sophie had been about her family not finding out. She turned to Max. "You can't tell anyone. This is personal."

"Wouldn't dream of it," Max said. "This is your business, not mine."

And a smile slowly slid across Tilly's face. Because if it was only a question of what she wanted, the answer was a very simple one indeed.

CHAPTER NINETEEN

Sophie's eyes were sticky and her head was bleary and she seriously, seriously regretted opening the second bottle of wine. Not that alcohol was an excuse. She should have known better. She did know better. She'd just got carried away in the moment and...

"Here."

The smell of the coffee sent a message straight to her brain to wake up. She blinked and saw a hand offering her a mug. She struggled to sit up and then took it, cradling it in her hands and eagerly taking a sip.

"So," Tilly said, sitting down in the chair opposite her.

Sophie wanted to close her eyes again, wanted to block all of this out. "I know," she said. "I know. I'm an idiot and I deserve whatever it is that's about to happen to me. I'm mortified. The only thing I can do is apologize."

"Mr. McKeefe seems to think that you were just indulging in some kind of hijinks," Tilly said. "His word, not mine."

With a sigh, Sophie looked up and for the first time saw Tilly's eyes, soft and blue and crinkled at the corners. She looked... not entirely angry. "No hijinks," she said. She cleared her throat. "This is all my fault though, I mean, if Jules and—"

"We've already sent them home," Tilly said. "McKeefe isn't pressing charges. Though he is interested in learning some of the lyrics that the four of you were singing last night."

Sophie groaned. "I'm just so embarrassed." She could feel it aching in her stomach, like a weight she'd never get rid of.

"What were you doing?" asked Tilly.

"Looking for car thieves," Sophie said. She looked at Tilly again. "We just thought… I just thought… Never mind."

Tilly leaned forward a little, almost like she was going to take Sophie's hand. Not that she would. Not that she ever would now. Sophie was more than aware of the fact that she'd blown it, that there was no way in hell that Tilly would have anything to do with her now. Not that she could blame her.

"I'm sorry," Sophie said. "I'm just…" She blinked away tears. "I get it. I get why you don't want anything to do with me and I'm sorry." There was a long silence, and Sophie could feel the sadness building up inside her.

"I'm sorry."

"What?" That didn't make sense.

"I'm sorry," Tilly said again.

"What do you have to be sorry for?" asked Sophie, very confused. Her hangover wasn't helping matters, but she was pretty sure she wouldn't know what was happening here even if she was stone cold sober.

"I'm sorry because I reacted badly," Tilly said. She took a breath. "Sophie, I didn't know who you were and when you told me, I was shocked. Shocked and… and, to be honest, afraid. Afraid because this is who I am. This job. It's all I've ever wanted and for a second there I saw something that might compromise me and I blamed you for that. Blamed you for something that wasn't at all your fault."

"No," Sophie said, swallowing down her tears again. "No, you were right. I should have told you. I… knew that you were looking into the garage, into dad, I just didn't really put two and two together and… Well, it's not like we've spent a whole lot of time together, is it?"

There was another silence. Sophie studied Tilly, the way the light hit her hair, the long lashes that brushed her cheek when she thought. She was beautiful, Sophie thought. Beautiful and fragile and very, very desirable.

"Can we start again?" Tilly said.

"What?"

"You heard me," said Tilly, straightening up. "Can we start again? Hear me out here. We've only met a handful of times. Maybe those times shouldn't count. Maybe we both screwed things up a bit and we should get a do-over."

"How did you screw things up?" asked Sophie.

"I over-reacted when you told me who you were so that you had to go out drunkenly trespassing in people's barns," Tilly said. "Which, now that I say it, sounds completely insane."

"It does," Sophie agreed. "But you have a point. I mean, I can't help who I am. I'm sure that my dad doesn't have anything to do with your car thefts, but he's no lover of the police. I don't want to compromise your career. That's the last thing I want."

Tilly held up both her hands. "I get it, I get the obstacles. But if we just put those aside for a second..." She took a breath. "Sophie, I really like you."

"You do?" Sophie's heart leaped in her chest. "Um, I mean, I like you too, if that's what we're doing here."

"Mmm, police stations aren't the most romantic places in the world." Tilly scratched her nose. "And we've both been up most of the night, not sure we're looking our best."

"Do we get a do-over on this, too?" Sophie said with a small laugh.

"No," Tilly said. "No, we don't. This gets done once and I might be messing it up already." She took a deep breath. "Alright, here goes. You're the most interesting, prettiest, nicest woman that I've met for a very long time. I like you. There."

Sophie smirked. "Can I just say the same?"

"No," Tilly said. "No, you have to tell the truth. We're in a police interview room. Those are the rules."

"Fine," said Sophie. "Fine. You're the most interesting person that's come to town in forever and the first time I saw you, I fancied you. Happy?"

It was Tilly's turn to smirk. "Alright, so we've got that

part sorted out. Now let's deal with the obstacles. I should not assume things about you because of your family. Actually, I shouldn't assume things about your family either. I'm a police officer. I work with evidence. And other than drunken trespassing, I've no evidence at all that you or your family have done anything wrong."

"Thank you," Sophie said. "That means a lot." She sighed. "But we can't pretend that my family isn't an obstacle. They won't be pleased about any of this. But they'll be far more displeased if they learn that I'm involved with a police officer."

"Involved with," Tilly repeated.

And Sophie had a sharp pain in her heart. Had she assumed too much?

"We barely know each other," Tilly said, looking at her with deep blue eyes. "We have no idea where this is going or what it is. All we do know is that we have to sing together and that there are some feelings swimming around."

Sophie bit her lip.

"I'm just saying… I'm saying that maybe we don't have to be so official yet. It's not like we have to announce things to your family. There might be nothing here. We could… wait a while."

A warmth was growing inside Sophie's stomach. "We could wait a little while," she agreed. "And, um, your job?"

"Max knows," Tilly said. "Don't worry, he's not going to spill the beans. But he's my boss, and he knows that there are, um, feelings. So I think that helps a little. And as long as you're not going to be robbing any banks or anything, I think we're alright."

"A life of crime is not for me," Sophie said quickly. "I think we've firmly established that."

"Good," Tilly said. "But I can't promise you that my investigations won't lead me to your garage. I have to do my job and if that means—"

"I don't need to hear about it," Sophie interrupted. "Your job is your job and you need to do it to the best of your ability. It has nothing to do with me, and if you show up at the garage, then I accept that you're just doing what you have to do."

"You'll trust me?" Tilly asked.

Sophie nodded. "I know you're not out to get them. And I know they're not doing anything wrong. If you need to investigate, then go ahead."

"Okay then."

"Okay then." Sophie coughed. "Um, should we be signing some kind of contract here?"

Tilly laughed, and the sound hit Sophie right in the heart. "I know this isn't the most romantic thing that's ever happened."

"No," Sophie said. "No, it's... It seems right. It feels good. We're both on the same page, I like that. I like..." She grinned. "I like you. Whatever it takes to get to see more of you."

Slowly, Tilly reached her hand across the table, and equally slowly, Sophie took it. Until their fingers were entangled together, until Sophie could feel the touch all over her skin, could feel the shivers as Tilly's fingers moved.

"I'm glad," Tilly said softly. "I'm glad because I actually don't want to be without you. I look forward to seeing you. I've never looked forward to seeing anyone before."

"I hope you're going to be seeing a lot more of me," Sophie said, blushing as she realized what she implied.

But Tilly's eyebrow raised just a millimeter. "Is that an invitation, Ms. Farmer?"

"Would you like it to be one?" Sophie responded. Her mouth was dry, and she didn't think it was just the hangover.

"I can't think of anything I'd like more." Tilly's voice had deepened, grown huskier.

Sophie was contemplating getting up, wondering if there was anything illegal about making out in an interview room, thinking that maybe, just maybe she might be about to throw caution to the wind, when the sound of her father's voice rang through the station.

"I demand to see my daughter."

She snatched her hand away from Tilly's, straightening up, starting to feel sick again.

"It's fine," Tilly said. "You're free to go."

Sophie nodded. "I'd better, um, better get out there then, before he does something he regrets."

Tilly stood up and gestured toward the door. "I'd probably better stay out of sight."

Sophie's hand was on the door handle now. She glanced back at Tilly. "Soon?"

"Soon," Tilly smiled.

And Sophie's heart lightened as she stepped out of the interview room.

Her father was standing in front of the wooden counter, his hair a mess, his face far too red. Max was trying to placate him.

"Dad, I'm fine," Sophie said, stepping around the counter. "And I'm free to go. Let's get out of here."

He glared at Max as Sophie took his arm. "Police harassment," he said.

Sophie sighed. "Think about your heart, your blood pressure," she said, pulling him toward the door.

"Maybe you should have thought about that," he grumbled, but he let himself be ushered out.

Sophie turned at the last minute and saw Tilly's pale face watching as she left. And her life felt suddenly so much brighter.

CHAPTER TWENTY

When Tilly woke up, she felt lighter than she had for weeks. She grinned to herself before she was even out of bed.

This was really working. She allowed herself the pleasure of imagining Sophie's face next to hers, of imagining her dark hair splayed out on the pillow. And she felt all the right tingles. It was just as Max had said. Communication was key. Not only in police work, but in relationships too, it turned out.

If that was all she had to do, be open and honest, she was going to be just as good at being a girlfriend as she was at being a police officer.

Being a girlfriend? Where had that come from?

But the more she thought about it, the more she liked the sound of it. Not that she was going to go asking Sophie about that right now. No. She'd take her time, take things slowly. She wouldn't be more than a few months in Whitebridge, but that meant she had some time to play with.

And when she left? Well, either she'd be leaving Sophie behind, hopefully after a mutually agreed upon break up, or, potentially, taking her along. Either way, there was a lot of scope here. And Tilly liked scope. She also liked being good at things.

Speaking of which, there was a choir rehearsal tonight. So she'd be seeing Sophie sooner rather than later.

Her body shuddered at the thought of it, at the memory of

Sophie's lips, at the thought of just seeing her smile.

There was a problem, though. They couldn't go on casting lingering glances at choir rehearsal and sharing secret kisses in the village hall. They weren't sweaty teenagers. There had to be some private time, and some romantic time.

She wondered if she could persuade Max to lend her the police car to take Sophie out to dinner somewhere outside of Whitebridge?

She'd have to work on that.

Despite the long night, she had a bounce in her step when she walked down the stairs and into the main house. Enough of a bounce that she almost didn't hear the argument that was happening in the living room.

But Mila's voice caught her attention.

"Be realistic," Mila said, sharply.

Tilly stopped in her tracks. The living room door was firmly closed.

"I am being realistic," Max said. "We've never had a problem before. I don't see why it should be one now."

"Because no matter how hard I try, I just can't get all this to add up," said Mila, sounding frustrated and a little bit like she might be crying

"Mil, there's no point crying about a fait accompli," said Max, sounding exasperated.

"And what am I supposed to do, then?" wailed Mila. "We don't have any choices here."

"There are always choices," said Max reasonably. "You just don't like any of them."

"Well, do you?"

There was a silence, then a snuffling sound as Mila sniffed.

"Something will turn up," Max said. "Really, I'll figure something out."

"When?"

Another exasperated sigh. "Later," Max said. "I have a ton of paperwork to finish."

"It's always work, work, work," Mila said.

Tilly closed her eyes. She shouldn't be listening to this. But then, she didn't really need to be listening to this. She'd heard it all before. Heard it from her mum and dad when she was not much older than Ag was now.

A sadness welled up inside her. Not just for her parents, but because she'd thought that Max and Mila had everything figured out, that they were the proof that relationships between police and civilians could work.

Except maybe they weren't. Maybe they had their problems just like everyone else.

She leaned against the wall, hearing Mila crying, Max obviously comforting her now. Would she end up like this? Would she end up comforting a crying Sophie as she came home late again? As she rushed to a crime scene again? As she missed a dinner or a birthday or Christmas again?

"Trust me," Max said. "Just trust me, Mil. We can make this work. Together, we can make this work."

"I know." Mila sounded tired. "But sometimes I want to hide under a table until the world goes away."

Max laughed. "Go for it."

"I would, but there's dropped cereal and all sorts under the kitchen table," said Mila. She sighed. "We'll make it work."

Tilly swallowed. She sincerely hoped that whatever the problem was that Mila and Max would make it work. Together. That was the key word, wasn't it? Together, they probably could. Maybe that was what it took, two people ready to work for the same thing.

Two people on the same page.

And weren't she and Sophie on the same page?

She felt her mouth twitching up into a smile again. They were, she knew it. She knew that if they could just keep being honest about things, keep talking, then they could stay on the same page. She took a breath. They could do this. She could do this.

She couldn't go around assuming every relationship was doomed to failure just because of her job. She wasn't making choices that denied her a life of her own. She was going to be a career police officer, and she was going to have a personal life. Plenty of other people managed to juggle both.

Her phone was in her pocket and she pulled it out. She had Sophie's mobile number, not that she'd ever used it for anything other than setting up a rehearsal meeting. But now she thought she should send something.

With quick fingers, she typed a brief message. *Thinking of you.* That was all. Simple, sweet, and true. She sent it and immediately her phone vibrated.

Me too, was the answer.

She felt warm inside as she slid her phone back into her pants pocket and left Mila and Max to their conversation. She was hungry and needed a late breakfast.

When she walked into the kitchen, Ag and Dash were at the table, still in pajamas, their faces sticky with cereal, and a pool of spilled milk on the counter.

"Did you two make your own breakfast?" Tilly asked.

"Mum and dad are arguing," Dash said.

"Not arguing, they're having a discussion," said Ag. "Mum says that's different because it means that you don't have to win. Which sounds boring because winning is important, isn't it?"

Tilly considered this. "Yes," she said finally. "But it's not always the most important thing."

"Why not?" asked Dash.

"Um, because sometimes other things are important," Tilly said. She looked at Ag. "Like when you play in your piano competitions, sometimes having the experience is important, sometimes just playing in front of people is important, it's not all about winning."

"Yes, but I'm going to win," Ag said. "Probably even a grand piano, but I'm definitely going to win a place at the conservatory."

"I thought that a conservatory was for plants," Dash said thoughtfully.

"It is," Ag said. Then she frowned. "But it's for pianos too."

"They're different things," said Tilly.

"Like how a barn is for pigs but also for cows," said Dash.

Now it was Tilly's turn to frown. She wasn't at all sure about the comparison. "Maybe?" she hazarded. She paused and listened. No sign of Max or Mila. "Do your mum and dad have a lot of... discussions?" she asked, fully aware that it was none of her business.

Ag shrugged. "No, mostly they do kissy stuff when they think no one's looking. And then they do working stuff because being a policeman is important and being a bookseller is equally important because people need to be safe but also they need to take breaks and relax for their mental health."

"Have you considered switching to a wind instrument, or a brass one?" Tilly asked. "Like a trumpet maybe?"

"Why?" Ag asked, eyes wide and blue.

"Because you don't seem to need to take a breath when you're talking," said Tilly. "I think that'd be an advantage for a trumpet player."

Ag tilted her head to one side. "I'll think about it," she said. "Do you want some cereal?"

"Yes," said Tilly. "But first I think we'd better clean up all this milk, don't you?"

She was instructing Dash on how to clean up, given he was the one that had made the spill, when Max and Mila came into the kitchen.

"I'm cleaning," Dash announced.

"You're a miracle worker," Mila said to Tilly. Her eyes looked a little red, but she was smiling and relaxed. "I can't even get him to pick up his toys."

"I'm only going to take them out again," Dash grumbled. "I don't see the point in putting them away."

"I'm going to fry some bacon," said Max. "Anyone for bacon sandwiches? They're the best breakfast."

"Yay," said Dash.

"Tilly?" asked Max.

"If it's no trouble."

"No trouble at all," he said. "Why don't you come out to the meat freezer in the garage and help me get the bacon?"

He was giving her a look that told her he wanted to talk to her in private, so she followed him out to the chilly garage, where he opened up a chest freezer and took out some bacon.

"Got a call this morning," he said quietly. "Someone wanted to talk to you, heard that you were investigating the car thefts. They'll be in tomorrow morning, so make sure you're at the station bright and early."

"A source," Tilly said.

Max grinned. "You're already getting a reputation around these parts," he said. "Well done. Just make sure the info's good before you do anything about it."

"Will do," Tilly said as Max closed the freezer up.

She followed him back into the kitchen with a grin on her face. Now she had two things to look forward to. Moving her investigation forward tomorrow morning, and far sooner, seeing Sophie in just a few hours.

CHAPTER TWENTY ONE

"Never again," Jules said. "I swear."

"I'm not buying that," said Sophie as they walked along the cool street toward the village hall. "Especially if Cass and Amelia are around."

"They're a bad influence," Jules agreed.

"They're certainly not a good one," said Sophie. She sighed. "But I was all in, and they were just trying to help. I'm not entirely sure how we ended up locked in McKeefe's barn, though."

"He thought we were cattle rustlers or something, you know how much *Yellowstone* he watches. He didn't press charges though," said Jules. "And it was your idea to go up there. You said we should revisit the scene of the crime. Anyway, it all worked out alright in the end, didn't it?"

Sophie grinned. "It might have," she said, not wanting to jinx anything.

"Oh, come on, you and the Constable are getting on like a house on fire now. You've got an arrangement, right?"

"We do. She does her job, I stay out of it, she doesn't hold my family against me, we don't tell them anything. Simple. Now all we need to do is figure out some way of actually seeing each other at some point, and we'll be fine."

"The pub has a back room," Jules offered. "You could have a drink in there. It's a bit cold though. But at least you get to sing together. You're getting quite the reputation. Billy won't stop going on about this damn carol that the two of you are singing. I'd got no idea you could actually sing."

"Me neither," Sophie said. "But dad said that mum liked to sing."

Jules reached out and squeezed her hand. Not having a mum around was something that they had in common. Jules's mum had disappeared when she was young, leaving her with her grandfather and sister.

"We're going to be late if we don't get a move on," Jules said. "Come on, I'll race you."

Sophie rolled her eyes as Jules started running toward the village hall. She sped up a little, but not too much. She was still trying to take in everything that had happened. She'd gone from depressed to drunk to locked in a barn to under arrest to having a 'state of the relationship' talk literally overnight.

Her father wasn't pleased with her, it went without saying. She'd had a stern lecture and warnings to stay away from McKeefe's and not to get involved with the police. And it had been all she could do to stop Gio filing some kind of police harassment report he was so sure that Sophie was being targeted because of her name.

It was all worth it, though. Worth it because as she approached the village hall, she could feel the tickling fingers of anticipation on her spine. Her stomach flipped, her blood started to pound, and she was going to see Tilly at any minute.

Jules was already in through the front door, shedding her jacket as Sophie went in herself. She got three steps inside before someone slid out of the shadows. She jumped, startled, then smiled. "Oh, it's you."

"Sorry, have we met?" Tilly said innocently.

"Ye—wait, what?"

"I'm Tilly Ware, I'm the new constable up at the police station," said Tilly, holding out a hand.

Sophie stared at it uncertainly.

"Do-over," Tilly hissed.

"Oh, right," said Sophie, catching on. She grinned wider. "I'm Sophie Farmer. I'm an accountant and receptionist at a garage down the street that is occasionally suspected of not being on the right side of the law. Even if it is."

Tilly grinned back. "That should about cover introductions, then." She cleared her throat. "You are very attractive Sophie."

"Um, thank you, you too."

Another grin. "I was wondering if perhaps you wouldn't like to go out for a drink sometime?"

Sophie laughed. "Alright, alright, point made. I would love not to have a drink with you."

Tilly stepped in, her hand sliding into the curve of Sophie's waist. In the hall, they could hear Billy start to call things to order. "I'd like to do a lot more than not take you for a drink," Tilly whispered.

The hairs on Sophie's neck stood on end. She shivered, a delightful heat pooling between her legs. She let one of her hands stray to Tilly's chest, felt her breath, felt the warmth of her. Then Tilly's head was tilting and Sophie's breath was coming faster. Their lips brushed and Billy shouted from the hall.

"Oh Christ," Tilly said. She stepped back. "Okay, time to sing."

It took Sophie a second to catch her breath again after losing it so suddenly. Tilly's eyes were dark with desire, her lips already swelling. For an instant, Sophie was about to suggest that they just leave. Go anywhere. Outside, a hotel, not that there was a hotel in Whitebridge. Or perhaps the garage. There was that big storage shed out back. There were no windows there, perhaps…

"We'll have time," Tilly said. "Let's do this properly. Come on, in we go."

ACROSS THE PIANO Sophie could watch Tilly as they sang, the whole choir together. It was a simple carol, and she didn't have to concentrate too hard. Giving her all the time she needed to drink Tilly in.

Her golden curls, her blue eyes, the way her nose wrinkled a little as she sang. And Sophie's heart was singing too. There was definitely something here, and even though it had only been a couple of weeks, she knew it was something special.

Something that could turn into something even better.

There were big feelings here, ones that she was afraid of, but that she couldn't deny. Tilly's had been the first face she'd thought of when she woke up, and she was so deep into thinking about her right now, she didn't care if the whole damn hall caught fire.

She could imagine, if she let herself, waking up next to her. Eating opposite her. Holding hands and shopping and doing all the banal everyday things that made up a life with her.

The only thing she couldn't factor into the picture was her family. She dreaded to think what her father would say when he found out, and Gio would be just as bad if not worse. And then what? Because as much as she could imagine her life with Tilly in it, she couldn't imagine one without her family there.

Yes, they irritated her, yes, they ruined things sometimes, but they were hers, an indelible part of her. She was achingly aware that at some point she might be forced to choose. And she could hardly bear to think about it.

The song came to an end. "Alright, alright," Billy said, clapping her hands together. "Not bad. You've got the sheet music to everything now, there'll be nothing else new. The concert is set for the second Saturday in December, which gives us less than four weeks to prepare everything. Now, let me hear my soloists, up to the front."

Sophie walked up to the piano and felt Tilly come up behind her, close enough that they were touching, close enough that Sophie's blood started to pound in her veins again. They patiently waited their turn, with Sophie leaning back into Tilly, feeling the support of her body.

Heat started to creep around her core. One of Tilly's hands

was on her waist again, hidden from the others by their position. Sophie's breath came faster. She closed her eyes, took as deep a breath as she could, and stepped away. She glanced up at Tilly, who was grinning. "Not here," she mouthed.

Tilly winked at her, but before she could say anything, it was their turn to sing.

"Not bad," Billy said when they were done. "You need a lot more practice, though. Can you commit to seeing each other outside of rehearsal?"

Sophie choked back a laugh as Tilly agreed rather too enthusiastically.

"Good," said Billy. "In fact, you can stay here now if you like. Just be sure to turn out the lights when you're done. The hall will be open until ten."

She dismissed the rest of the choir and they left, Jules dropping a lascivious wink in Sophie's direction as she went out.

And then they were alone again.

"Ours until ten," Tilly said, taking a step forward.

"That's only fifteen minutes," said Sophie, not quite daring to reach out and touch Tilly.

"That's plenty of time for what I had in mind."

Sophie laughed and shook her head. "Not here. It's cold. It's… just not here."

Tilly nodded. "Fair enough." She stepped forward again anyway, putting her arms around Sophie's waist. "Do you know I've only kissed you once?"

"Ah," said Sophie, her eyes fixated on Tilly's rosy lips. "That means it's my turn to kiss you, doesn't it?"

She didn't wait for an answer, leaning in, letting her lips brush Tilly's, driving the kiss, putting more pressure on, until her hands were on Tilly's face, until Tilly's hands were pulling at her waist, pulling her in, closer.

She stumbled and Tilly took her weight for a moment, lifting her, positioning her until she was backed up against the piano and she could feel Tilly's body pressed up against her own, could feel the firmness of her breasts, the sharpness of her hip-bones.

It was Tilly that stepped back, taking a gasping breath. "Jesus," she said. "Jesus." Another breath, slower this time. "Not here, right?"

Sophie shook her head. Anyone could come in. And she didn't want things to be this way. She did want Tilly, however. "I'm sorry."

"Don't be sorry. We're adults, you're right, we shouldn't be fumbling around in public places. I'm a police officer. I don't need a public nudity charge."

Sophie snorted a laugh. "Naked in the village hall."

"Not a good look."

"Even if you're very attractive?" Sophie asked.

Tilly didn't answer. "Listen, the night after tomorrow, I'm babysitting at Max and Mila's. Why don't you come over? I'll text you when the kids are in bed. I'm sure Max and Mila won't mind, but I'll ask them, anyway. We could have a little privacy, have some dinner maybe. No expectations, I promise."

Sophie bit her lip and nodded immediately. "No expectations," she said. But her head, her stomach, her core were all swimming with expectations. She shivered against the cold. "It's a date," she said.

Tilly smiled. "Good. Now, do we need to leave separately?"

"Maybe?"

"You go first," Tilly said. She leaned in and brushed Sophie's lips with her own. "Best go before I change my mind."

And Sophie ran off, warm and, for the first time in a long time, happy.

CHAPTER TWENTY TWO

Tilly was in such a good mood that even Ag banging out a rousing rendition of her concert piece at six thirty in the morning didn't bother her in the slightest. "Nice job, Ag," she called through to the living room as she went into the kitchen.

"It's the zillionth time I've heard it," Dash was moaning as she went in.

"Your sister has to practice," said Mila.

"Why? We don't have room for a stupid grand piano," said Dash. "And she's not a plant, she can't grow in a conservatory."

"Eat your cereal," said Mila, rolling her eyes at Tilly. "Can I get you something?"

"I'll just grab some cereal, if that's okay," said Tilly. She tilted her head to better take in Mila, who was looking very tired. "But if you want to sit down, I can get us both something? Make some coffee maybe?"

Mila laughed. "No time for breakfast. I've got to get these monsters off to school. And you don't have time to take care of me. Max has left already."

"This early?"

"He's catching up on paperwork," said Mila. "Or hoping for a promotion."

Tilly smiled and poured herself some cereal. She didn't know what Max's chances of a promotion were, but they couldn't be high. Not if he wanted to stay working in Whitebridge. It was only when she was halfway through her cereal that she remembered that she had a big day coming up.

Her first informant. She wondered who it could be and what they could want to tell her. She was determined not to get her hopes up. Unlike her hopes with Sophie. They were very firmly up. Which reminded her.

"Mila, I was wondering if I could ask you something?"

"Anything," Mila said, wiping up the mess that Dash had made.

"Absolutely feel free to say no, but I was wondering if it was alright to invite Sophie over tomorrow when I'm babysitting? After the kids are already asleep, obviously."

Mila snorted a laugh. "Of course, it's fine," she said. "And don't worry about the kids being asleep. They both know Soph. Although if you're still wanting to keep things quiet, you'd do better waiting until they're out for the count. Ag never stops talking and Dash doesn't see the point of secrets."

"What's a secret?" Dash asked, looking up.

"None of your business," said Mila. "Now go and find your coat, please." He hopped off his chair and disappeared. Mila turned back to Tilly. "I know that the accommodation situation isn't ideal," she said. "But you should feel free to bring friends home. Even, um, special friends. You've got your own entrance, your own little flat up there. Who you invite is your own business."

"Thanks," Tilly said, feeling herself blush slightly.

"Max even did some soundproofing, so feel free to get loud," Mila said with a naughty wink.

Tilly blushed even further, bolted the rest of her cereal, and decided to beat a rapid retreat. She had the feeling that Ag and Dash's lack of filter was probably hereditary.

IT WAS HALF past ten when a man walked into the station. Tilly was sitting behind the desk getting some paperwork done. Writing parking tickets was all very well, but there was always so much follow up to do after. She looked up and smiled before she recognized the man as old Mrs. Dodds' son.

"Oh dear," she said. "Is it your mum? Is she alright?"

"Great," he said. "Those new locks have really set her mind at rest. She's a lot better now. Thanks for coming over."

"Not a problem," Tilly said, getting up and coming to the counter. "So, what can I help you with today, then?"

He reached up and scratched his nose. "Well, it's more a case of what I might be able to help you with," he said. "Max said you were working on this car theft thing?"

"Oh," Tilly said, surprised. "Oh, right, yes. You'd better come through. Let's go into one of the interview rooms so we'll have some privacy. Coffee? Tea?"

"A cuppa would be lovely," he said. "I'm Len, by the way. Len Dodds."

"Pleasure to meet you, Len. I'll be right with you."

She hurried to make the tea, wondering just what she'd expected. Probably someone shadier, someone more... criminal looking, to be honest. Definitely not someone clean-cut and respectable, like Len Dodds. She sighed to herself. She really needed to stop judging people like that.

It was a lesson to be learned, she told herself, as she carried the cups into the little interview room.

"Right then," she said, once they were settled. "Why don't you just tell me what you know in your own words?"

"Okay," he said, picking up his cup. "The thing is, mum doesn't sleep so well anymore. She's up and down all the time and rarely sleeps past about four." He paused and looked at Tilly. "I look after her, see? I moved in after she had her first stroke."

"Right," Tilly said, pen paused over her notebook.

"I'm telling you that so you know why I might be up at odd

hours is all," he went on. "And the other thing you should know is that my mate Dougie is one of the ones that had his car stolen, so I know that there's been a problem."

McKeefe again, Tilly thought. His name was coming up a lot. "Okay."

"Anyway, I don't know if it's anything, but it's happened a few times now and that's got me thinking that it might be something."

"What's happened exactly?" Tilly asked, starting to get impatient.

"Cars driving down past the back window at odd times of night. The house doesn't back onto a main road or anything. It's Moore Street if you want to check. There's usually not much traffic there at all. But for the last few weeks, I've been seeing and hearing cars down there. Usually late, around one or two."

Tilly nodded. "Alright, okay, that's... helpful information. Thank you." Her mind was already buzzing. There might be cameras down there, she might be able to see the registration plates of cars. On the other hand, it could be nothing. Maybe there were roadworks somewhere and people were avoiding them, for example.

"Just wanted to say," Len said. "Cracking tea, thanks."

"You're very welcome," Tilly said, but she was already getting up. "I'm going to have to get that information checked out. Feel free to stay until you've finished your tea." And then she was gone.

Five minutes later, she knew that there were no cameras around Moore Street. But she also knew something else. Moore Street ran parallel to the main street through town. Which meant it ran right along the back side of the Farmer's garage.

IT WASN'T THAT she didn't consider Sophie. It was that this was her job, and they had an agreement and Tilly had honestly thought that they could both handle it.

But when she and Max walked through the door of the garage,

the smell of oil and petrol hitting her nose, she could see by the look on Sophie's face that this wasn't going to be as simple as all that.

"Paul," Max said with a nod.

"What do you want?" Paul Farmer said. His son, Gio, was standing right behind him, a large wrench in his hand.

Max sighed. "Don't make this difficult," he said. "We've had some information about cars being spotted around these parts."

"It's a garage. What do you expect?" Paul sneered.

"Late at night, when there shouldn't be cars," Max went on calmly. "Now, it's only a bit of information. I could apply for a warrant. But I thought you might let me have a little look around, keep things quiet and off the record for now."

Gio stepped forward. "So you can plant something?"

"He wouldn't do that," said Tilly.

Max waved a hand at her to quieten her. "You're welcome to be with me every step of the way," he said. "I just want to have a look at what's out in the open. Just make sure everything's alright." He paused. "Or I could get that warrant."

Paul Farmer shook his head at his son. "Let him look," he said. "We've got nothing to hide."

Sophie stepped out from behind her desk. Tilly's heart skipped a beat, and it was all she could do not to smile at her.

"They've done nothing," said Sophie, determinedly looking at Max and not at Tilly.

Tilly took a breath. Maybe she shouldn't have come, but this was her case.

"I hear you," Max said. "But I'd like a look around, anyway."

"I live with them both," said Sophie. "I'd know if they were out at night chopping up cars, and they're not. You've got my word. They're not doing anything."

"Stay out of it," Paul said to Sophie. "Let the bastards have a look around." He nodded to Gio. "You go with them, make sure they don't leave anything behind."

Max and Tilly began looking around the garage, followed closely by Gio. Max had already told her the rules here. They weren't to touch anything, they could only look at what was in plain sight, so no opening any drawers or cupboards. As they wandered around the place, looking for any signs that any of the stolen cars might have been here, Tilly could feel Sophie's eyes on her.

It felt like a long time, but it was only around ten minutes or so, before Max stopped, turned back to Paul Farmer, and thanked him.

"Told you you'd find nothing," Paul said. "Go on then, get out of here. And next time, bring a bloody warrant."

"Hopefully, that won't be necessary," Max said, leading Tilly out of the garage and back to the street.

Tilly looked back over her shoulder, desperate for one last glimpse of Sophie, but Sophie was hidden behind her computer.

"Not a sausage," Max sniffed when they got back out onto the street. "Which only means that they're clever enough not to leave anything in plain sight." He sighed. "I don't think we've got enough for a warrant, though, not without more than Len Dodds seeing the odd car at night."

"Agreed," Tilly said. "It was only a thought."

"Not a bad one," Max said. "But let's keep our options open, shall we? And you did the right thing. We had to have a look."

But Tilly wasn't so sure. Not now that she'd seen Sophie's face. She had an uncomfortable feeling that she and Sophie were about to have an unpleasant discussion.

CHAPTER TWENTY THREE

Paul Farmer slammed down the hood of the car he'd been working on and patted it. "Good as new," he said. He turned to Sophie. "You can give Ad Park a ring and tell her that her car's ready to be picked up."

"Right," Sophie said, writing a post-it and sticking it on her computer. "And then I've ordered the parts you wanted. They'll be in on the sixteenth."

"Good. I'll just go and wash my hands." He disappeared off into the bathroom.

Sophie sighed.

This wasn't what she'd wanted to do with her life. Sitting at a tiny desk in a cramped garage, smelling of oil and ordering car parts. Alright, she did some accounting, but this wasn't what she'd trained for.

Not for the first time, she thought about applying for other jobs. At the beginning, this had all been temporary. Her dad had needed the help, and she'd just finished school. But over time, it had turned into an expectation.

Which was why she couldn't apply for another job. Her dad would be so hurt.

"What you thinking about, Soph?" he asked as he came back in. He perched on the edge of her desk. "Not still worried about the police thing, are you?"

How was she supposed to answer that? Of course she was. She'd tried to file it away in her mind, tried to forget about it, but of course she was worried about it. Her love interest had raided her work-place.

Okay, that was a bit of an exaggeration, but it was kind of true, too. And yes, she knew that Tilly had a job to do, but she could have sent a text or something instead of just turning up like that. There was more to it, though. Like the fact that she'd been sitting there at her desk while Max and Tilly were walking around, expecting them to find something at any moment.

She'd been so sure that Gio and her dad hadn't done anything. Right up until the police arrived. Then she'd just been waiting for the piano to fall on her head.

They weren't going out at night, she was sure of that. She was relatively sure that they had nothing directly to do with the stolen cars. But… but there was that little sneaky suspicion in the back of her head. That worry about why Gio had a new car, about the raises they'd been promised.

"You don't need to be worried about the cops," her dad said now. "They're just giving us a hard time. It'll clear itself up."

"Right."

"We haven't done anything, you know that, don't you?"

She nodded. Her dad reached over and took her hand, giving it a squeeze.

"You do a good job here, Soph," he said, his eyes blue and a bit misty looking. "And I've been meaning to talk to you about it for a while now. I know that this isn't your dream job."

"But—"

"Nah, let me finish," he said. "I know it's not what you've always wanted to do. But I also know that you've got a good head on your shoulders and, well, I'm not getting any younger, am I?"

"You're fine," Sophie said. "And you'll stay fine as long as you take your meds."

"I can't stay fine forever," he said, squeezing her hand again. "And it's important to have things sorted out." He rubbed his nose with his hand. "Here's the thing. I know you can be trusted. So when I go, I want to leave the garage in your hands."

She opened her eyes wider in shock. "Me? I always thought—"

"Gio's a good boy and he's good at his job, but he can't run the place and both you and he know it. I'll expect you to keep him on and pay him a good salary, but the actual day-to-day running of the place, well, that'll be down to you. I'll talk to Gio about it. Not now, but closer to the time."

Sophie swallowed, nodded, unsure of what she was supposed to say.

Her dad stood up and stretched. "Right, after a day like today, I'm off for a pint. Gio's probably already propping up the bar. You coming down the pub?"

"No," Sophie said. "Not yet. I've got a few invoices to finish and then I need to do some choir practice."

"I tell you what, I'm looking forward to this concert of yours," her dad said with a grin.

She smiled back. "It won't be long now."

She bent her head down and got on with some work while her dad finished putting tools away and then bid her goodbye. She waited until he was truly gone, door closed, before she sat back in her chair and looked around.

She didn't think they'd done anything. But thinking wasn't enough. Not if this place was going to be hers one day. If she was going to own the garage, she wanted to know that everything was legal. She wanted to make sure there was nothing to find here.

And she had one advantage over the police. She could go anywhere she liked.

She started with the large tool boxes with their pull out drawers.

IT WAS ALMOST eight, and she'd found nothing when her phone started to ring. Tired, dirty, and aching, she went back to her desk, flopped onto her chair, and answered the phone without thinking.

"I thought we were going to sing."

Sophie sighed. "I thought we had an arrangement."

"Me too," said Tilly. "To sing. But you're not here?"

She'd been avoiding this conversation, she realized. Okay, so she had wanted to check the garage for possible contraband. She'd wanted to make sure that if the police came back, they found nothing. But, more pressingly, she'd wanted to avoid seeing Tilly. Because she was angry.

"That's not what I meant."

"Ah," Tilly said. There was a silence on the other end of the phone. When Tilly spoke again, her voice was soft but clear. "I'm not going to apologize, Sophie."

"You could have rung."

"No," Tilly said. "No, I couldn't. That was police work. I had information that led me to believe the garage could be involved in the stolen car ring. I could not inform you, the daughter of the owner, that we were preparing to come and have a look around. How would that have looked in court?"

"We're not in court," Sophie said stubbornly.

"Listen, we agreed. I have a job to do. You have a complicated family. Those two things are going to coincide at points. There's nothing I can do about that. What would you have liked me to do?"

"I'd have liked some warning."

"You're being unreasonable." There was a pause. "Sophie, I know that you know this."

She did know it. She was being unreasonable. "I suppose."

"These things are going to happen. I'm not going to compromise my job for you. And in the same way, I don't expect you to compromise your family for me."

Sophie bit her lip. Tilly was right, she knew she was right. "It was just… it was a shock, that's all. To see you here, to see you so soon, just… just looking."

"Looking and finding nothing," Tilly reminded her. "And just so you know, no matter what your brother might think, neither

Max nor I would ever plant evidence."

"I know that," Sophie said. She did know it. She instinctively trusted Tilly. She sighed, the sound louder through the phone than she'd intended. "Have I messed all this up?"

"What?"

"This. Us. Have I been unreasonable and messed it all up?"

Tilly laughed a little and Sophie's stomach eased. "I don't think so. There are bound to be misunderstandings sometimes, aren't there?" Tilly said. "And whilst I won't apologize for doing my job, I will apologize for taking you by surprise like that. It wasn't my intention, just an unfortunate side effect."

"Right," Sophie said. "Um, and I apologize for being weird about it."

"We all get to be weird sometimes," said Tilly. "What about this singing business?"

"Yeah, sorry about that too," Sophie said. "I got caught up in some paperwork and forgot the time." Partially true.

"It's a bit late now," said Tilly. "I think we're doing okay, though. We can miss one practice." She cleared her throat. "What about tomorrow?"

"Tomorrow?"

"Babysitting?"

Sophie stared at her computer screen. She'd been shaken when Tilly and Max had shown up. She'd made her promises in the village hall, thinking that the matter was mostly closed, thinking that there was no way anyone could really believe that Gio and her dad had done anything. The reality of it hit a little different.

The reality of dating someone like Tilly.

A police officer.

"You absolutely don't have to come," Tilly said. There was a slight catch in her voice, something Sophie hadn't heard before. "I mean, if you don't want to, or it's too soon, or, or whatever."

Still, the police had been now, hadn't they? They'd seen that there was nothing here. They surely wouldn't come back. She was being silly. She looked around at the half-darkened garage.

The garage that would be hers one day.

"Yes," she said. "Yes, I'll be there."

"Brilliant," Tilly said, and she sounded like she was sixteen, so young, so innocent. "I've already talked to Mila about it. She says it's fine. We can order a pizza or something if you like. How about around eight? I think the kids should be asleep by then."

Sophie stretched her legs out, thinking about Tilly's hand on her waist, thinking about the firmness of her lips. "How about around seven?" she said.

"Eager, are we?"

"I want to see you." The raw desire in her voice took even Sophie by surprise. She took another look around the garage, wondering if she could stand another full day of working before she saw Tilly again.

"I want to see you too," said Tilly. "I... I was worried that you weren't going to want to see me anymore after today."

"But you did your job anyway," Sophie said.

"I did. It's important to me."

"More important than I am?" Sophie couldn't help but ask.

"That's not a fair question. I've only known you for a couple of weeks. And we have an arrangement."

"We do," Sophie said. "Yes. You're right. We do." She closed her eyes and could see Tilly's face. "Alright, I'll be there tomorrow."

"I can't wait," Tilly said.

"Me neither."

CHAPTER TWENTY FOUR

"You don't have to worry," Mila said. "Ag will tell you what to do. You know what's she's like. Just make sure they're in bed by seven. Dash can read for a half hour, Ag can read for an hour."

"Fine," said Tilly. Honestly, she was a police officer. She was trained to deal with drunk and disorderly adults. Surely she could handle two small children.

"You're not allowed to use handcuffs, pepper spray, or your baton," Max said, reading her mind. "That makes it a whole lot more difficult."

"I'll be fine," said Tilly. "You just go out and have a nice time."

"We won't be late," Mila said.

"We're only going for a meal," said Max.

"Just have fun," said Tilly, ushering them out of the house.

The next hour was taken up with getting the kids dinner and getting them to actually eat it rather than talk through it. In the end, Tilly had to institute a no talking at the table rule, which Dash neatly avoided by simply getting out of his chair every time he had something to say.

By the time the doorbell rang, Tilly hadn't had a second to be nervous about Sophie coming. Normally, she'd have been panicking by now, straightening cushions, brushing her teeth multiple times, wondering if she was going to make a good impression.

But she opened the door with spaghetti on her shirt and a lock of hair falling over one eye.

"Is that blood or ketchup?" Sophie asked, leaning in to see Tilly's face better in the light.

"Ketchup," Tilly said. "Probably." She wiped her arm across her face. "Sorry."

"Don't be," laughed Sophie. "I know Ag and Dash of old. They're a handful."

"What's a handful?" Dash asked, strolling out of the kitchen with a large bottle of coke in both hands.

"You are," said Sophie. "And I've got a feeling that you're not supposed to have that."

"I'm not going to drink it," Dash said, as though the very thought of it was unbelievable. "I'm going to throw it out of the window upstairs 'cos Ag says it's going to explode."

"It will explode," said Ag, following her brother out of the kitchen. "Do you want to watch?"

Tilly shared a look with Sophie. "Um, that's probably a mum and dad activity, so maybe wait until tomorrow?" she said. "Ag, why don't you play your concert piece for Sophie? Soph's in the choir, you know?"

"Yay," Ag said. She took Sophie's hand. "Come on. You can tell me about Billy. I mean, Ms. Brooke. She's my piano teacher and your choir teacher."

"Sorry," Tilly said. "Let me just get Dash clean and I'll be in to rescue you."

"We'll be fine," Sophie said, laughing as Ag dragged her away.

DASH RAN DOWNSTAIRS in his pajamas, Tilly following him, hoping that Ag hadn't talked Sophie to death.

"You're going to sing for us," Ag announced as Tilly went into the living room.

"We are?" asked Tilly.

"Hurray," Dash said, bouncing on the couch.

"Sorry," Sophie said. "But Ag insists on hearing it. Is it alright? I thought we could do with the practice, and Ag can play the accompaniment."

"Fine by me," Tilly said. "But Dash can only listen if he sits down quietly."

The boy immediately crashed down onto the couch, crossed his legs and arms, and pressed his lips tightly closed.

"Are you ready?" Ag asked.

Tilly glanced at Sophie and shrugged. "I suppose."

The first notes rang out from the piano and Tilly took a breath. She was a bit wobbly at first, but after a bar, Sophie joined in, and suddenly singing was easier than breathing. There was something about doing it together that just made it natural.

She edged closer to Sophie, wanting to hear better how their voices melded, and by the time the final note was hanging in the air, she was feeling a warm buzz.

"That was really good," Ag said, closing the piano.

"Yeah, it was great," agreed Dash. "You two should get married now."

"What?" Tilly said at the same time as Sophie said, "Dash!"

"You can't tell people to get married," Ag told her brother.

"Why not?" he grumbled. "They could sing all the time together then, couldn't they? Isn't that what married people do?"

"Sing?" asked Tilly, slightly confused.

"No, be together," Dash said. "Except when they're at work." He tilted his head to one side in thought. "Sometimes they do arguments."

"Discussions," corrected Ag.

"Right," agreed Dash.

Tilly pinched the bridge of her nose between her finger and thumb and sighed a deep sigh. "I really think it's time for bed," she said. "Sophie, can you order some pizza while I get these two upstairs?"

"Glad to," Sophie said, collapsing down on the couch and

pulling out her phone.

HALF AN HOUR later, and the doorbell rang again. Tilly, exhausted by now, jogged down the stairs, paid for the pizza, closed the door, and turned around to find herself face to face with Sophie.

"Jesus, sorry," she said.

"It's fine," said Sophie. "Kids okay?"

"In bed, reading, and about to go to sleep, I think." Tilly frowned. "I'm really sorry. Maybe this was a bad idea. I had no idea how tiring all of this was going to be."

"It's a baptism by fire," Sophie said, taking the pizza from her. "You know, if we ever think we want kids, we can look back on tonight and make an informed decision." She'd been walking down the hallway, but she stopped suddenly. "Um…"

"It's alright," Tilly laughed. "You didn't scare me off."

"I didn't mean want kids together or anything," said Sophie. "I just meant individually. Or, you know, together, or whatever, or —"

"Maybe we should start in on that pizza before it gets too cold?" suggested Tilly.

"Right," Sophie said, carrying the box into the kitchen.

"I'll get some napkins," Tilly said, finding a roll of paper towels.

"Do they argue much, Max and Mila?" Sophie said, sitting down at the table and opening the box. "They don't look like the type."

Tilly rolled her eyes and sat down. "That's just Dash talking out of school. I mean, they have had a few discussions while I've been here. But I'm not sure I'm the greatest judge of what's normal and what's not in that regard."

"Oh?" Sophie took a slice of pizza.

"Child of divorce," Tilly explained. "My mum and dad argued like it was a competitive sport. Then, um, then my mum left."

"You stayed with your dad?"

"It was my choice," said Tilly.

"I grew up with my dad too," said Sophie. "My mum died when I was little."

"I did hear that." Tilly looked over at Sophie's calm face. "I'm sorry."

"I barely remember her," Sophie said. "I'd like to, but I really don't. It's hard to miss someone that you never really knew. I think probably I miss the idea of a mum more than I miss my actual mum." She grimaced. "That sounds heartless."

"No, it sounds honest," Tilly said. "I'm not sure if I miss my mum at all, if I'm going to be honest. My dad and I always got along really well. We're similar people. He's in the police, too."

"Ah," said Sophie.

"Ah what?"

She shook her head. "I was just thinking, amateur analysis and all that. Missing mums explains a bit, doesn't it?"

"Does it?" asked Tilly, taking a bite of pizza.

"Well, you're job focused in an effort to prove yourself to your policeman father, and I'm family focused in order to please my widowed dad. We both had to grow up pretty fast, I'm guessing. And we're probably both a little too concerned with pleasing people."

Tilly took that in. "I suppose. I'm not sure my dad would have been angry if I didn't join the force, though."

"Mine wouldn't be angry if I left the garage," Sophie said. "But he would be hurt. And somehow that's worse, isn't it?"

"Yes," Tilly said. "Yes, it is."

"And this has now turned into a pity party, oops," laughed Sophie. "Sorry about that. Didn't mean to get so deep so soon. Want to talk about football or music or something?"

Tilly shook her head. "No, no, I don't mind." She smiled. "I feel like we always jump in with both feet. It's kind of... us."

"So there's an us?" Sophie asked, taking another slice of pizza.

"Is there not?" Tilly's heart beat a little faster, her hands got sweaty. "Am I overstepping?"

But Sophie laughed. "I'm teasing you," she said. "I know what you mean. All of this has been quick, but then I don't see how it couldn't be. You know, my mum and dad got married after three weeks."

"Three weeks?"

Sophie nodded. "My mum needed the visa to stay in the country and my dad didn't want her to leave. He always says that when you know, you know. I didn't really understand. Until now."

"You know?"

"Do you not?"

It was Tilly's turn to laugh. "I'm kidding now. Yes, I know. This has never happened to me before, but I suddenly don't want you not to be in my life. Which is weird, but it's how it is."

"Same," said Sophie, putting pizza crust down on her plate. "But I'm fully aware that this isn't... normal. That there are things standing in our way."

"Who's to say what's normal?" said Tilly. "We can do things our own way if we like. I don't see how it's anyone's business but ours."

She looked across the table at Sophie's smile, at the curve of her cheek, at the light on her skin, and her heart filled so full that she could barely breathe. There was an us. She could feel it, could feel the connection between them.

"Tilly?"

"Mmm?"

"How would you feel about perhaps going upstairs?"

"Upstairs?"

"You do have a bed here, right?" asked Sophie, dabbing at her lips with a piece of paper towel.

"I do."

Sophie looked at her with large, dark eyes and Tilly's pulse beat under her skin. "So?"

"So," said Tilly.

And going upstairs seemed like the most natural thing in the world.

CHAPTER TWENTY FIVE

Tilly's flat was a tiny little oasis of calm after the bustle of the main house. The walls were white, the bed was neatly made, and there was a little line of shoes by the front door, all paired and clean. Just the sight of it made Sophie smile.

The whole place smelled of her, a clean, soapy kind of smell, and Sophie sat demurely on the edge of the bed waiting. She wasn't nervous. This all seemed like it was ordained. When she heard Tilly's footsteps on the stairs, her heart started to beat harder.

"Okay, they're both asleep," Tilly said. "And I left a note for Mila saying that I'd gone to bed. So... we should have some privacy."

"Finally," Sophie said.

"Finally," said Tilly, leaning against the doorframe. She ran a hand through her blonde curls and bit her lip. "We said no expectations."

"We did," Sophie agreed.

"You look very beautiful sitting on the bed." Tilly looked down at her feet, cheeks going pink.

"You look very beautiful propping up the doorframe," said Sophie. She got up and walked toward Tilly, reaching out her hand. "We don't have to do anything if you're nervous."

"Me? Nervous?" Tilly took her hand, palm warm. "I thought you were…"

Sophie shook her head. "Not in the slightest."

"So, um…" Tilly swallowed. "So, everything is consensual?"

Sophie grinned. "How about I let you know if I want to stop? That way, you won't have to ask for consent every step of the way." She had a feeling that Tilly would if she needed to. Maybe that was why she felt so safe here.

"Thank god," Tilly muttered.

Then she was pulling at Sophie's hand, dragging her closer and turning, closing the front door and pressing Sophie up against it in one graceful move.

"Thank god?" Sophie asked. "Why would you do that?"

"Because I've been wanting to do this all evening," Tilly groaned.

Her hands skirted up the sides of Sophie's body until there was a palm on either side of her face and then Tilly leaned in, pressing her lips against Sophie's, parting her lips, exploring with her tongue as Sophie grew increasingly breathless.

She let her hands take Tilly's waist, pull her in even closer, until she could feel every possible inch of Tilly pressed up against her. Until she had to break the kiss. "This is no good," she muttered.

Tilly jumped back an entire foot. "Sorry, I'm sorry," she said, looking shocked and pale.

Sophie watched her, shaking her head. "Okay, we need to establish something here. I want to be here. I want to be with you. In fact, what I was just complaining about was the fact that we're both wearing far too many clothes, not about the kissing or anything else it might lead to."

"You were?" Tilly's color came back.

"Very much so."

Tilly started to smile. "Okay, right, sorry, I just…"

"Bit nervous?" Sophie asked.

Tilly nodded. "I don't know why. I've definitely done this before. Just this time seems a bit more important somehow."

"Because there are feelings involved," Sophie said, stepping forward to take Tilly's hand. "It makes the stakes a bit higher, doesn't it?"

Tilly nodded again.

"But I have your full consent, right?"

Another nod.

"Good," Sophie said. With steady, cool hands, she started to unbutton Tilly's shirt. She slid the material off her shoulders, pausing to kiss Tilly's sharp collarbone before moving downward. Dropping to her knees, she unbuttoned Tilly's pants as Tilly's hands started to curl in her hair.

Sophie felt the familiar bubbling between her legs, the heat in her stomach as Tilly pressed her head toward her underwear. She could smell her, the damp scent of her, and her mouth started to water.

Carefully, she reached up and pulled Tilly's underwear down. Even more carefully, she leaned in, dropping a kiss on Tilly's tight curls. Then she took a deep breath, drinking in Tilly's scent, and stood up. Slowly, she had to do this slowly. Even if she wanted to throw Tilly straight onto the bed and have her way with her.

"What..." started Tilly.

Sophie silenced her with a kiss and then tugged off her own t-shirt and shucked off her jeans and knickers as quickly as she could. Until she and Tilly were standing in front of each other, Sophie in her bra, Tilly in her bra and shirt.

She heard Tilly gasp as she reached behind and unclasped her bra, taking it off and throwing it to the floor. She saw Tilly start to reach out and then stop herself. So she reached out, arms snaking behind Tilly's back and undoing her bra, letting it drop, so that they were both completely naked.

Tilly was so pale, her legs long and muscled, her stomach flat and rippled. Sophie swallowed, trying to take it all in, comparing Tilly's obvious fitness to her own rounded belly, her own full breasts, her own dimpled thighs and coming up lacking until Tilly groaned.

"You're so beautiful."

"Me?" Sophie asked, surprised.

"Christ, yes," mumbled Tilly.

Sophie held her head a little higher and stepped forward until the tips of her breasts were touching Tilly's. Tilly snatched in a breath and finally, Sophie allowed herself to kiss her. Allowed herself to press up against Tilly, to feel every inch of her soft, naked skin, every curve and point of her.

She molded her body against Tilly's until they were both panting and beginning to sweat, until she could bear it no longer, until she pushed backward and Tilly fell onto the bed. She dropped to her knees this time, determined not to deny herself anything.

Tilly's hands came back to her hair, tangling her fingers there as she directed Sophie's head between her legs. Sophie's hands parted Tilly's firm thighs and her lips kissed up the inside of sensitive skin. She took a deep, shaking breath and breathed in all of Tilly's scent, and Tilly said just one word.

"Please."

It broke Sophie. She could restrain herself no longer. She pressed herself against Tilly's sex, feeling wetness on her chin and mouth as she used her tongue to part Tilly's folds and Tilly's fingers tightened around her hair, pulling her ever closer.

Tilly was already wet, already swollen and waiting and ready. Sophie found her hard bump and sucked at it, tracing her tongue around it in tight circles as Tilly raised her hips up to meet her mouth.

Sophie let her fingers trace up the inside of Tilly's thigh and was rewarded with a gasp that deepened into a moan as those same fingers slid up inside Tilly's wetness. She pushed her hand to the hilt as Tilly rose to meet her, pressing her tongue hard against Tilly until something crashed over her and Tilly was moaning and shaking and clutching at Sophie's hair.

She waited until Tilly was still again, until the heartbeat against her tongue had settled, and then she moved back. "Okay?"

Tilly laughed. "Okay? That was slightly more than okay, I should think." Then she looked worriedly down at Sophie's face between her legs. "Wasn't it?"

Sophie licked her lips slowly and then smiled. "Oh, I should say so."

Tilly groaned again, eyes dark with lust, and reaching down, took both Sophie's hands, pulling her up and on top of her until Sophie was astride her hips on the low bed.

Tilly never broke eye contact, her eyes never wavering as she ran both hands over Sophie's thighs, as she reached the center point and parted Sophie's folds with her thumbs.

Sophie gasped at such close contact. So close and yet not enough. She shifted her hips.

"Patience," Tilly whispered, still gazing into her eyes.

"I don't have any."

Tilly smiled a small, secret smile. "I've heard it's a virtue."

"I definitely don't have any of that," Sophie said, breath coming faster as Tilly slid a hand down between them.

"I can see that," Tilly said with a lazy grin. "I find it quite appealing, to be honest."

Then she was curling her fingers up so that they slid inside Sophie, so that she could impale herself down on them, as her thumb curved upwards to rub against her. Sophie pressed herself against that thumb and then, slowly at first, very slowly, began to move her hips.

She stared down into Tilly's eyes, hips moving, warmth building up inside her, breath coming faster, pulse starting to pound, determined to watch the desire spreading across Tilly's face. Determined to see the redness of her cheeks, the sparkle of her eyes, the way her lips swelled, determined to drink her in.

But she couldn't control herself, couldn't stop her hips moving faster, couldn't stop the explosion that was so inevitable.

Tilly reached up with her free hand, letting her thumb graze Sophie's dark nipple. Sophie bit her lip, but Tilly continued, pinching her nipple and it was more than Sophie could take.

Again and again she crushed herself against Tilly's hand, again and again until the stars exploded and her eyes slammed shut and she could control herself no longer.

She cried out, shuddering and shaking against Tilly's hand, aware of nothing other than the sensations running through her, washing over her, taking over her.

At the end, Tilly sat up, her hand still in place, her other arm holding Sophie against her, her cheek pressing against Sophie's stomach, holding her until her breath started to even out, until she was finally able to form words again.

"Jesus," was the first word that came out.

"Don't think he had much to do with this," Tilly said, tilting backward so that Sophie could see her face.

"No," said Sophie with a grin. "No, probably not."

"Are you tired?" Tilly asked.

"Not a bit."

"Oh good."

"Why?" asked Sophie.

"Because I don't think I'm done yet,"

Sophie swung her leg back over Tilly's body and snuggled down so that she was lying beside her, head on her chest. "I'm not sure that I am either," she said. Her tongue snaked out and licked the tip of Tilly's pink nipple.

Tilly gasped. "Glad we're on the same page," she said.

"Glad we're finally on the same bed," said Sophie. Then she busied her mouth doing things that weren't talking.

CHAPTER TWENTY SIX

Tilly held Sophie close, listening to her breathing, perfectly content until Sophie finally stirred.
"It's half ten."
"Not quite," Tilly said. "We've got a few minutes yet."
Sophie snuggled closer again. "Okay, but just a few minutes. Don't let me fall asleep."
The flat was littered with the remains of an Indian takeaway and smelled of spices, but Tilly was happier than she'd been for months, perhaps ever.
Every other night for the last few weeks, Sophie had come in through the back door after work, sneaking home again as it got late. It was all Tilly could do to get through the workday so that she could rush home.
Okay, so things couldn't stay this way permanently. She got that. But for right now, it was working. Any doubts that she'd had about her feelings for Sophie were long gone. This was what she'd been waiting for, this sense of complete familiarity even in someone she'd just met. This comfort.
She put her chin on Sophie's head, letting one naked arm pull her a little closer. "I like you a lot," she mumbled.
"Careful," Sophie said with a laugh in her voice. "That almost turned into a bigger L word."

For a second Tilly felt a squeeze of anxiety, but she shook it off. So what if it did? She was allowed to have feelings, wasn't she? "Should I not be using that word yet?" she asked.

Sophie moved now, propping her head up on one hand so that the duvet fell off her shoulder, baring her creamy skin. "I don't know," she said. "Should we?"

"We? So you might have some big L energy going on too?" Tilly teased.

Sophie bit her lip and looked down. "There might be some feelings swimming around."

Tilly nodded, her heart tripling in size. "Well, okay then. As long as we both know where we stand. We don't have to say it just yet."

Sophie looked up. "We can wait for the right time."

Tilly grinned at her. "Patience is a virtue." She reached out and tucked a lock of hair behind Sophie's ear. "How's it going at home?"

"So-so," Sophie said. "You know, once this choir concert is over, I'm going to be all out of excuses. I can't say that I'm going to practice every other night so that I can come over here."

"We'll think of something," said Tilly, rubbing Sophie's arm. "Don't worry about it."

"We could," said Sophie. "Or..." She took a deep breath. "Or maybe we could, um, we could tell them."

Tilly almost sat up in shock. "Really? I thought..."

"We don't have to if you don't want to." Sophie looked a little stung.

"No, that's not what I meant." Tilly settled down again. "I just meant that, well, this is a big thing for you. I don't want to rush anything. Not if it makes life harder for you."

"I didn't want to make waves at the beginning," Sophie said. "There was no point if this wasn't going anywhere. And Gio has a habit of ruining anything that I try to start. I just... I wanted a chance to make something for myself, you know? It's not that I'm trying to hide you or anything."

"I know that," Tilly said. "And I know that telling your dad and

Gio is going to be difficult. I just want you to be sure that you know what you're doing." She grinned down at her. "If I had my way, I'd be shouting all this from the rooftops, you know that."

"I do." Sophie smiled back. "And I know it's going to be tough. They're not going to be happy. I'll have to tell them in the right way, and they still won't like it much. But this... this is turning into something, Till. I need to tell them. I want to tell them. I want everyone to know."

"I'll do whatever you think is best," Tilly said. She stroked Sophie's bare shoulder. "Would you like to come and meet my dad?"

"The Chief Superintendent? That sounds a bit scary."

"He's lovely," said Tilly. "And he'll love you. As long as you don't commit any crimes. But on the whole, I'm certain that he'll think you're as wonderful as I think you are."

"Okay then," Sophie said. "Yes. I'd like to meet him." She settled down again, snuggling against Tilly's chest in a way that made Tilly want to keep her there forever. "This is getting very serious, isn't it?"

"Only if you want it to be." Tilly stroked her arm. "But I do like you a lot. And I'm ready to move things on if you are."

Sophie nodded against her chest. "Yeah, I think I am. I know that the fallout might not be pretty, but I don't like lying to my family and I think it's time that they knew. I'll tell them this weekend. Maybe make a nice dinner and do it."

"Do you want me there?"

"Maybe you could come for dessert?"

"Whatever you need," Tilly said, starting to get drowsy in the warmth.

"What about Max and Mila?" asked Sophie. "They must surely suspect something by now."

"They know that we're... interested. They know that you've visited. But Mila told me that who I invited up here was my own business. Besides, I think they're too involved with their own stuff right now."

"Oh yeah?"

Tilly sighed. The last couple of weeks had been a little more strained around the Browning household. "I don't know what's going on. They're stressed about something, but they clam up anytime I'm around or the kids are here. Not that it's any of my business, but I'd like to be able to help them."

"You're the great detective," Sophie said, her hand warm on Tilly's stomach. "Surely you've figured out something?"

"It's something to do with money, I'm pretty sure. I don't want to pry, but I think money is at the heart of things, which I'm guessing is why they don't want to talk to me about anything."

"Could be," said Sophie. "Max works full time and Mila owns half the bookshop though, they haven't seemed to be struggling in the past."

Tilly shrugged. "I can't tell you. I honestly don't know much more than that."

"You know basically what they're arguing about," said Sophie. "I told you that you're a great detective."

She was kidding and Tilly knew it, but that didn't stop her stomach clenching at the word detective.

The car theft case was going nowhere, and she was pretty sure that Max had already written it off as a cold case. No more cars had been stolen in the local area, but at least once a week, one of the surrounding areas reported a theft. No one else seemed to be getting anywhere either, which took some of the sting out of her failure. But still. It wasn't nice thinking that she'd got nowhere.

And a little bit of her wondered if perhaps she hadn't been so distracted by Sophie she might have got further in her investigations.

Not that she could bring herself to regret any time spent with Sophie.

"I'd better get going," Sophie said, sitting up. She leaned to drop a kiss on Tilly's forehead.

Tilly pulled her down, kissing her properly before letting her go again.

She watched as Sophie pulled on her clothes, first her underwear, then her jeans, and looked around for her top.

She hated watching her go. But if everything went to plan, then after this weekend, all this could be hers. She could watch Sophie dress every morning if she wanted to.

The thought caught in her chest, spreading warmth through her whole body.

The idea of her and Sophie actually being together, living together, building a life together.

Sophie tripped over a container of rice and then snorted a laugh. "Sorry about that. It's a bit cramped in here. Let me clean it up."

"Leave it," Tilly said. "Let's move in together."

"What?" Sophie stopped and looked at her.

Tilly flushed but stuck to her guns. "Let's move in together. After you've told your family, once everything's out in the open. Let's get a place together."

Before she knew what was happening, Sophie was back in her arms, littering her face with kisses.

"Okay, okay," said Tilly, fending her off. "You have to go. You're going to be late."

But she was secretly pleased that Sophie was as enthusiastic about the idea as she was.

THE WEATHER HAD turned even chillier over the last week or so and it was firmly the beginnings of winter. There was no snow yet, but it couldn't be far away. Tilly could smell the sharp bite of coldness in the air as she walked to the police station.

"Morning," Max said as she got in.

"How long have you been here?" she asked in surprise.

"I like an early start," he said. "I needed to catch up on some paperwork. Besides, it's nice to have a bit of quiet in the morning sometimes."

Tilly grinned. "The kids giving you hell?"

"I love them to death," he said. "But I don't know where I got two such chatterboxes from. Mila agreed to deal with them this morning and she's going to get a lie in tomorrow when I take them to school."

"Seems very fair," Tilly said, thinking how nice it must be to have someone to take half the responsibility from you at times. She smiled to herself. She did have someone. Or almost.

"You're looking in a good mood," Max said. "Let me guess, Sophie Farmer?"

Tilly hesitated, then nodded.

"Glad to see that someone's happy," was all he said before turning back to his paperwork.

It was on the tip of Tilly's tongue to say something, perhaps to ask if Max would like to talk, or to say that she'd noticed there was stress in the house, or something. But she was rescued by the front door opening.

"Hello," she said, turning around to see Len Dodds. "What can we do for you this morning?"

Len came to the desk. "It's about… the same thing as before."

Tilly sighed. "I know, but there's nothing we can do about cars using the road behind your house, Len."

"I know that," he said. "And I know that you needed proof that something was going on." He reached into his pocket. "So I got proof." He laid a USB stick on the wooden counter between them.

CHAPTER TWENTY SEVEN

Sophie tried to concentrate on her computer screen and failed miserably. Partly, she was tired. Spending every other evening with Tilly was exhausting. Not that she regretted it. Partly, she was distracted. In a good way.

The idea of moving in with Tilly was so new, so brilliant, that she hadn't quite digested it yet. She knew that she wanted it, knew that she desperately wanted it. But she wasn't quite sure she believed it yet. Like it was a lottery win or something like that, something that was so good it wasn't quite real yet.

"What's with you?" her dad asked, passing by her desk and doing a double take. "You're sitting there grinning like the cat that got the cream."

"Nothing," she said quickly.

Paul Farmer hesitated, then crossed his arms and came closer to the desk. "Sophia Isabella, don't you tell lies to me. I've known you your whole life and if anyone knows there's something going on, it's me."

She sighed. "Dad, it's really nothing, not yet."

He perched on the edge of her desk. "Nothing? Is that what you call going out every other night and coming home with a smile all over your face? It's not singing that's done that. I'm not an idiot, you know."

Oh dear. "I know that, dad."

"And you're an adult now. I can't forbid you from going out to see people." He looked down and gave a sniff. "And, um, I know I wasn't always great about the gay thing."

"You did threaten to throw me out of the house," Sophie said, getting her feet back in the conversation.

He looked up at her. "I did. And I've apologized and will forever regret saying it. You're my daughter, and it took me a while to get used to things being different. I'm sorry, really, truly sorry."

"I know, dad." He was sorry. It had taken some time. It had been a rocky patch, but she knew that she was accepted.

"I love you."

"What?" The words took her by surprise, not that he never said them, though he rarely did, but because he was saying them here and now.

"I love you," he said again. He rubbed his face. "You're my daughter and I love you to death. I might not always have done the best job, especially without your mum around. But I love you and all I want is for you to be happy." He sniffed again. "Your mum'd be proud of you."

"Would she?"

He nodded. "She liked an independent woman, one that no man could boss around. She used to drive me crazy sometimes. It took me a while to get used to that too, to being ordered around by this little slip of a girl." He smiled at the memory of it. "I'd have done anything for her, though. If…" Another sniff. "I'd have gladly gone instead of her."

Sophie's eyes filled with tears and for a second she couldn't speak. She had to blink and gain control of herself. "Dad…" she said finally.

"Oh, I know. I'm being a soppy old fool," he said. He patted her hand. "But I just wanted you to know that when I fell in love with your mum, I shouted it from the damn rooftops. I couldn't believe that someone that perfect could love me, and I told as many people as I could just in case she tried to change her mind.

I just wanted the world to know that for an instant I was good enough to be loved by someone like that."

"Dad," she said again.

He patted her hand again. "No, hear me out. If I've put you in a position where you feel like you can't tell me news as important as that, where you think I'd be uncomfortable or angry or somehow disappointed, I want you to know how very, very sorry I am. I want you to be happy, Soph. That's all I've ever wanted."

"I know."

"So, is there anything you want to tell me?"

Sophie exhaled, rolled her shoulders, then nodded. This was hardly the time or the place, and not exactly what she'd imagined, but she had to do this. "There's a woman," she said, the words barely sounding real.

Her dad grinned. "Yeah?"

"Yeah."

"She's nice and kind? Gentle when she needs to be and bossy when she has to be? She treats you well and puts that smile on your face?"

Sophie thought about Tilly and nodded. "Yes, she's all those things."

"Then that's all that matters, isn't it?" he said, standing up. "She sounds lovely. When you're ready, bring her over for dinner. Or we can go out to lunch. Whatever you think would make the right impression."

She had to take another breath. "Thanks, dad." She scratched her head. "Um, actually, there's something—"

"Dad!" Gio yelled from across the garage. "A hand, please!"

"Bugger," said her dad. "We'll talk about this later, alright?" he said to Sophie, then he ran off to see what Gio needed.

That wasn't so bad, was it? Sophie breathed, calming herself. It hadn't been so bad. It had been… touching. Sad, a little. But also hopeful. Okay, so she hadn't exactly told him everything, but she'd made a good start and so far things had gone well.

She felt lighter, like part of a weight had been lifted off her.

Her smile came back as she wiggled her mouse and got back to work.

* * *

"You've got your vest on?" Max asked for the fifth time.

"Yes," said Tilly. "I'm fully equipped and ready."

Max checked his watch and then peered out of the window of the police station. "Where are they?"

"Should be here any minute, sir." Waiting for backup had been his idea, not hers, and she'd bowed to it, both because it was protocol and because... Because she kind of hoped that with more people around Sophie would be less likely to see her.

Which was ridiculous, of course, but she could hope.

Not for an instant had she considered not acting on this information. Not for a second had she considered not doing her job. But she had wondered if perhaps she shouldn't be the one doing this, if maybe she was too compromised.

It wasn't a feeling that she liked. She knew in her heart that she'd done nothing wrong, but nothing about this felt right.

There were consequences to every decision. But these consequences were going to be personal ones, and she really didn't want to think about what they would be.

"It's going to be alright," Max said, putting a hand on her shoulder.

"Is it?" Her voice sounded small.

"Probably." He sighed. "I can't promise. But you're doing the right thing, and you're an incredible police officer."

"Weren't you the one that told me to remember that there are people involved here, that it's not just about the laws?"

Max nodded. "But then, sometimes people get hurt, Till. It's the nature of life, the nature of the job."

"Are you telling me that you'd go to Mila's bookshop and arrest her and her partner?"

Max looked at her and sighed. "Yes," he said simply. "Yes, if I had to, I would. Because as much as I might not want to, at least I could ensure that they were treated properly, and they got a fair hearing. It's cold comfort, but I'd do what I had to."

There was the sound of rumbling from outside.

"Looks like our back up's here," Max said. "You ready for this?"

Tilly wasn't, but she nodded. Max was right. She had to do her job.

They went in through the open front of the garage, shouting and yelling and in the confusion hoping that no one reached for a weapon.

Max himself took down Paul Farmer, grabbing his arm and bringing him to his knees to cuff him on the floor.

Gio spat and swore and ended up bent over the bonnet of a car with a police officer holding his head to the metal as he too was cuffed.

Tilly didn't know how it happened. One minute she was right behind Max, the next she was turning around and seeing Sophie. Maybe she'd tried to run, maybe she'd tried to fight, Tilly didn't know. But somehow she'd ended up splayed across the concrete floor, blood coming from her nose.

"Get off her," Tilly shouted.

The officer who was cuffing her looked up in surprise.

"She's bleeding," Tilly said.

"She's cuffed," said the officer gruffly.

Tilly reached into her pocket and found a tissue before she strode over to where Sophie was lying. She pulled at her arms, got her into a sitting position, and then used the tissue to blot the blood from her nose.

"I'm so sorry," she said, not knowing whether she was apologizing for the bloody nose, the raid, or the fact that she was here at all.

"Right." Sophie's face was hard.

"I'm just doing my job. We had an agreement," said Tilly. "You'll be out in no time as long as you've done nothing."

"You don't know that I've done nothing?" Sophie said, eyes flashing now. "You think that I could have had anything to do with anything? How could you? How—"

"Three vehicles found in the back," said an officer, coming in through the rear door. "There's a storage area out there."

Tilly turned to Sophie, who'd gone pale now. "I didn't... We didn't..."

Tilly's stomach turned itself into a knot. She'd been so worried about this, it had torn her up inside. And now, now it turned out that it was all true, that she never should have trusted Sophie in the first place.

She felt physically sick.

"Tilly," Sophie said. "We didn't do this."

"Then tell me who did."

"Don't talk," Paul Farmer yelled at his daughter. "Don't talk without a solicitor. Don't even say a word."

Sophie looked at her dad, then looked back at Tilly.

"Tell me who did this if you didn't," Tilly said.

Sophie took a breath and swallowed. "I want my lawyer," was all she said.

CHAPTER TWENTY EIGHT

The problem with police interview rooms is that they're so small, it's impossible to walk off anger. Sophie tried to pace, but ended up looking ridiculous, so she slumped on the chair and let her anger ferment instead.

Anger at herself, at Tilly, at her father, her brother, at the world. Anger that bubbled and writhed inside her but that had no real target, because she didn't know who to blame. She was angry and, she realized, scared. She didn't know what was happening.

What she did know was that Tilly had been there. Tilly had looked her in the eye as she'd been arrested. No warning, no nothing. Just a bunch of idiot police showing up in riot gear like they were raiding a mob boss's lair or something.

And then this. Nothing. Sitting in a room for hours on end with nothing to look at, no one to talk to, just her thoughts and nothing else.

When the door finally did open, Sophie whipped around, sure for a moment that it was going to be Tilly, sure that she was going to get a target for that anger and that sadness and that fear. But instead she saw Max's familiar face.

"Tea?" he asked kindly.

"That's it? That's the best you've got? An offer of tea?" It wasn't often that she felt Italian. Her mum hadn't been around long enough for it to matter. But there were times when she felt very un-English, and this was one of them.

"Coffee?" Max tried.

Sophie glared at him and he nodded before quietly coming into the room and closing the door behind him.

"Why don't you have a seat?"

For a second she considered not sitting, even thought about spitting at him. She was so angry. Max's face was so familiar, but the tone of his voice wasn't. He was firm, not to be argued with, business like. She came to a compromise; she kept glaring, but she took a seat.

"Right," said Max, taking a seat himself. "First, I'm sorry that you've had to wait. There's only two of us. I was busy interviewing your dad and, well, it didn't seem appropriate for Constable Ware to be in here."

Sophie felt her skin flush. She swallowed and said nothing. What would she have done if Tilly had walked into the room, she wondered.

"I needed to get more information from your dad before I came and talked to you," Max went on. "But I think I've got the lay of the land more or less now."

She wanted to protest, wanted to scream that she knew her dad and Gio hadn't done anything. But the police had come. The police had seemed so sure, and now she was less sure. They hadn't done anything, surely they hadn't?

Her mouth was dry. She wished she'd accepted the tea now. "What happened?" They weren't the words she wanted to use, but they were the ones that came out.

Max sighed. "Well, your dad and Gio are both protesting innocence, but that's to be expected."

Sophie stared at him, and he pressed his lips together and closed his eyes for a second. When he opened them, he seemed to have come to a decision.

"Alright, let's be honest with each other, shall we?"

"I never considered being anything else," Sophie said because she really hadn't. She was worried now, worried that maybe her dad and Gio had done something. She just couldn't figure out what and how and the logistics of it all.

"Okay," said Max. "In that case, your dad and Gio are both saying they haven't done anything, and you're backing them up. We, however, got solid proof that at least three stolen cars have been driven down that back lane toward the rear door of the garage."

"Proof?"

"Video," Max said. "Indisputable. That's what gave us cause to come in like that." He paused, collected his thoughts, and went on. "We found nothing in the garage."

Sophie's stomach jumped. Max held up a hand.

"But we found plenty in the storage shed behind the garage."

"We haven't used that place for years," Sophie said without thinking. She sat up straighter. "Max, seriously. I don't remember the last time I set foot in it."

Max looked at her long and hard, and then grinned in relief. "I was hoping you'd say something like that," he admitted.

"Like what?"

"That you didn't know what was inside. It's exactly what your brother said. And I believe you both. Your dad, on the other hand, was a bit less forthcoming."

"He hasn't been in there," Sophie said, desperately racking her brains to think of answers. "The shed came with the garage, but dad and Gio can only work on so many cars at once. They keep two in the garage and then whatever else there is gets parked out front for convenience. No one goes in there, really."

"That's what your dad said," said Max. "And then he admitted to renting the place out under the table."

The truth suddenly all came together. Sophie closed her eyes and shook her head. The extra money that was lying around, her dad was collecting illegal rent. Property prices in Whitebridge were horrific. He'd have been raking it in. "Shit."

"Perhaps," Max said as Sophie opened her eyes. "Or perhaps not." He eyed her. "I think the lot of you are telling the truth. You and Gio are innocent. Your dad's guilty of being a bit stupid. But on the whole, I've found my chop shop but I haven't found the car thieves."

Sophie's whole being filled up with relief. "So what happens now?"

Max scratched at his chin. "Your dad and Gio are staying here. At least overnight. We need to check out their stories. I want to make sure that there's plenty of evidence of other people being in that shed. As soon as I'm comfortable, I'll let them go. Though I'm expecting your dad to help with inquiries."

Sophie sniffed at that. Max might be expecting it, but she didn't think her dad would be thrilled with the idea.

"You can go though," Max said. "Unless there's anything you want to tell me?"

Sophie shook her head. "Nothing, except I've definitely not been in that shed for yonks. I'm sure the others haven't either. And Gio and dad have definitely not been spending nights chopping up cars, I can swear to that."

"Sure you can swear to that? You've been spending half your nights in my granny flat," Max said, a little twinkle in his eye.

"Yeah, well, I won't be any longer, will I," Sophie said, standing up. "So I'm free to go then?"

Max looked like he wanted to say something, but in the end he just got up too. "Jules is here," he said. "I thought you might want a bit of moral support, and she was bringing sandwiches from the pub for the boys anyway."

"Yeah, thanks."

Max stopped by the door. "This is the second time you've been in the station this month," he said. "Let's not make a habit of it." He opened up and Sophie walked out into the main station.

Jules was standing by the counter. "You free to go?"

"She's free to go," Max said. "Keep her out of trouble."

He and Jules shared a look that Sophie caught but didn't make immediate sense out of. Then she realized that they must be talking about her and Tilly and she felt a deep spike of pain in her insides. Tilly. She looked around but saw no sign of her.

"Come on then," Jules said. "Want to stop for a pint on the way home?"

Sophie shook her head.

"Alright then, let's get you back to yours, shall we?"

Jules looped her arm through Sophie's and escorted her out into the crisp freshness of the evening. Sophie shivered and Jules held her closer.

"You alright?"

"Yeah."

"Want to talk about it?" Jules asked.

"Not really."

"Your dad and Gio gonna be alright?"

Sophie nodded. "Yeah, I think so."

They started to walk down the road, the fresh air on their faces. "And what about Tilly?" Jules asked, finally.

They kept walking, feet crunching on the pavement, the burning smell of autumn in their noses. "Tilly," Sophie said eventually, even the name seeming hard to say and strange in her mouth.

"She was just doing her job," said Jules.

"Yeah." Sophie breathed the air in. It hurt to breathe. Was it supposed to hurt to breathe? She couldn't remember. "I know she was."

"So?"

"So nothing," said Sophie. "It's over."

"But—"

"I really don't want to talk about this."

Jules sighed. "Yeah, alright. Sorry." She pulled Sophie a bit closer so that their shoulders bumped as they walked. "Fancy a sausage sandwich when we get back?"

Sophie sighed. She wasn't hungry, but Jules was trying to be nice. "Yeah, alright then."

IT WAS STRANGE being in the house alone. It was quiet, too quiet, and Sophie almost wished that she'd asked Jules to stay.

She couldn't bring herself to go to bed alone, so she was lying on the couch, the TV playing silently as she lay there in the dark.

Everything was a mess in her head. She was angry at her dad for making stupid decisions. Angry at him for not telling her and Gio what he was up to. She was angry at herself for not being more aware of things, for not checking where the money was coming from.

Most of all, she was angry at Tilly.

She knew Tilly was doing her job; she knew that they had an agreement. But it didn't seem to make any difference. Tilly had seen her be arrested. Tilly had stood there and watched it happen. She might not have wanted to, but she had.

It was just her job, a little voice in the back of Sophie's head kept saying. But the problem was, the job would always be there. The job would always come first. Sophie didn't know if she could deal with that.

And her family definitely couldn't deal with it. She'd lied to them enough. It was over now. She'd taken her eye off them for all of a second and look what had happened. Her dad and Gio were both spending the night at the police station.

No, this all had to come to an end now. It had already come to an end.

It was over.

CHAPTER TWENTY NINE

Tilly walked out of the police station into the cold night and didn't know where to go. She couldn't stand to be in the station any longer, and as much as the kids were sweet, she couldn't handle them at home tonight. Even the thought of sneaking into her own flat made her heart hurt. There were too many memories of Sophie there, she couldn't do it yet.

In the end, she made her way down the road to the pub, because where else could she sit undisturbed with her thoughts?

She'd seen it on Sophie's face the second she'd turned around. She'd known that there was no getting out of this, that she'd sacrificed whatever they'd had or were going to have in order to do her job properly.

And now she felt like she was torn in half. One half hating the other. Her chest felt heavy and tight, and she didn't think anything was going to set things right again.

Jules was not behind the bar, which was the first good thing that had happened all day. She ordered a gin and slimline tonic and took it to a table as far away from the bar as she could get. She just wanted to sit in the warm until she was tired enough that she thought she might be able to fall asleep.

"So," Billy said, pulling out a chair opposite Tilly. "How is the practicing going?"

Tilly looked up in alarm. She hadn't seen Billy coming and on the list of things she really didn't want to deal with right now, talking about the winter concert was fairly high. "I, uh, I was just leaving," she said, ignoring the full drink on the table in front of her.

"No, you weren't," said Billy. "You literally just got here." She put her own glass down on the table. "We don't have to talk about choir if you don't want to. But if we're not going to, then I'd just like you to know that you can sing. I'm very happy with what you and Sophie have done with your solos. You're going to be the stars of the night."

Tilly knew that she'd blushed when Sophie's name had been mentioned. And, she supposed, she was going to have to deal with things sooner rather than later. She sighed. "About that."

"Oh no," Billy said. "You can't pull out now."

"I don't want to," Tilly said, stung at the idea that she might be unreliable.

Billy narrowed her eyes. "What is it then?"

"I... there's been a development," said Tilly weakly.

"Is this about you and Sophie sleeping together?"

Tilly looked up in shock and Billy shrugged.

"Jules said not to say anything, that it would be more diplomatic. But honestly, it was pretty obvious. You two have been making eyes at each other across the room since you met." She paused. "Um, there's no rules against it or anything. In the choir, I mean, if that's what you're worried about."

"It's absolutely not what I'm worried about," said Tilly, who hadn't even considered it. "It's more the fact that I'm pretty sure Sophie currently wants to kill me and she definitely never wants to see me again. So you can see how singing together might be a bit tough."

"What did you do?" asked Billy, picking up her beer.

"Arrested her."

Billy burst out into laughter. "You're kidding?"

"Nope."

"Huh. Well, I can see how she might be a bit cross. I'm assuming that there was some kind of misunderstanding or something? I can't see our Sophie as a master criminal."

Tilly pulled a face.

"What happened?" asked Billy.

"I can't—"

"Psh. Tell me. It's my concert at stake here, I've got a right to know. Besides, you look like you could use a friendly ear. I'm offering. It won't happen again, so if you're going to tell someone, then you'd better get started."

Tilly found herself spilling the whole sordid tale to Billy, though she hadn't intended on telling anyone at all. When she was done, Billy shook her head.

"Tough choice," she said. "I don't really see what you could have done differently. I'm sure that when Sophie's had a chance to think about things, she'll see the same thing."

"I don't think so," Tilly said. "She chose her family over me, and I can't blame her for that. And it's not like I can apologize and say I'll change. I'm not going to. My job is important to me." She sighed. "I just wish it could be different."

"Maybe she's not the one for you then," Billy said. "I should know. Before I married Jules, I was in another relationship for years. I was so sure that we were supposed to be together that when we broke up, I thought I'd never love anyone again. Look how that turned out."

"Maybe," Tilly said. "I suppose you're right. If we can't see eye to eye on the important stuff, then I suppose it wouldn't have worked out in the end, anyway."

"You're not saying that like you believe it." Billy drank another mouthful.

"It's just that… well, my life was better with Sophie in it," Tilly said.

"Why?"

"What?"

"Why?" asked Billy. "It's easy to say stuff like that, but do you really mean it? How was your life better with Sophie in it?"

Tilly thought about this. "It just was," she said finally.

"That's the easy answer, and it's bullshit," said Billy. "Find the answer to that question and you'll know whether or not you two can work together. If you can't find an answer, well, it was doomed to failure."

"I'm not sure you should be walking around giving advice like that," Tilly said, starting to get irritated.

"I'm not an agony aunt," said Billy. "I never pretended to be one. But I am happily married after being a disaster myself. I put my career ahead of everything, I ruined relationships, I've been in your shoes."

"I'm no disaster," said Tilly.

"Fine," huffed Billy. "You're not a disaster. You're miserable, though, and not especially pleasant company."

"I never asked you to sit here."

"True." Billy picked up her drink. "These things have a tendency to work out in the end. You have to have patience. Let me know by the end of the week whether the two of you are capable of singing together. If you're not, I'll have to work something else out."

She got up and wandered back across the pub toward the bar.

Tilly eyed her gin and tonic. Would this all work out in the end? Could this all work out? She didn't see a way. Sophie hated her, and who could blame her? She tried to put herself in Sophie's shoes. How would she feel toward an officer that arrested her father?

But the thought of her dad being in trouble with the law was so far outside her experience that she couldn't truly empathize.

In the end, she supposed, there wasn't much she could do to change things. She'd done what she had to do, and Sophie had made her decisions. But as she finished up her drink and decided to risk going home, her shoulders were heavy. And the world outside the door was just a bit darker than it had been before.

Things had changed. Everything had changed. And Tilly really, really wished that it hadn't.

THE PHONE RANG at five to ten and Tilly answered it without looking at who it was, desperately praying that it was Sophie, but not wanting to jinx her luck by seeing a name on the display.

"Matilda," said her father when she picked up the phone.

"Dad." Her heart sank back down into the soles of her feet. Not Sophie then. She never should have hoped.

"Don't sound so pleased to hear from me."

She took a breath and forced herself to smile, hoping that he'd hear it through the phone. "I am glad to hear from you, always."

"I just phoned to say well done," he said. "I've heard about the arrests, and I'm proud of you."

Her heart sank even lower, like it was trying to physically escape through the bottom of her feet. "Actually, the arrests aren't going to stick."

"Not procedural," he groaned.

"No, no," she said. She sighed. "The garage was being used, but only a big storage shed out back. We arrested the owner, but it turns out he was illegally renting the place out. So we've got a location, but we still don't have the actual thieves."

"There's nothing wrong with that," said her father stoutly. "That's still good police work, and that's what counts. You'll get there in the end. Slow and steady wins the race, eh?"

She had a genuine smile then. It was a small one, but still. She'd forgotten how her dad could put a bright face on things, how he could make her feel better. "Yeah, we'll get there."

"Is everything alright down there? You're sounding a wee bit glum."

She'd also forgotten that he could read her like a book. "All fine," she said, hoping he was going to leave the issue alone.

"Ah, right." He was quiet for a minute. "I was thinking about maybe coming for a visit. Saturday afternoon if you're not too busy? I'd like to see you." He was quiet again for a second. "I, uh, I miss having you around."

She cursed at herself. She'd been so involved in her own life that she hadn't even thought about her dad rattling around alone in that big house. Maybe having him here was what she needed. A reminder of how important the job was, and a friendly face around for a few hours. "I should have invited you," she said.

"No, no, you've been busy."

"No, I should have invited you. And I'm officially inviting you now. Would you like to come over on Saturday and have a tour of Whitebridge? We can make a day of it."

Her father chuckled. "I'd like that," he said. "I'm looking forward to seeing you."

When she put the phone down, Tilly sighed. Life had to go on, she supposed. But that didn't mean that she was going to be happy about it.

She had the feeling that she was never really going to be happy again.

CHAPTER THIRTY

Sophie stood outside the village hall and looked at the very closed door. She really didn't want to do this, but Jules was her friend and she couldn't let her down.

"No," Jules had said. "I'm definitely not telling Billy that. You know how she gets about her music."

They'd been sitting in the pub. Sophie had had to escape the house once her dad and Gio had come home. The two of them had been at each other's throats all day. Gio, quite understandably, slightly upset that he'd spent the night in jail due to his father's burgeoning property empire.

"Come on, you're married to her, please?" Sophie had asked.

"Absolutely not. If you don't want to sing, and I can see why you might not, you need to go and tell her yourself," Jules had said adamantly.

Which was pretty fair, Sophie knew, but still, she wished she wasn't standing here right now. She sighed, stood up straighter, and walked in.

Straight into Tilly.

"Jesus," Sophie said, rubbing her head where it had hit Tilly's.

"Crap, sorry," said Tilly, rubbing her head where it had hit Sophie's.

Sophie took a step back, unsure what to say, her stomach cramping and her skin prickling.

"Sorry," Tilly said again. She pressed her lips together

nervously. "I, uh, I was just coming in to see Billy."

"Yeah, me too."

"Right." Tilly swallowed audibly.

"About the singing."

"Absolutely," Tilly agreed.

"We can't..."

"No."

They stood there, facing each other, the world continuing to turn even though everything seemed so very, very still.

Then Billy pushed open the big front door. "What are you two doing in here?" she asked. It was a good twenty minutes before the choir rehearsal was supposed to start.

Tilly eyed Sophie, who nodded at her. "We, um, need to talk to you."

Billy glared at them both. "No," she said finally.

"No?" said Sophie.

"No," said Billy. "Just no."

"But—" began Tilly.

"No," said Billy. She sighed. "I won't have it. I know exactly what's gone on. This is a small town. I know exactly why you're here. And the answer is no. You've both made a commitment. Now stick to it. Whatever happened in your personal lives, I'm not asking you to make out on stage or anything. You're adults, you can sing a thirty-second solo together, end of story." She swept past them into the hall itself.

"Well," Tilly said, watching her go.

"Quite," agreed Sophie.

There was silence for a second until Billy began playing scales on the piano. Sophie took a breath.

"Okay," she said reluctantly.

"Okay?" asked Tilly.

"She's right," Sophie said. "We're adults, we agreed to do this, we shouldn't let other people down because... well, because we can't make things work between us."

Tilly exhaled and nodded. "Alright."

"We can sing?" asked Sophie.

"Yes," Tilly said. "We can sing."

Sophie checked her watch. They were so early that there was no point going in yet, but it was late enough that there was no point going anywhere else.

"Your dad's helping us with our inquiries," Tilly said.

"I'm well aware of that." It was odd being close to her. Odd to feel the familiar tingling sensations in her body. But then, Sophie supposed that you didn't just stop responding to someone, even when that person wasn't your person anymore.

"I just meant, well, I meant that he was helping us, that's all," said Tilly, flushing slightly. "He's unlikely to face any charges."

"Right."

Tilly exhaled again, the sound loud in the little entrance hall. "Listen, Sophie—"

Sophie held up her hands. "I know," she said, because she did know. "I know that you were just doing your job, I know that in the end nothing terrible happened. I know that none of us are in prison and you had no choice, and we had an agreement and all the rest of it."

"Then…" Tilly shook her head. "Alright. You get it."

Sophie turned to her now. "The job will always come first," she said. "I don't think I can do that. I don't think I can be second all the time. And I can't disappoint my family like that. They're everything I've got, you have to understand that. They wouldn't have been pleased under the best of circumstances, but now…"

"Now they'd hate you as much as they hate me," Tilly said numbly.

Sophie had an overwhelming urge to reach out, but she kept her hands to herself. "It just wouldn't work," she said.

Tilly looked at her for a long minute, her nose upturned, her hair mussed by the wind, her eyes deep and blue, and Sophie longed to kiss her. But again, she kept her lips to herself. "Okay," she said finally. "Alright."

Sophie decided she might as well go into the hall. It would be warmer there and she was afraid that if she stayed here, she might do or say something she might regret. Whether that would be something good or bad, she really wasn't sure.

She could feel Tilly's eyes on her as she walked toward the door. She pushed it open, the sound of the piano coming louder, and turned at the last second. "I don't hate you," she said before she went inside.

And she didn't. Not that it made a difference. But it seemed important that Tilly know that much, at least.

SHE WALKED HOME alone in the cold night, the air nipping at her nose and her whole body sad. Singing with Tilly had been… fine. They'd got the notes out. They'd managed to stand next to each other, but it had infected Sophie with a flood of sadness that she just couldn't shake.

They could have had so much, could have been so perfect. But it hadn't worked out. She supposed that it had been doomed from the beginning. She also supposed that having Gio around lurking behind all her previous dates might not have been the bad thing she'd always imagined.

At least that way she hadn't had the chance to get in too deep before things ended. This way, her way, hurt. It hurt seeing Tilly. It hurt not seeing Tilly. It just hurt.

By the time she walked into the house, she just wanted to go to bed to lick her wounds, to try to sleep and forget about the world for a few precious hours.

She closed the door behind her and everything was quiet. She frowned. She'd left both her dad and Gio at home. It was strange that things were so quiet. Uncomfortable. She was just starting to panic, just starting to imagine all the things that might have gone wrong, when her father called her name.

She walked into the kitchen to find him sitting at the kitchen table. She didn't even get the chance to speak.

"A policewoman." It wasn't a question. "A fucking policewoman. Are you kidding me?"

She felt a sharp pain in her chest, felt her face heat up. "Dad, it's not—"

"Don't you tell me that it's not what I think. It's exactly what I think. You've been sleeping around with a policewoman, with that new one, and now your chickens are coming home to roost."

"Dad—"

He scraped his chair back and stood, knuckles on the table. "What did you tell her?"

"Nothing, dad—"

"What did you fucking tell her?" His eyes were flashing and he spat when he talked.

"Nothing!"

He took one step closer to her, his fists balled at his sides, his face red. "I swear to god, Sophie."

"I didn't tell her anything," she practically screamed. "I swear to you. I didn't. I didn't say anything."

"A daughter of mine going with a copper, a daughter of mine lying down with filth," he spat. "And then we all get arrested. A bit too much of a coincidence that, isn't it?"

She swallowed. He was getting closer. She'd never been afraid of her father. He'd never laid a finger on her. Not ever. But he was angry, angrier than she thought she'd ever seen him. "I didn't tell her anything. There was nothing to tell."

"Sophie." There was a warning growl in his voice.

She did the only thing she could think of. "I didn't tell her anything. I swear on mum."

He stopped, took a breath, his face paling slightly. "On mum?"

"I didn't tell her anything, dad," she said more quietly now. "We had a... a thing. We did. I kept it from you because I knew you'd be angry. But I never talked about you, never talked about the business. Even if I did, it was all fine. We haven't been doing anything wrong."

He grunted.

"The raid, the arrests. That was all her, nothing to do with me."

"You'd better be damn sure of that, girl."

"It wasn't. We never talked about her job, either." Sophie swallowed. "I swear to you, dad."

He looked older now, more worn, his skin more gray, his forehead sweaty. He lifted a hand, pointed a sharp finger at her. "You'd better—"

She interrupted him before he could give her ultimatums. "It's over," she said flatly.

His eyes widened slightly.

"It's over," she said again, more quietly. "There's nothing between us. It's… she's… it's done. I swear."

He looked at her for a second. "It had better be."

"It is."

They stood in the kitchen face to face for a long minute, then he nodded. "Alright then. I'll believe you." He sniffed. "Best not tell Gio. He'll lose his shit."

Sophie nodded. "Right."

"Go on then, off to bed with you. I don't want to see you tonight." He turned back to his chair, a can of beer beside it.

Sophie thought about saying something, but what was there to say? She turned and walked away, climbing the stairs slowly to her room.

She'd told the truth. It was all over. Even if it hadn't been before, it definitely was now. Because even if there was a small, tiny chance that she and Tilly could make things work, her father would never stand for it. And she couldn't stand to lose him.

Her heart hurt in ways she couldn't describe, and it was a long time before she fell asleep.

CHAPTER THIRTY ONE

On Saturday morning, Tilly woke up early. It was only when she was already in the shower that she realized that actually, she was excited about her dad coming to visit. The last few days had admittedly been terrible. She thought of Sophie all the time, and singing next to her was pure torture.

But that didn't mean that a tiny part of her couldn't be happy that her dad was coming. A familiar face, someone she didn't have to try hard with. Someone who could give her a hug and tell her everything would be alright even if it wouldn't.

It was early enough that she snuck down the stairs, not wanting to wake anyone else in the house. A quiet breakfast and then she'd go down to the station and meet the train.

She was silently creeping down the stairs when she heard the sniff. Confused, she looked back up the stairs, but no, the sound was coming from the living room. She hesitated, not sure whether she should go in or not, but then Mila had always been there for her, and the sniffing couldn't be anyone else.

She knocked quietly on the door before she went in, and Mila was hastily wiping her eyes, blue hair tucked behind her ears, cheeks pink.

"Sorry to intrude," Tilly said gently. "But I wanted to check that you're alright. Is there something I can do?"

Mila gave her a watery smile. "No, love. No, I'm just being a bit silly, that's all."

Tilly sat down on the couch next to her. "I'm sure you're not," she said. She thought about all the discussions she'd heard, she thought about Dash saying his parents argued, she thought about her own break up, and she sighed. "Want to talk about it?"

"It's nothing, really," Mila said.

"You've got a free listening ear," said Tilly, smiling. "I won't tell a soul anything. You can rely on that."

Tilly smiled back. "Yeah, you're right about that. Max says that you're by the book, that you never break a rule."

"That includes the rules of friendship," said Tilly stoutly.

Mila shook her head. "It's just... Well, to be honest, it's money."

Tilly frowned. "Money? It's not... You're not... You and Max?"

Mila laughed. "Me and Max are fine, but I suppose you've overheard some things over the last few weeks. We've argued a bit, I'll admit that, but mostly because we need to figure some things out."

"Like what?"

"Like how we can afford a bigger house and private school fees," Mila sighed. She rubbed at her eyes. "Ag's talking about bringing a grand piano home. She stands a good chance of getting into the conservatory. Dash's room is basically a cupboard. God knows where we're going to fit a new baby in."

Tilly's mouth dropped open. "A... a baby? You mean... you?" She started to laugh. "I had no idea. Congratulations."

Mila looked pleased. "Yes, well, the little one might be sleeping in a drawer at this rate. Property prices around here are ridiculous. We can't afford to move."

"I'll keep an eye out," Tilly promised. "Something will show up. I'm sure it will."

"Thank you," Mila said. "We haven't really told people yet, so, you know..."

"My lips are sealed," Tilly said.

"And there's you supposed to be an up-and-coming detective," said Mila with a grin. "You didn't even guess?"

"Not a clue, your secret's very... secret." Tilly sighed again, if only because her image of Max and Mila as the perfect couple was restored. She was glad, she found, that they weren't having relationship problems. She was glad that at least one couple in the world got everything right.

"Can I return the favor?" Mila asked, reaching out and taking Tilly's hand.

"How?" Tilly said, a little confused.

Mila squeezed her hand. "Relationships are hard," she said. "Don't ever let anyone tell you otherwise. But then, anything worth having is hard work."

"Ah." Tilly cleared her throat. "Sophie and I—"

"Broke up, I know," Mila said. "But I can see that it's not ended for you. I can see that you still have feelings. I'm not trying to interfere. I'm really not. I'm just telling you that if you know something is right in life, then you act upon it. Whether that's a law, a moral, or just a feeling. You fight for what's right. You're a police officer, you should know that."

It was a nice thought. Tilly smiled a little. "Thank you," she said. "But I don't think Sophie wants to talk to me, let alone be in a relationship with me. I did what was right. I made the arrests. Perhaps now I have to let things go."

"You won't know until you try to talk to her," Mila said, getting up. There was a bump overhead. "And that'll be Dash. He's an early riser like his mum. I'd better be getting on with breakfast. Eggs for you?"

"Only if I'm making them," Tilly said. "You go and get Dash. I'll start cooking for us all."

Mila went off upstairs, and Tilly went to the kitchen. She was truly pleased for Mila and for Max, too. She was sure something would work out for them. But she thought Mila was wrong. Happy endings didn't belong to everyone, and she was sure that Sophie wouldn't want anything to do with her.

Fighting for what was right was one thing. She did that at work enough. But it was time to let things go.

SHE WAS PROUD to show her dad around Whitebridge. It was a neat and clean town, law abiding and prosperous. He nodded in satisfaction as she showed him the small police station. He and Max spent a few minutes catching up, but then he took Tilly's arm and escorted her out of the station.

"You could have stayed for longer," she said. "You haven't seen Max for ages."

"I came to see you," he said. The air was crisp and cool, the day pleasantly sunny if a little cold. "And if I'm spending time with my daughter, I want to give her my undivided attention."

Tilly grinned at him. "That's sweet."

"Why don't we go for a walk?" he asked. "There's a nice footpath that goes over the fields and around the town. Max says it finishes at the pub, so we could get an early dinner before I get the train home."

"Sounds perfect," said Tilly, keeping her arm in her father's as they began to walk to the outskirts of town.

Her father updated her on everything that was happening with his own career, and by the time they were out into the countryside, Tilly was feeling more relaxed than she'd felt in days. Until her father cleared his throat.

"Alright," he said. "Out with it."

"Out with what?" she asked in surprise.

"Whatever it is that's bothering you. And don't pull that 'it's nothing' trick. I'm not only your father, but I was quite a passable detective in my time. I'm here to make sure that everything's alright, and it obviously isn't. So what's wrong?"

Tilly clenched her jaw and waited for another answer to come to her, but when it didn't, she sighed and began to tell him everything.

To his credit, he kept his reactions to a minimum, even though she was sure that she saw a glimpse of disapproval in his eyes.

"And that's it," she said, when she was done.

He said nothing for a while as they tramped through the fields, cold nibbling at their ears. Until they came to a stile, and he stopped.

With clear blue eyes, he looked at her. "I'd do it differently," he said. "If I could do it again."

"Do what differently?" she asked.

He looked down at his gnarled hands. "Your mother always told me that I put the job first. And I thought it was the right thing to do. Maybe it was. Making the world a safe place to be, that's important. So I worked nights, so I went up for promotion, so I left her alone more often than I should, and we argued."

"Dad, this isn't about—"

"Just hear me out," he said, still looking at his hands. "We didn't work out. Maybe we never would have, even if I'd been around all the time. But I don't know because I never got the chance to find out. She left. She had every right to. I was no husband to her." He looked up now. "But I'd do it differently if I had another chance, just so you know."

Tilly tried to digest this. He'd do it differently? Her father? The most career-minded person she'd ever met? Her role model?

He looked out over the fields. "The thing is," he said. "It's lonely being alone. And the job doesn't keep you warm at night. It's an important job, it really is. But there's more to life than just the job."

"I'd have thought that you'd be the first to tell me what an idiot I've been," Tilly said.

"Why? Because you got mixed up with someone who might not be the perfect choice?" He laughed. "The heart wants what the heart wants, girl."

Tilly bit her lip. "I just want to make you proud."

"You can. You do." He sighed. "But if you really want to make me proud, then don't make the same mistakes I did."

Tilly took her dad's hand. "I don't think she wants me anymore," she said quietly.

"Do you want her?"

She closed her eyes. "My life was better with her in it," she said. "It was lighter, brighter. I didn't want to stay at work all the time. There was something waiting for me."

"See?" he said. "That's the thing. The job means more when you're doing it for someone. For me, that person was you. I told myself every day that I was making the world a safer place for you. You need to find your person. Because without that, the job's just a job, same as any other."

Tilly squeezed her eyes tight shut for a second, then opened them to blinding brightness. "I do want her," she said. "I'm not ready to let her go."

"Then, for god's sake, tell the woman," her father said, shaking his head. "Or I really will think you're an idiot."

He squeezed her hand, let it go, and began to clamber over the stile. Tilly watched him for a second, then started to laugh. Was it all really that easy?

CHAPTER THIRTY TWO

"Soph, Soph, wake up." Gio was hammering on her bedroom door. "Get up."

"Jesus, Gio, give me a minute to get my head straight." She pulled one arm out of bed to check the time, just gone seven thirty. She hadn't gone to sleep until after one, sitting up and thinking about life, about love, about Tilly.

"No, get up now," Gio said.

For an instant, she considered telling him where to go with his insistence, but there was something in his voice. She jumped out of bed and opened the door. He was white, his face looking sick. "What is it?" she said.

"Dad."

"What?"

"Just come downstairs."

She followed him down to find her father sitting at his usual place at the head of the table. He was gray, his breath coming harder than hers, and she'd just run down the stairs. She looked at Gio. "How long has he been like this?"

"Since he came down," said Gio. "What do we do? He's refusing to have the doctor out."

"We'll see about that," Sophie said.

"He is right here," gasped her father. "And you'll not be

wasting the doc's time on me. Go and get that garage opened and I'll be there in half an hour. Let me just catch my breath."

Sophie looked at her brother, nervous and pale, and at her father, sick and gray, and shook her head. She wasn't doing this, wasn't going to play silly masculine games. She took a breath, straightened her shoulders, and took charge.

"Gi, call the surgery and get the emergency number. See if we can get Lydia out here before her morning starts."

"Right," Gio said, picking up the cordless phone.

"No," said her father. "I'll have no fuss."

"You'll do exactly as I tell you," Sophie barked.

"What about the garage? I've got a business to run."

"Gio's going to go and open as soon as he's done on the phone," Sophie said. "Now come on, let's get you to the couch."

"I'm not sick."

"Fine, you're not sick, but at least that way you can watch telly while you're waiting for the doc."

That seemed to placate him and she helped him into the living room, his weight heavy on her arm. She settled him and went back to the kitchen.

"Lydia's on her way over," Gio said.

"Good, now go on and open up the garage."

"But—"

"No buts," she said firmly. "He's not on his deathbed, and you know what he's like. He'll worry a lot less if he knows the garage is open. Go on, I'll give you a ring as soon as Lydia's come and I know more." She needed Gio out of the way. He'd panic. He was terrible in an emergency. It would be better for him to keep himself busy.

She ushered him out of the house and went back to her father. He was looking a little better now that he was lying down. His color was slightly pinker.

"There's nothing wrong," he grumbled as she came in.

"Did I say there was?" she said, sitting down next to him on the edge of the couch. "And if there's not, well, it won't be a problem, will it? Lydia will check you out and you'll be right off to work."

"I will be that," he said.

"Or she'll give you a sick note and you can stay home and watch the telly all day. Sounds like a win-win to me."

He grinned a bit at that. "Doesn't sound bad at all, put like that." He took a wheezing breath and then reached out to take her hand. "Only don't..."

"Don't what?"

He looked up at her, his face pained. "Don't let them take me away."

"Why would I do that?" she asked, thinking that an ambulance to the hospital would be the most sensible thing she'd heard in a long time.

"They took your mum away," he said, turning away from her. "She wanted to stay, but they took her."

"Dad..." She took a deep breath. "Dad, you're not mum. You don't have cancer. If Lyd needs you to go to hospital, it'll only be for tests. Try not to worry so much. I'm right here with you."

She squeezed his hand tight and knew that he was afraid. It was hard to stay angry with him, hard to imagine that he was the same man that had been so angry with her just last night.

Unless that had something to do with this. Unless she'd worried him into this with her stupid decisions and her stupid heart.

"I'll be at that concert tomorrow," he said, turning back to her with a grim smile. "You want to bet on it?"

She laughed. "It's only a concert, dad. It's not important."

"You're in it. It's important to me. I don't want to miss it."

"Well, you'd better do what the doctor says then, hadn't you?" she said, patting his arm just as the doorbell rang.

LYDIA PUT HER stethoscope back into her case and closed it up with a click. "I'd really prefer that you go into hospital," she said.

"No," said Paul Farmer. He was looking better, to be fair. His cheeks were pink again and his breathing was better. "I'm feeling alright now. I don't want to be waiting around until all hours at the hospital. I've got a family and a business to run."

Lydia laughed. "I'm sure that Sophie and Gio can take care of themselves."

Paul just grunted at this, and it occurred to Sophie for that first time that her father still thought he had to look after his children. He's spent a long time caring for them alone, she thought. It must be a hard habit to break.

"Well, if you're sure," said Lydia. "You've got your pills, and if there's any sign of anything else, I want you to call an ambulance immediately, no waiting for me to get here. Tightness in your chest, trouble breathing, pain in your chest or in your arm, you call nine-nine-nine immediately, is that clear?"

"Clear as glass," Paul said with a sniff. "I'll be back at work this afternoon, though. You wait and see."

Lydia flashed a look at Sophie, who said, "No."

"What?"

"No, dad," she said. "You're having the rest of the day off, at least. If you want to come to the concert tomorrow, then you need to stay home today and get some rest. No arguments. Right, doctor?"

"Sounds fair to me," said Lydia, with a nod at Sophie.

Paul sniffed again. "Worrying women," he said, but he was already settling back onto the couch with the remote in his hand. Sophie showed Lydia to the door.

"Is he really alright?" she said.

Lydia sighed. "For now, yes. But he needs tests, a thorough checkup. If you could persuade him to go to the hospital, it'd be far better."

"I'll work on it," Sophie said. She already had a plan. Her dad and Gio would come to see the concert tomorrow and ten-to-one Gio would be in his shiny new car. He practically drove it to the shop at the end of the street. She'd persuade her dad to ride home with them in Gio's car, and instead they'd take him to the hospital.

Lydia nodded at the plan. "I'll give the cardiac clinic a ring," she said. "Make sure they know he's coming in tomorrow afternoon. Maybe that might speed things up a bit."

"Right," said Sophie. "I'll make sure that he takes his meds and doesn't do anything too strenuous. Thank you."

"It's my job," Lydia grinned. "And you're very welcome. A large part of the battle with patients like your dad is getting them to take things seriously. They've spent a long time having a stiff upper lip and pretending that nothing is wrong, so getting them to make serious changes is difficult."

Sophie opened the door to let Lydia out and was more than surprised to see Tilly walking up the garden path.

"I'll get out of your way," Lydia said, looking from Tilly to Sophie and then back again before scurrying off.

Sophie gritted her teeth and pulled the front door shut behind her. Tilly wasn't coming into the house. She couldn't risk her dad finding out that she was here. "What do you want?" she hissed.

"To talk to you," said Tilly.

"There's nothing to say." Which wasn't true. There was too much to say, that was more the problem.

"Please, Sophie," said Tilly. "I just want a few minutes of your time. Let me say my piece and then I'll go if you want me to, I swear."

For just a second, Sophie almost said yes. She wanted to hear what Tilly wanted to say. She wanted to be close to her, even if it was just for a minute. She couldn't help how she felt, even though she knew she shouldn't feel that way.

Then her dad coughed inside and she shook herself out of her thoughts. "No," she said shortly.

"Please." Tilly moved a step closer and Sophie could smell the scent of her, her mouth watering at the warmth of having her so close. "Just a few minutes?"

Sophie bit her lip, then sighed. "Not here, not now," she said finally.

Tilly's face lit up. "Okay, where and when?"

"Soph?" her dad called from inside. He sounded whiny, not in pain.

"Tomorrow," she said hurriedly. "After the concert. Five minutes only."

"Anything you say," Tilly said.

"Right then."

"Soph?" called her dad.

"Is everything alright?" asked Tilly, face frowning in concern, she looked over to where Lydia was disappearing around the corner of the street.

"It's fine," Sophie said firmly. "I've got to go."

Tilly stepped back again. "Right, yes, course. Um, until tomorrow."

"Tomorrow," Sophie said, taking one last long look at Tilly before she turned around and went back inside.

"Soph?" her dad called from the living room. "That you? Want to bring me a bacon sandwich?"

She closed the front door and sighed. "No dad, no bacon, we've talked about this. I'll get you a nice salad instead and some eggs."

There was the sound of grumbling from the living room, but she ignored it as she went into the kitchen. Most of her mind was worried about her dad. A tiny part was wondering just what Tilly wanted to say to her. Her heart beat a little harder. Tilly had looked nice, worried, relieved a little. Would Tilly always make her feel this way?

CHAPTER THIRTY THREE

Sophie had agreed to talk. That was step number one. What Tilly was worried about now was step number two, the actual talking part. What was she going to say? Her heart told her to keep it simple, her head told her to go into vast amounts of detail. She was torn between the two as she walked along the high street.

At the corner before the police station, a fancy black car slid into half a parking space by the curb. Tilly stopped. The car's rear end was sticking out over the line. She waited to see if the driver was going to move, and when he didn't, she changed direction and walked over.

As she approached, Dougie McKeefe got out of the driver's seat. Tilly took a deep breath. People policing, she told herself. "Not the best parking job there, Dougie," she said, proud of herself for keeping her cool and not being too formal.

Dougie looked down, swore, and got back in the car. He straightened up as Tilly waited, then got out again. "Better, constable?"

"Much," she said with a grin. "Nice car, new is it?" She walked around the front. The tax sticker was there and valid.

"Well, that's one of the advantages of having your old vehicle stolen, isn't it?" Dougie said. "At least the insurance pays out and you can treat yourself to something new."

Tilly raised an eyebrow. "I don't think your insurance paid for all of this, did it?"

Dougie looked a little hang-dog. "Happen I had to put in a bit myself," he agreed. "Is the parking alright now?"

Tilly looked up and down the street and then nodded. "Perfectly fine," she said.

Dougie sighed in relief, bid her goodbye, and starting walking down the street toward the pub. Tilly watched him go, her brain ticking. Her eyes kept flicking back and forth between the car and Dougie as she thought.

The idea was brewing, getting bigger, stronger, but it was a full minute before she marched back to the police station and threw herself into the chair opposite Max's desk.

"The thing that's been bothering me is the shotgun," she said.

Max looked up from his paperwork. "Morning, Tilly," he said. "How are you?"

"Fine, fine," she said. "But the shotgun."

"What shotgun?"

"Dougie McKeefe's," she said.

Max pushed his chair back from the desk a little and crossed his arms. "You've lost me. You're going to have to start from the beginning."

"When Sophie, Jules, and Amelia got caught up at McKeefe's farm, he pulled a shotgun on them."

"He's a farmer," shrugged Max. "He's probably always got one around, for foxes and the like."

"But he knew they were people. In fact, he probably even knew it was Sophie, Jules, and Amelia, given he could hear them singing. But he still kept them locked up in a barn with a shotgun trained at them."

Max narrowed his eyes. "Yes, he did."

"But why?" pressed Tilly. "If he knew who they were, if he knew they were harmless and drunk, why keep them locked up like that?"

Max tapped his fingers on his desk. "Because... he didn't want them loose around his farm."

"Right," said Tilly. "Which makes me think that there's something at the farm that he didn't want them seeing." She leaned forward. "I've just seen McKeefe in a shiny new car. Definitely pricier than his insurance would pay for."

"Alright," Max said. "And what are we going to do about at this?"

Tilly thought for a moment, then nodded. "We need evidence, clearly. Getting a warrant based on a gut feeling is a practical impossibility. My guess would be that our best bet is surveillance."

"Agreed," Max said. He was already reaching for his phone. "I'll collaborate with the surrounding forces and we'll see what we can do."

"I can—" Tilly started.

"No, you can't," Max interrupted. He paused, looking at her. "And why can't you?"

She was about to lose her temper, about to tell Max that she wasn't involved with Sophie anymore, that this had nothing to do with the Farmers anyway. Then she saw that his lips were twitching in a smile.

"Crap," she said.

"You've already worked an extra shift this week," said Max. "I don't have the budget for the overtime, I'm afraid. But if it's any consolation, you won't have to sit in a cold car all night watching a dark farm."

Tilly nodded. "Understood. You'll keep me posted, though, right?"

"Of course I will," Max said. "Let me get all this set up. I'll have a brew if you're making one."

She heard him on the phone as she was making tea. She had no idea if he knew that Mila had told her about everything, and, she was ashamed to admit, she'd been so preoccupied with her own problems that she hadn't had time to think about Mila's.

Not that she was rolling in cash and could give it away to anyone who needed it. Still, though, a fresh pair of eyes might find a solution that Max and Mila hadn't thought of yet.

"All done," Max said as she bought tea to him and sat down again. He looked at her thoughtfully. "That was some quick thinking."

"It was just… lucky," she said. "I happened to be standing there when McKeefe was parking and once I saw him I started thinking about the gun again and, well, it all sort of started to make a bit of sense in my head."

"We'll have to wait for confirmation, of course," said Max, picking up his cup. "But I think you could be on to something here. Good work."

She felt herself blush. "Thanks."

"That's exactly the kind of thinking that gets you promoted," Max said. He looked a bit sad at that. "I should know. I don't think like that at all."

Tilly was surprised. "You're not saying you're a bad officer, are you?" she asked. "Because you're really not. You're amazing. When I see you with people around here, how you communicate, solve problems, you're brilliant at your job."

He grinned. "We can't all be high-flying detectives. And I'm just feeling a wee bit sorry for myself, that's all." He sighed. "No promotions in the near future for me, I'm afraid."

"Oh," Tilly said. "I'm, um, I'm sorry."

His eyes twinkled. "I know that you know. You don't have to walk on eggshells. Mila told me that she talked to you." He drank some tea. "And it'll all work out, I'm sure. It usually does. If need be, I'll move Ag into one of the cells here. As long as she's got a piano in with her, she'll be alright."

Tilly laughed. "I hope you're kidding."

"I very much am, don't worry." He looked back at his paperwork. "Alright, back to work. I'll let you know as soon as I know something."

She stood up. "Great, and, um, don't forget—"

"That you've got the afternoon off tomorrow for your concert," Max finished with a grin. "Billy would kill me if I forgot. Mila's dying to hear you as well, not to mention Ag and Dash.

They've really taken a shine to you."

Tilly remembered again that she needed to plan what to say to Sophie. Her stomach clenched. She only had one shot at this, she was sure.

IT WAS LUNCHTIME on the following day when Max put down his phone with a satisfied look on his face. "We've got 'em," he announced.

"Got who?" asked Tilly, trying desperately to finish her round of paperwork before she left and still distracted by the thought of what she was going to say to Sophie.

"Who do you think?" Max said. "McKeefe and his cronies. They ran surveillance last night and saw two cars go in the farm gates that were reported stolen. They must be using one of the barns up there to store the vehicles now that they can't use Farmer's garage anymore."

Tilly's face split into a grin. "Hallelujah," she said. "You know, that's my first real case?"

"Which is why you should be there for the arrests," said Max.

She bit her lip. There was little that she wanted more. Well, there was one thing.

"I know, I know," Max said. "It's your concert and you can absolutely go. I just wanted to give you the opportunity to change your mind if you wanted to, that's all."

Tilly seriously thought about it. The buzz of making an arrest, the satisfied knowledge that it was her intel that had cracked the case, the implications for her future career. She wanted to see the car thieves arrested so badly she could almost taste it.

In the end, the decision wasn't that difficult, though. "No," she said carefully. "Thank you, but no. I've got a concert to sing in." And a woman to persuade to love me, she added in her head. She wasn't about to make the same mistake again. She wasn't going to put her career ahead of Sophie.

"That's fine," Max said cheerfully. "I don't like putting on all that gear, anyway. Stab vests itch and those hard helmets ruin my hair."

"You're going though, right?" Tilly asked.

Max looked at his watch. "I'll see. I'll check in with Mila first and see if she needs me for moral support. I might pop by for a while, but I don't want to miss your first concert."

Tilly swore. She was very close to being late. "I've got to run," she said.

"Good luck," Max called after her as she left.

She was practically running, though she wasn't that late. She still didn't know what she was going to say to Sophie. And it was only because she was thinking of Sophie at all that she glanced toward the Farmer garage as she passed it.

She made it four or five steps past the garage gates before she realized what she'd seen.

She stopped. Had she seen what she thought she had?

She glanced at her watch again, swore quietly, then turned around and went back to the garage.

Something was off and she couldn't put a finger on what. Cautiously, she stepped through the gates, peering into the darkness of the open garage doors.

Only then did she really understand what she saw. Paul Farmer was lying on the concrete floor, his lips blue, completely still.

CHAPTER THIRTY FOUR

Sophie took a deep breath in and then out again.

"You'll be fine," Jules said. "Easy peasy. Just imagine everyone naked."

"Not sure that's going to help," Sophie said, peeking through the curtains to see half the town sitting in the audience.

"You could have a drink?" Jules offered.

Sophie glared at her. "Do you not think that drinking's got us into enough trouble?"

"I'm not sure whether you can blame the drink for that or Amelia and Cass. I love them both dearly, but they have some kind of magnetic attraction when it comes to trouble." Jules peeked out of the curtain next to Sophie. "There they are. They're very supportive, I'll give them that."

With a sigh, Sophie let the curtain fall back. "Where is she?"

"Who?" asked Jules, still surveying the audience.

"Um, Tilly?"

"Oh, right. I'm sure she'll be here." Jules had taken against Tilly ever since the arrest. "If she has to be."

Sophie started pacing the stage. She couldn't sing the solo by herself. What was she supposed to do?

She gritted her teeth, annoyance building in her chest. She should have known better than to trust Tilly. So much for them talking after the show. So much for whatever compromise she had thought they might be able to make.

* * *

Paul Farmer's body was heavy and she couldn't move it. The best she could do was drag at his feet to get him vaguely flat as she yelled into her phone to have the ambulance sent.

"Stay with me," said the responder. "There's an ambulance on the way."

Tilly's heart was pounding in her chest as she ripped Paul's shirt buttons off, baring his chest. The ambulance might be on its way, but it was going to be too late unless she did something about it.

"Is the patient breathing?" asked the tinny voice from her phone.

"No," she said, clasping her fingers together.

"Then stay calm. I'm going to lead you through the process of doing CPR," said the voice, sounding quite bored by the whole ordeal.

But Tilly was already pushing down on Paul's flabby chest, closing her eyes, bringing her training back. "I'm a police officer," she shouted at the phone. "I know what I'm doing. Just get me some help."

She pushed deep into his chest, deeper than she thought she had to. That's what her instructor had always said. She'd never done this before on a live person and was horrified to hear the crack of ribs breaking. For an instant, she was going to stop.

"Just keep going," said the phone. "You're doing a good job. It's normal to hear those noises. It means you're doing it right."

She pushed harder, trying to keep the rhythm, looking around, praying for someone else to come, someone else to help take the responsibility off her shoulders. She could feel tears in her eyes, could feel panic wanting to come.

"You're doing fine," said the phone. "Let me count you through it. Come on, we'll do this together. One and two and three. One and two and three."

Tilly clung to the voice on the other end of the phone as her arms started to ache.

❊ ❊ ❊

"This is ridiculous," Sophie muttered.

"She'll be here," said Jules, who was busy painting some lipstick on.

"Warm up in ten minutes," Billy called, clapping her hands.

Sophie snorted in annoyance and, turning on her heel, walked out of the little practice room behind the stage.

She had to come; she had to be here. She wouldn't leave her to do this alone, would she? Not after everything that they'd been through. She had to know that if she didn't show up, then… then there'd be nothing left. No trust. No connection. No hope.

Sophie went around the stage, coming out into the tiny hall and pushing through the people there to get outside.

What had she been expecting?

She hadn't let herself think about it, she hadn't let herself hope. But now that Tilly wasn't there, she realized that she'd been expecting her happy ending. That as much as she knew this couldn't work, as angry as she'd been at Tilly, as much as her father had been furious, she'd still, deep in her heart, thought that there could be a happy ending.

"There still can," she whispered to herself. But only if Tilly showed up.

All of it was ridiculous, she could see that now. Could see, now that Tilly wasn't here, that her life without Tilly in it simply wasn't as good. She missed her, which sounded pathetic, but it was true.

"Sophie!"

She turned and something small and fast crashed into her legs.

"Dash, don't do that," Mila said, rolling her eyes at Sophie. "Sorry, we're still working on personal space."

Sophie forced a smile. "Not a problem. Hello, Ag."

"Hello," Ag said. She tilted her head to one side. "You look pretty. Almost as pretty as when you were at our house with Tilly. I like your trousers. I'm here for your concert. Are you going to come to my concert? It's in two weeks, except it's not really a concert, it's a competition and actually I don't know if people can just come and watch or if it's only judges that watch that kind of thing but—"

"Ag," said Mila warningly.

"Sorry," said Ag.

"Why don't you take Dash and get us some seats?" Mila suggested to her daughter. Ag and Dash chased off happily through the crowds. "Honestly," Mila said, shaking her head. "I don't know how I'm going to cope with three of them."

Sophie was peering out onto the street, searching for any sign of Tilly, so the words took her a second to figure out. "Three?" she said, turning back to look at Mila.

Mila pulled a face. "I thought Tilly might have told you already," she said. "But yes, three. And I've already used my two favorite crime writers to name Dash and Ag. Goodness knows who the next one will be named for."

"You'll have some time to decide," Sophie said.

"There's plenty of things to decide," sighed Mila. "Like whether or not Ag can go to a conservatory, and where we're going to keep a grand piano if she wins one."

"I'd keep it in the village hall," Sophie said, looking back out to the street. "The acoustics in a private house probably wouldn't be great, anyway."

"Huh." Mila grinned. "That's not a bad idea, actually."

Sophie turned back to her. "No Max today?"

Mila shook her head. "They're making the arrests for that car theft ring this afternoon," she said.

Sophie's stomach plummeted. She turned all her attention back to Mila. There was no point looking out on the street, Tilly wouldn't be there. She wouldn't be coming at all. Sophie felt sick. Tilly's job had come first again. Of course it had.

* * *

"We've got a pulse," said the male paramedic.

"It's alright, love," the female paramedic said to Tilly. "It's alright, we're here now, you've done brilliantly."

Tilly's arms felt like they were made of stone and her back ached with the stress of it all. But she looked over and saw Paul Farmer's skin was turning pink again instead of that horrible, ashy gray. For a second, she closed her eyes and lay her head on the paramedic's shoulder.

"You did wonderfully," the paramedic said, patting her back and drawing away. "But we've got to get him to the hospital now."

"Right, yes, of course," Tilly said, pulling back.

"Do you know who he is? Who his next of kin are?"

Tilly felt nauseous. How was she supposed to tell Sophie this? But she nodded.

The paramedic looked at her for a moment. "You're police, right?"

"Yes."

"Want to come in the van with us?" she offered, eyes kind. "The hospital's not far. You can help keep an eye on things, and you can call his next of kin from in the back, if you want? He's starting to come round, might even be able to talk to them himself to keep them from worrying."

"Yes," Tilly said. "Yes, that sounds like a good idea."

"Hop in then, love," said the paramedic, turning around to help her mate roll the stretcher into place.

With a heavy heart, Tilly followed the stretcher into the ambulance, wondering just what she was going to say. Paul was starting to stir, saying something behind his oxygen mask.

"Sir, stay still, sir," said the male paramedic.

But he kept squirming, finally reaching up to take the mask off his face. "Call. Gio." Two words.

Tilly nodded.

* * *

The job, the job, it was always going to be about the job. Sophie was so angry she could spit, but was simultaneously so scared that she could faint. What was she supposed to do?

"I can sing the solo with you," Jules suggested.

"You're not a soprano," said Sophie. "Also, you haven't exactly practiced."

"Fair point."

"Alright, everyone around the piano, please," Billy said. "A two minute warm up and then we're on." She eyed Sophie. "Where's your partner in crime?"

"Not here," Sophie said, swallowing down her anxiety.

Billy's nostrils flared. "If she doesn't show up, there's going to be trouble."

Tell me about it, thought Sophie. She turned to look at the door even though she knew that there wasn't a chance in hell of Tilly turning up. No, she'd be making her arrests, she'd be doing her job just like always, putting it before everything and everyone else.

Except… the door was opening. Sophie's heart galloped.

"No, no," Billy said. "Choir only."

"It's an emergency," Gio said, his face as white as paper, his hands trembling.

The choir parted so that Sophie could get to him, could take his hands, could look into his eyes.

"Soph," he said, voice strangled. "It's dad."

CHAPTER THIRTY FIVE

The doctor looked tired, but she was smiling and for the first time in what felt like hours, Sophie felt her muscles relax just a tad.

"First, you can see your dad in just a minute," the doctor said.

Sophie heard Gio let out an enormous breath.

"We're about to send your dad in for surgery. The arteries in his heart are narrowed and we're going to put in a stent to open them up," said the doctor, obviously putting things simply for their benefit. "The operation isn't without risks, but he got here quickly. He's got a strong pulse at the moment, and we're optimistic. Do you have any questions?" She looked from one to the other.

Sophie shook her head. She had a million questions, but nothing she could articulate. More than anything, she wanted to see her father.

"Then I'll let you in to see him for a few minutes," said the doctor. "Please try not to excite him, and he's going to be a bit tired. But he's been a very lucky man."

"What do you mean?" Gio asked.

The doctor shrugged. "The number of people whose hearts stop and get restarted outside of a hospital is… negligible at best. The chances are incredibly slim. Your dad just happened to be around someone who knew what they were doing."

"Who?" asked Sophie.

"I don't have that information," smiled the doctor. "Now, if you want to go and see him, just go through that door right there. Only a few minutes, mind."

Sophie felt Gio reaching for her hand, something he hadn't done since she was a child. He pulled her through the door and on the other side, she found someone she hadn't expected to see in her wildest dreams.

Tilly was sitting on a plastic chair, a styrofoam cup of coffee in her hand.

"What—" Sophie began.

"No," said Tilly. "Not now. Go to your dad first. Go on."

And she had no choice. Gio was pulling her into the room and then he was there, pale and weary looking, but smiling, his eyes sparkling.

"Didn't think I'd go without giving you some trouble, did you?" he said.

Sophie collapsed onto him, hugging him as gently as she could while tears fell from her eyes.

"No, no," her dad said. His voice was weak. "Sit up, both of you. I need to talk to you before… before."

"Dad, I should have been there," Gio said.

"No," said their father. "I should have taken better care of myself. And I'm going to. You've not seen the back of me yet. Gi, I'm proud of you. I might not say it enough, but I am. You're a good lad and you're a brilliant mechanic. Better than I ever was. I love you, son. Don't forget that."

Gio nodded and turned away, not wanting his tears to be seen.

"And you," he said, turning to Sophie. "I was wrong."

"About what?"

He closed his eyes. "Life's short, Soph. Life's short and shitty and there's the occasional glimpse of sunshine." He opened his eyes again. "You know what makes it all worth it?"

She shook her head.

"Love. That's it. The only thing. Love for your kids, love for your pets, love for your friends. And love, real love. It doesn't come along often, but when it does, you need to grab it with both hands like a bloody life raft."

"I don't understand," Sophie began.

"She's out there," said her dad. "She saved my life. And I know you love her. I've known you your whole life. I can read your face as well as my own. You're angry at her and you're confused about things, but that doesn't take away the fact that you've fallen in love with her."

"Dad—"

"Tell her," he said, eyes closing again. "If I wake up from this damn operation and you're still single, there's going to be hell to pay."

Sophie squeezed his hand, and the door opened, admitting a nurse. Sophie bit back a sob.

"Enough of that nonsense. I'm going to be fine," her dad said. "Now, off with the two of you, I'll see you on the other side of this."

She and Gio waited as her father's bed was wheeled out.

"I need to move the car," Gio said when he was gone.

"Go on then," said Sophie, knowing that he wanted to be alone for a while, wanted to shed some private tears.

She let him go and took a deep breath before she walked out into the corridor.

Tilly was still there.

"Sophie," she said, standing up.

"No," said Sophie. "Sit down, be quiet, and listen to me."

Tilly sat.

Sophie took a second to gather her thoughts.

"You're right," she said, finally.

"About?"

"Your job is important," Sophie said. "I've been thinking that it put me in second place, but this is your job, saving lives, making people safe. You putting your job first means that I get to hug my dad again. I was being selfish and stupid, thinking that an intelligent, decent person only had time for one thing in their life."

Tilly watched her silently, eyes blue as the ocean.

"What I mean is," said Sophie. "Is that we're different, you and I. We're different and that's okay. We have different priorities about things, and that's fine. You might not always love my family, and they might not always love you, but sometimes, just sometimes, we have to put ourselves first. And that's what I'm doing."

"Are you?" Tilly asked doubtfully.

Sophie sighed and sat down. "I'm doing a terrible job of explaining things. Okay, let's try again. Thank you for saving my dad's life."

"You're welcome."

"And I understand that your job is important and that it's important to you. I don't want to stand in the way of that."

"Okay."

She took a breath. "And what I'm saying is... well, is there a chance for us? I'd like there to be a chance for us."

Tilly was silent.

Sophie felt her heart start to crack. "I don't want to be without you," she said, more quietly. "I want to wake up with you. I want to see your smile when I come home. I want to feel you next to me when I'm sad and laugh with you when I'm not. I can't imagine a world that doesn't have you and me in it together."

Tilly reached out and took her hand.

"When you asked me to move in with you, it felt... right," said Sophie. "Like the world just clicked into place like a big Rubik's cube, all the colors in all the right places. I don't think I realized at the time what that was. It was so quiet, so understated, so perfect in its normality. But I know now."

"What was it?" asked Tilly, equally quietly.

"It was me falling in love with you."

Tilly took a shaky breath. "You're right," she said. "My job is important. But people have been trying to explain to me for a long time why it's important. It's not the job, it's the people. Max keeps telling me that policing is for the people. And I don't think

I really understood before."

Sophie stroked her thumb on Tilly's palm.

"It sounds stupid, but it's easy to forget sometimes that people are who they are. This afternoon I was doing CPR on this man and I wasn't thinking that he was a patient, a body, a potential criminal, someone who hated me. The only thing I was thinking was that this was your dad."

Sophie gulped, but managed not to cry.

"My job is only important if I have someone to do it for, someone to give it meaning," said Tilly. She looked up. "And that person is you."

"Me?"

Tilly nodded. "I didn't plan on falling in love. I didn't plan on compromising my career. Honestly, I didn't think it was possible. But these last few weeks with Max and Mila have made me realize that who you love is important. Who you come home to is important. Who you build a life with is important."

"I think it is," agreed Sophie.

"And for me, that person is you." Tilly gave a small laugh. "I have no idea when it happened. I think the first time I saw you, I knew that there was something different. But it all crept up on me, this slow, stunning realization that actually, you are the other half of me. You're right, we're different, but that's a good thing. It means we can complete each other, be stronger together."

There was a long minute of quiet.

"What I'm trying to say is that I love you too," Tilly said, finally, her voice cool and strong in the empty hospital corridor.

Sophie bit her lip. "Are we going to make this work?"

"I'll always ask before I take any overtime," Tilly said.

"I'll try to remember that you're saving the world before I get angry that you're not home for dinner," Sophie said with a grin.

"There is one more thing," Tilly said. "Your family."

Sophie sat up straighter. "My family are grown adult men who are more than capable of looking after themselves. You saved my dad's life, and he'd better be grateful for it. As for Gio, well, he can like it or lump it. But if he wants a decent home-cooked meal every now and again, he'd better get used to things."

"You sure?" Tilly asked, gripping her hand.

Sophie nodded. "I'm sure. I need to live my life for me. And for you."

Tilly smiled a crooked smile, and it was more than Sophie's heart could take. She leaned in and brushed Tilly's lips with her own and then deepened the kiss until her arms were around Tilly's neck and time stood still.

Until she could feel Tilly's heartbeat in her lips and feel the muscles of her neck relaxing. Until she could feel the perfection that they made together.

Until the corridor door swung open and Gio strode in. "What the hell?" he shouted.

And Sophie began to laugh. "Gi, meet my girlfriend."

"We've already met. When she arrested me," he growled.

Sophie rolled her eyes and took Tilly's hand. "Better behave yourself then. She's got handcuffs in her back pocket."

Then both she and Tilly were laughing at the wide-eyed shock on Gio's face.

EPILOGUE

"What exactly am I supposed to do with this?" Sophie said, looking down at the writhing bundle that Tilly had passed her.

"He's my god-son, not a this," Tilly said.

"But I don't know anything about babies," Sophie wailed.

"You know about as much as I do," said Tilly. "Besides, look how small he is. It's not like he can be that much trouble. It's for, what, a couple of hours tops?"

Sophie looked at Art. His face was smooth and small, his eyes were closed now, and he appeared to be falling back to sleep. "Alright, if you think so," she said doubtfully.

"I could put him in a baby seat in the back of the police car?" offered Tilly. "Max does it all the time."

A pungent odor began to rise from the baby. "Mmm, I'm not sure that's a good idea. What do I do with him now?"

Tilly choked back a laugh. "Change him, I'm guessing. There's nappies in the bag over there, there's bottles in the cool bag. Max's mum had to catch the first train this morning, his dad's had a fall. Nothing major, but she needs to get home. So we're on duty."

"Until you meet the plane," Sophie said, reminding Tilly for the umpteenth time.

"I'm not going to forget them," said Tilly, putting on her uniform cap. "Max and Mila's plane gets in at eleven thirty. I'll be at the airport to pick them up. Easy peasy."

"Max and Mila's plane gets in at eleven," said Sophie.

Tilly grinned and dropped a kiss on Sophie's cheek. "I was kidding." She walked toward the door and Sophie followed, redolent Art still in her arms.

"I thought babymoons were supposed to happen before the baby was born."

"Technically, I think they are," agreed Tilly. "But then, little Art came so fast. And you can't fly when you're heavily pregnant. Plus, I mean, Mila obviously needed the break now. With three kids around the house, I'm thinking a weekend away was just what she needed."

Sophie stopped in the middle of the hallway. "Oh my god, where are the other two?"

Tilly laughed. "At school, where they're supposed to be. I dropped them off on my way back here. Will you stop worrying?"

She was leaning against the doorframe, relaxed and confident in her uniform, and so beautiful that Sophie still couldn't believe she was allowed to touch her. Even after a year together.

They'd been lucky getting the small cottage on the outskirts of Whitebridge, and luckier still that Tilly's next assignment had left her within commuting distance. At the time, Sophie had been worried. But as Tilly said, there wasn't really room in Whitebridge for two police officers.

"It's going to be fine," Tilly said again.

"It had better be," said Sophie. "The house is almost finished, dad's over there doing a final look-around and Gio's wandering around with a paint can getting the last patches. The builders have collected their stuff, so unless the entire extension falls down immediately, I think we should be alright."

"Do you think Mila knows it's going to be finished?" Tilly asked.

Sophie laughed this time. "Knowing Max, probably. I mean, it was practically done before they left, and I know he wanted it to be a surprise that it was done a week early, but you know what he's like. I really don't think he can keep a secret."

"I can keep secrets," Tilly said with a broad wink. She tipped her cap until it was rakishly over one eye.

Sophie's breath left her body for a second. "As long as you don't keep them from me," she said. Then she glimpsed the clock by the door. "And as long as you don't miss that damn plane."

"Alright, alright," Tilly said. She took a step toward Sophie and kissed her cheek. Then changed her mind and kissed her lips.

Sophie felt the familiar warmth running through her veins at Tilly's touch. She shivered.

"Sorry," Tilly said. "But you have to change the baby. He's not going to smell any better. I'd help but…"

"You've got a plane to meet," Sophie said, holding Art with one hand and pushing Tilly toward the door with the other.

❈ ❈ ❈

Tilly pulled the car onto the motorway and relaxed a little. She liked driving. It was calming. More calming than home had been recently, anyway. What with Gio dropping by at least once a day, and Paul coming almost as often, with Mila visiting with the baby and the kids running around, it was sort of nice to get a moment to herself.

Not that she begrudged a moment that she spent living with Sophie. She loved her to death. But now that she was about to take over the garage, she was on edge and worried all the time. Which was odd, because Tilly knew she could handle it. She'd been practically running the place for years. And it wasn't like Paul was going to leave her to run it alone. He was bound to be in there every day for a few hours.

The phone rang and Tilly touched the hands-free button. "Ware."

"It's me," Sophie said. Tilly could hear the cries of the baby in the background. "He won't drink the milk."

"Did you warm it?"

"Did you tell me to warm it?"

"Maybe?" hazarded Tilly. "Max's mum said you're supposed to put it in a cup of hot water for a few minutes and then pour some milk on the back of your hand to make sure it's not too hot."

"Ooo-kay... Right, yes, alright, I can do that."

"Relax, you're doing a good job," said Tilly encouragingly. "You'll be fine."

"I'm not so sure about that. He keeps crying. Just... just get that plane, okay?"

"I'm on my way," Tilly said, ending the call.

So much stress. She sighed and settled back in to driving. With Paul retiring, she'd bought up the idea of retiring to her own father. He'd laughed at her and told her he'd die on the beat, which she hoped he didn't mean literally.

She had persuaded him to start dating again, which was progress. She'd been pretty happy with herself for that, up until her dad had announced that he now had a girlfriend. She wasn't sure how she felt about that. Not a real, serious girlfriend. But Becca had proven nice, sensible, and a fellow police officer.

She'd be moving into Tilly's childhood home next month, something that Tilly knew she should be happy for, but also made her a little nervous. She couldn't control her dad's life. She could just hope that everything went well.

So many changes. So much was going to be different. Life just kept moving onward, and she knew that it had to, but she worried sometimes that she didn't have time to enjoy things before they were gone.

She was so busy thinking about this that when the silver car jetted past her, she reached up and switched on the lights and siren without really thinking about it. And then she had to chase it down. She had no choice.

*　*　*

Sophie bounced the baby in one arm. He gurgled, and she

smiled. "See? It's not so bad, is it?"

He gave another gurgle and then spat up what seemed like half the milk he'd drunk.

"Crap." She grabbed a tea towel and cleaned him up before checking the time. "You know what, why don't we go and see Uncle Gio?" she asked.

Her dad would be there. He was well-versed in babies. And they were supposed to be at the house for the house-warming party in an hour or so anyway. That part was a secret. Even Max didn't know about it. It had been her idea, and she was proud of it. A welcome home present for Max and Mila, and a chance to christen the new part of their house.

She bundled Art back into his pram, picked up everything that had come with him, and got out of the house. Babies seemed to come with a lot of accessories, she hoped that she hadn't forgotten anything.

* * *

Tilly looked from the data on her in-car computer to the man handcuffed by the side of the car to the clock on the dashboard. Damn it all. She hadn't intended for this to happen. He'd been speeding. It should have been a ticket and a stern talking to, and that was it.

How was she supposed to know that he had an outstanding warrant? She gritted her teeth as she called it in.

"Back up on its way," growled the dispatcher.

Tilly eyed the clock again. She could still make it on time if she left in the next ten minutes.

* * *

"Aw, look at him," Gio said, peering into the pram. "He looks like Winston Churchill."

"All babies look like Churchill," said their father.

Art took this personally and started to grumble and then cry. Sophie looked at her father in desperation.

"Here we go," Paul said, lifting the boy up and cradling him over his shoulder. Art stopped crying immediately. "See? Easy."

Sophie sighed. Everyone seemed to think that everything was easy nowadays. She wasn't so sure. For a start, as of next week, she'd be the official owner of the garage. "What about that mold in the toilet?" she asked, remembering that she'd meant to ask about it the day before and forgotten.

Her dad rolled his eyes. "Use some mold cleaner to clean it up. Easy."

There was that word again.

"Hello, dear," Sylv said, bustling through into the new extension. "We're almost all set up here. People will start arriving soon and then we'll just be waiting for the guests of honor."

"Right, Tilly's on that," said Sophie, checking her watch. Or at least she hoped Tilly was.

* * *

Tilly breathed out through her nose and in through her mouth, trying to calm herself down as she checked the rear-view mirror. No sign of another police car. There was a disgruntled-looking man in her back seat, but he was safely cuffed.

A lot safer than she'd be when Sophie found out that there was no chance of her making that plane now. She groaned out loud.

"What's wrong?"

She eyed the mirror again. "Nothing for you to concern yourself with."

He pulled a face. "No, go on, we've got to sit here, anyway. What's wrong? You look like you've sat on a pile of thorns."

"Charming," said Tilly. "If you must know, I was supposed to pick someone up at the airport and I'm going to be late."

He thought about this for a second. "You could always let me go," he suggested.

"Ha ha. Not going to happen."

"Be like that then. Anyway, whoever it is will wait for you," he said.

"Yeah, but my girlfriend will kill me. She's always worried that I put the job first," Tilly said, without really thinking about who she was speaking to.

The man in the back seat shrugged. "Then arrange for someone else to do the pickup from the airport. I'm married myself. You just have to make sure that your responsibilities are taken care of, even if it's someone else doing them."

She looked into the rear-view again. Huh. That made sense. That way, she could do her job and Sophie would still be happy. She grinned. "Cheers."

"Don't mention it," said the man. He sniffed. "You gonna let me go now, then?"

"No," said Tilly, picking up her mobile. "But you've got my thanks, if that counts for anything?"

* * *

"I can't believe it's finished," Mila said, her eyes aglow. She turned to Max. "Did you arrange all this?"

He nodded and blushed as his wife kissed him.

"We helped with the party though," Ag said, pushing through the little crowd in her conservatory uniform.

"That was Sophie's idea," said Dash, cake already smeared around his mouth.

"Thank you," Mila said. "Um, not to be picky or anything, but I'm pretty sure I have three children now?"

Sophie laughed and nodded over to a corner where her father sat in a chair asleep, Art on his chest. "You might have found yourself a new babysitter," she said. "He's going to be bored now that he's retiring. He'll need something to do."

"I could use the help," said Mila. "I kept Ag and Dash under the counter at the shop, but Art hates it there. He wants to be up front and center where he can see people all the time."

"Can't blame him for that," Tilly said, finally arriving.

Sophie raised an eyebrow. "Strange, given that you were picking Max and Mila up, I sort of assumed that you'd be arriving at the same time as them?"

"Give her a break," Gio said as he walked past. "I was glad of an excuse to drive the car on the motorway."

"Thanks," Tilly said. Gio gave her a high five and went off in search of a beer.

"Come on," said Max, putting an arm around his wife. "Let's go and get something to eat."

"I'm sorry," Tilly said as Max and Mila left. "I know I was supposed to pick them up. But there was a speeder, and I made an arrest and, well, it all got a bit out of hand."

For a second, Sophie looked at her, then she smiled. "It's fine. They got picked up, no one was injured in the process, I didn't have to problem-solve to make up for you being stuck at work. It's not a problem."

"Really?"

"Yes," Sophie said. "Really."

"That's good," said Tilly. She looked down at her feet. "Because, um, there's something that I've been meaning to tell you." She looked up again, face pink. "Remember before when I said that I could keep a secret?"

Sophie's stomach dropped. "Yes."

Tilly came closer, put her hand on Sophie's arm. "I know you're worried. You're worried about taking over the garage, you're worried that I'm commuting and we won't have enough time together, and I just want you to know that you have nothing to worry about."

She looked up into Tilly's earnest blue eyes. "I don't?"

Tilly shook her head. "Nope. You're great at your job and you'll be brilliant at running the business. I've got no worries about that at all. As for the other stuff, well..." She blushed even deeper. "I had to wait until it was all confirmed, but... I'm coming back to work in Whitebridge."

Sophie stilled. "You are?"

"I am. The force is expanding our area and there are going to be three officers stationed here. And it's coming with a promotion. Sergeant Ware."

Sophie's face split into a grin. "That's brilliant, Till, well done."

Tilly pulled her in close. "I know things are changing. Things will always be changing. But we'll face the changes together, Soph. That's what couples do. Just look at Max and Mila."

Sophie looked over at where the couple were laughing with Paul, Max holding his new son on his shoulder as Mila ruffled Ag's hair. Dash was playing with Gio on the floor. She smiled. "They're a lovely family."

"And so are we," Tilly said. "Whatever that family ends up looking like, however big or small it becomes, as long as you and I are at the heart of it, then it will be perfect."

Sophie pulled back a little. "Babies?" she asked.

Tilly snorted. "Only if you get a lot more practice. You weren't exactly a natural with Art, you know?"

Sophie laughed. "Fair. I'm not sure about the whole baby thing."

"Then we'll adopt an older child. Or we'll have cats or dogs or llamas instead."

"Llamas?"

"Llamas," Tilly confirmed.

Sophie let herself be pulled in close again, let herself feel Tilly's scratchy uniform against her cheek, smell Tilly's familiar smell, let herself feel Tilly's heartbeat. "I love you."

Tilly tilted her head. "I love you too," she said, brushing Sophie's lips with her own.

"Song, song!" shouted Sylv. Billy was already sitting at the piano in the corner, Ag perched on the bench with her.

"Fancy a sing?" Tilly asked.

"With you?" said Sophie. "I thought you'd never ask."

Music curled into the air late into the night in a little town called Whitebridge. It wasn't until after midnight that a newly minted sergeant led her soon-to-be garage owner girlfriend home by the hand. It took another year before they adopted a cat. Then a dog. And five years before Sophie finally decided that a baby might not be so bad. Especially if Tilly was the one having it. They sang in the choir and Sophie opened a car parts shop that ran alongside the garage. Tilly became a Chief Superintendent, just like her dad. They never did get a llama though...

THANKS FOR READING!

If you liked this book, why not leave a review? Reviews are so important to independent authors, they help new readers discover us, and give us valuable feedback. Every review is very much appreciated.

And if you want to stay up to date with the latest Sienna Waters news and new releases, then check me out at:

www.siennawaters.com

Keep reading for a sneak peek at my next book!

BOOKS FROM SIENNA WATERS

The Oakview Series:

Coffee For Two
Saving the World
Rescue My Heart
Dance With Me
Learn to Love
Away from Home
Picture Me Perfect

The Monday's Child Series:

Fair of Face
Full of Grace
Full of Woe

The Hawkin Island Series:

More than Me

The Whitebridge Series:

The Queens of Crime
Teaching Hope
Play It Again, Ma'am
Changing Plans
Play Our Song

The Tetherington Hearts Series:

The Mended Hearts Bookshop
The Damaged Hearts Bargain

Standalone Books:

The Opposite of You
French Press
The Wrong Date
Everything We Never Wanted
Fair Trade
One For The Road
The Real Story
A Big Straight Wedding
A Perfect Mess

Love By Numbers
Ready, Set, Bake
Tea Leaves & Tourniquets
The Best Time
A Quiet Life
Watching Henry
Count On You
The Life Coach
Crossing the Pond
Not Only One Bed
The Revenge Plot
The Hotel Inspector
That French Summer
The Wedding That Almost Wasn't
Loving Jemima
(Not So) Mad About You
The Almost Bride

Or turn the page to get a sneak preview of The Almost Bride!

THE ALMOST BRIDE

Chapter One

It had taken two months to find the dress. Two months and four dress fittings and it slid on like a glove, clinging in all the right places like it was a second skin. As Mia smoothed out the creases, she caught her mother dabbing at her eyes with a tissue.

"Mum."

"I know, I know," her mother said, still dabbing. "It's just that… you look so pretty."

Mia, who had her reservations about this, nodded. It was all very well looking pretty, but what about feeling pretty? Or feeling anything, for that matter. Not that she was about to mention anything to her mum. What was she supposed to say, anyway? 'Oh, by the way, mum, I've started feeling like there's a rock in my chest and I'm a bit worried that maybe I've got heart cancer or maybe my heart fell out altogether and I don't know what to do.'

Her mother would just worry about the caterers.

"We're so proud of you, you know," her mother said, abandoning her tissue to come and finish zipping Mia up. She turned her, so that they were both facing the mirror. "Mind you, I shouldn't be surprised. You were always so dependable. Even when you were small, you never wrinkled a paper. Every time you had to bring home a letter from school, it was always pristine."

Mia could remember sliding everything into neat folders that pleased her. She liked it when things were put away and in place.

"And then those grades, good enough to get into Oxford, they said," her mother went on.

Not that Mia had gone to Oxford. She wasn't entirely sure why. Probably because she was a middle-class girl from a middle-class family and people like her didn't go to Oxford. But that wasn't important. What was important was that she *could* have gone. Instead, she'd gone to a very nice university and graduated with a first class degree, and no one had expected anything less of her.

"A perfect daughter, a perfect degree, and now this," her mother said, sniffing a little again. "A perfect wedding."

To Mikey, who was, after all, the perfect man. Blonde hair, firm jaw, good with children, on the fast track to a well-paid career in business, and funny and kind to boot. It was, Mia thought, almost sickening how perfect he was. Then she felt bad because Mikey was lovely.

There must be something wrong with her. That was the only thing she could think of. She looked herself up and down in the full-length mirror. Her long, blonde hair was loose around her tanned shoulders, descending in careful, artful waves. Her big blue eyes were expertly made up. Her skin was smooth, her teeth were straight without ever having been near an orthodontist. She was pretty and bright and fun to be around.

Which made all of this so much worse.

It had started a few weeks ago. She'd been in town, looking at bikinis for her upcoming honeymoon, when she'd seen a woman come out of a changing room, laughing. She'd been buxom, with love handles spilling out over the edges of her bikini bottoms, her eyes full of fun, her laugh deep and real, and Mia had stared so long and so hard that the woman had raised a questioning eyebrow at her.

Mia had made some excuse and run away, feeling hot and a bit sick at the thought of being caught staring. And then, on the way home, she'd stopped at the newsagent to pick up a bridal magazine that she'd ordered, and she'd done something so awful, so unlike her, that even now she could see herself coloring in the mirror at the very thought of it.

When the newsagent had turned his back to get her magazine from under the counter, she'd watched in horror as her hand darted out and grabbed a Snickers bar from the display. Quick as a flash, the chocolate had disappeared into her coat pocket and then the newsagent had turned back and it was done and couldn't be undone.

And the rock had set up shop in her chest and she hadn't taken a full breath since.

"That's everything then," her mother said, looking her up and down. "Perfect. Just perfect."

Which, to be fair, the outside definitely was. Plucked and preened and doted on. It was more the inside that Mia was worried about.

It was nerves. Cold feet. That was all. She told herself night after night that she'd feel better as soon as this was done, as soon as she and Mikey were married and off on their honeymoon. It was the stress of the wedding and loads of people must feel the same.

After all, who wouldn't want to be married to Mikey? He was, as her mother often reminded her, a catch.

"You'd better go, mum. You don't want to get to the church all sweaty." Her lips felt numb. It was hard to form words.

Her mother took her hand and squeezed it. "You'll be nervous," she said. "And that's alright, it's perfectly normal. But you and Mikey will have the rest of your lives together. That's what's important. Get this stressful wedding out of the way and then, well, then you'll get everything you've ever worked for. You deserve this, Mia. You truly do."

It might be different if she could just talk to someone. But who? She could hardly tell her two best friends, who were both bridesmaids and jealous as all get out. It wasn't like she could tell her mother. And Mikey... Well, up until a few weeks ago, she'd thought that she could tell Mikey anything. Then she'd seen a half-naked woman laughing and stolen a chocolate bar and her world had started to crumble from the inside out.

"I know, mum," she said, lips still numb.

"You'll be mum yourself, soon enough," her mother said. "What was it we said? Another year of working and then you two will start a family?"

A year, that was the plan. A year together, getting used to being married, getting used to living under the same roof, and then they'd start trying. And knowing her, she'd be pregnant within a week. And then she'd give birth to a perfect little baby, and then they'd wait two years and do it again, and they'd have a boy and a girl, the boy first, and…

"Mia?" her mother said sharply.

"Yes?" Her breath was coming too fast. She made a concerted effort to slow it down. "Yes?"

Her mother squeezed her hand again. "You're just a bit nervous, that's all. It's normal."

If it was so normal, then why hadn't she felt this way before? Why hadn't she hyperventilated while waiting to go on stage for her piano solos, or when she graduated, or when any one of a hundred other occasions had presented themselves?

"I'm fine," she said now, feeling anything but.

Her mum was about to question this, but then her mobile buzzed and she checked it and let go of Mia's hand. "That's your dad. He's on the way with the car. I'd better be going. I'll be there at the front of the church. I'll be the one with the hankie. You won't be able to miss me."

"It'll be fine, mum," Mia said, more to herself than to her mother.

"So beautiful," her mother said. She went to the door, took one last look. "So perfect." And then she was gone and Mia could collapse down onto the bed.

Now that she was alone, her breath was coming faster again. With this stupid rock on her chest, she couldn't get any oxygen at all.

And the thought of it all, of everything, of her entire life marching out in front of her with Mikey and babies and houses in the country and holidays and Christmas with her parents and Boxing day with his parents and dogs and parent-teacher nights and...

She slammed her eyes shut and saw the changing room woman. Saw her laugh, her front tooth crooked, saw her lightness, her joy, the life oozing from every pore. And never in her entire life had she been more jealous of anyone.

Her. Mia Tate. Top of her class, pretty and smart and everything in between. She was the object of jealousy, sure, but not actually jealous. Never jealous. She was too nice for that.

Her breath caught in her throat now, and she gasped, coughing, trying to get more oxygen into her lungs.

She couldn't die now, not like this. Her father would be here any second. Which somehow made things worse.

Her chest heaved, trying desperately to get the air that she needed. Her eyes flashed open, she was starting to panic. Her breath was still caught, she still couldn't breathe in. She looked around, desperate to find something, anything to help.

Then she saw them.

And her chest rose, oxygen flooding into her lungs.

Her hands were sweating, so wet that she almost dropped the keys when she tried to pick them up. She squeezed them tight in her hand so that they almost pierced her skin, and didn't even think.

Her father would be here any minute.

She tore the room door open, bounded down the stairs, keys in hand and not even a change of underwear to be seen.

Downstairs, she flung open the front door, slamming it behind her, and raced in her high heels over the gravel to her little Mini Cooper. Her hands shook as she unlocked it. She crammed herself in, pulling handfuls of wedding dress in after her, stuffing material down the sides of the seat, between her legs, anywhere she could until she could close the car door.

Her whole body was shaking now, shaking and sweaty as she

put the key in the ignition and turned it.

Any second, her dad was going to be here. Any second, a limo was going to pull into the driveway.

She slammed the car into reverse, screeched around until she was facing the entrance to the drive, then slammed the car into first and hit the accelerator. She slammed into second as she pulled out of the driveway, third as she careened down the street, and fourth as she turned the corner, catching a glimpse of a black limo festooned in white ribbons as she accelerated away.

She navigated the streets that she'd grown up in deftly, driving the speed limit, and finally, finally, spotting the ramp to the motorway. Pulling onto it, she joined the traffic, put the car firmly into fifth, and for the first time since she'd gone bikini shopping, she took a deep, full breath.

CHAPTER TWO

Luna hitched her duffel bag up on her shoulder and thanked the bus driver cheerily as she bounded down the steps.

"You know where you're going, love?" he asked.

"Yeah, don't worry." It was, even she had to admit, nice to be able to speak English with people again.

"That bag looks heavy," he said doubtfully.

"Nah, there's barely anything in it, promise." Which was true. She'd always depended on being able to shed things and pick things up when needed. Currently, she owed three full outfits, a small selection of t-shirts, two pairs of shoes, minimal underwear, her phone, and a wallet that was so empty she could slide it through the bus doors that were now closing.

The day was pleasantly warm, which wasn't what she'd been expecting. She'd thought that her arrival in England would be greeted by the normal rain. It looked like she'd lucked out. She was still wearing the same cotton trousers and shirt that she'd had on when she'd left Sri Lanka.

"Afternoon, love," an elderly man said, pulling his dog's lead so that they both skirted Luna.

"Afternoon." If there was one thing that could be said about Little Chipping, it was that the people were friendly. Luna should know. She'd spent a fair part of her life here. A part that had seemed very distant when she was in Malaysia or Mali or

Morocco, but all too close now that she was back. Things really hadn't changed at all.

"You're looking a bit lost there, love. Need any help?" The man with the dog had turned back.

Luna grinned. "Thanks for asking, but I'll be alright."

"There's a youth hostel up the top of that road," he said, pointing. He looked her up and down, taking in grubby hands and feet, messy dark curls, and clothes that hadn't seen an iron in forever. "Or a wee hotel down the other way," he added unsurely, as though he ought to give her the option but didn't think she could afford it.

She wished she could take him up on either of those offers. However, not only did she not have a penny to her name, having spent the last fifty pence she had on crackers at a shop by the bus stop, but her grandmother would find out sooner or later.

And she dreaded to think what Evelyn Truman would say if a granddaughter of hers was caught in a youth hostel in Little Chipping. Honestly, the president of the bridge club could hardly be associated with such a person.

Although, to be fair, Luna thought as she started walking, perhaps her grandmother had changed. Perhaps these few years on her own had softened her, made her nicer, friendlier, warmer.

It had been years. Years that had gone by faster than Luna could account for them.

She turned a corner and could see the house, all gray stone and gable windows and jolly flowers lining the path.

It wasn't like she had a choice. As she'd explained to the lorry driver that had picked her up in Dover. "The dosh just isn't there."

"You and me both, love," he'd said. "Explains why you're hitchhiking though. It's not safe, you know. Not for young girls like yourself."

"I'm twenty-eight," she'd said indignantly.

"And a wee thing, just look at you," he'd said right back. "Unless you know some of that Krav Maga or something."

Luna had looked down at her skinny legs and blown out a

breath. She did not, in fact, know Krav Maga. Or any other martial art, for that matter. But she'd always trusted strangers, always thought the best of people, and she didn't want to stop now. "I'll be fine," she'd said.

"As long as you get some cash," he'd said. He glanced over at her. "You got a plan, then?"

"I do," she'd said confidently.

"What's that then?"

"My business and not yours."

He'd laughed at that and offered her a jelly baby and for the rest of the ride they'd sung along to old Abba songs and he'd told her about his sons and his dogs, showing a clear preference for the dogs.

She did have a plan. Sort of. A plan that hinged on her grandmother having softened with age and loneliness.

A plan that, now that she was standing on the front step of the big, gray house, seemed slightly less realistic than it had seemed on the beach in Sri Lanka.

She took a deep breath and then rang the bell.

There was a brief second after her grandmother opened the front door when Luna thought that everything might be alright. A second when there was a glimmer of emotion in her grandmother's blue eyes, a slight sparkle of something that might have been love. Then she'd sniffed and raised an eyebrow. "You're back then." She turned and walked down the hall, leaving the front door open.

"I'm back," Luna said, coming inside and dropping her bag by the door.

"Don't leave that there," said her grandmother. "Put it away where it belongs. Upstairs. You weren't brought up in a barn."

With a sigh, Luna picked up the bag, hitched it over her shoulder, and carried it toward the stairs.

"There'll be tea in the drawing room," her grandmother said as Luna went upstairs.

WHEN SHE WAS six years old, Luna Truman's life had

changed for good. One moment she'd been a happy, dark-haired, normal school girl, the next she'd been living in a big, gray house afraid to drop crumbs from her toast.

Her room was just as she remembered it. So she shoved her bag under her bed and breathed in the stale air. Only then did she pick up the picture from her dressing table.

"It's been a while," she said.

Her mother didn't answer. Hardly surprising since she'd been dead for more years than Luna had known her, and Luna didn't remember what her voice sounded like. She did smile from the picture frame, though, and Luna smiled back.

"There's a lot to tell you," she said. "But I can't right now because if I'm not back downstairs in a minute, the old witch will come looking for me. And yes, I know she didn't have to take me in, and yes, I know that I should be more patient with her and she's an old woman."

Age had not softened her, though, Luna thought privately.

She put the picture down, looked in the mirror, ran her fingers through her short curls, decided things weren't going to get much better, and stomped off back down the stairs.

"Milk?" her grandmother asked, as Luna walked into the drawing room with its over-stuffed couch. She was holding a silver milk jug.

"No, thanks," said Luna.

Her grandmother eyed her outfit with disapproval. Her grandmother disapproved of a great many things. She disapproved of iced coffee, for instance. She certainly disapproved of her daughter becoming a single mother. It was hard to tell whether she disapproved of that more or less than the amount she disapproved of her daughter rudely dying and leaving her with a granddaughter to bring up. She definitely disapproved of said granddaughter.

"I suppose you'll be wanting to stay."

Luna tried her hardest to smile nicely. "It would be nice if I could."

"This is your home. Of course you can stay."

"That's kind." Luna rubbed at her nose and then accepted a cup of tea. This could work out for both of them, she reminded herself. She was sure that her grandmother didn't want her to stay any more than she wanted to stay. "Of course, I don't have to stay long."

Her grandmother paused, teacup half-raised to her mouth. "You don't?"

Luna took a breath. She'd practiced this on the ferry, mumbling the words to herself under her breath until the other passengers thought there was something wrong with her. It was harder here. Logical, she told herself. Cool and calm. They were both adults. "I think you know why I'm here," she said.

Her grandmother smiled coldly. "Do I?"

Ah, so she wasn't going to make this easy. Luna didn't know why she'd expected any less. "The, um, the money," she began, her words stumbling now.

Her grandmother put down her teacup quietly and gently and settled back in her chair with her hands in her lap. "Ah, yes, I thought it might come down to that."

Luna's lips were dry. "I'm twenty-eight," she began.

"And my opinion has not changed," said her grandmother.

"It's been seven years."

Her grandmother lowered her chin, but kept her eyes firmly on Luna's. "Exactly my point."

"How is that your point?" Luna asked. "I mean, I can see how handing over my inheritance when I was twenty-one perhaps wasn't a wise thing to do, but I'm a fully grown adult now."

"Are you?"

The clock on the mantle ticked in the silence that followed. Luna didn't know how to answer that question, short of pulling out her birth certificate and a dictionary to explain the meaning of the word adult.

Her grandmother took a breath. "I am the executor of your mother's estate," she said. "Your mother's money, the money she inherited from my mother, was placed in my care when your mother passed, with clear instruction that you were to receive your inheritance only once you became a responsible adult."

"But—"

"A *responsible* adult, not a *grown* adult," her grandmother interrupted. "A case of unclear wording, perhaps, and yet I intend to abide by my daughter's last will and testament."

"But I—"

"Disappearing for seven years and showing up like a dirty monkey in cheap foreign clothes does not a responsible adult make."

Luna opened her mouth to speak and then closed it again. She didn't think there was any point in continuing this conversation. She should have known better. The arguments that had sounded so good in the Asian sun suddenly didn't matter at all. What mattered was that her grandmother hadn't changed in the slightest.

Her grandmother picked up her teacup again. "You're welcome to stay as long as you like," she said. "This is your home, for better or worse. But you won't be getting your money until you have proven to me that you're a responsible adult."

Get Your Copy of The Almost Bride Now, Only from Amazon!

Printed in Great Britain
by Amazon